WITHDRAWN

THE OPPOSITE HOUSE

NAN A. TALESE

DOUBLEDAY

NEW YORK LONDON

TORONTO SYDNEY

AUCKLAND

THE

OPPOSITE

HOUSE

....

HELEN

OYEYEMI

PUBLISHED BY NAN A. TALESE
AN IMPRINT OF DOUBLEDAY

Published in the United States by Nan A. Talese, an imprint of The Doubleday
Broadway Publishing Group, a division of Random House, Inc., New York.

www.nanatalese.com

The Opposite House was first published in Great Britain by
Bloomsbury Publishing, May 2007.

DOUBLEDAY is a registered trademark of Random House, Inc.

Grateful acknowledgment is made to the following for permission to quote from
copyrighted material:
Reprinted by permission of the publishers and the Trustees of Amherst College:
excerpts from *The Poems of Emily Dickinson,* Thomas H. Johnson, ed., Cambridge,
Mass.: The Belknap Press of Harvard University Press, Copyright © 1951, 1955,
1979, 1983 by the President and Fellows of Harvard College.
Reprinted by permission of the publishers: excerpt from *The Letters of Emily
Dickinson,* Thomas. H. Johnson, ed., Cambridge, Mass.: The Belknap Press of
Harvard University Press, Copyright © 1958, 1986 by the President and
Fellows of Harvard College; 1914, 1924, 1932, 1942 by Martha Dickinson
Bianchi; 1952 by Alfred Leete Hampson; 1960 by Mary L. Hampson.

Book design by Gretchen Achilles

Library of Congress Cataloging-in-Publication Data
Oyeyemi, Helen.
    The opposite house / Helen Oyeyemi.—1st ed.
        p.   cm.
    1. Young women—Fiction. 2. Cubans—Great Britain—Fiction.
3. Santeria—Fiction. 4. Self-perception—Fiction. I. Title.
PR6115.Y49O67 2007
823'.92—dc22

                                                            2006036812
ISBN: 978-0-385-51384-5

PRINTED IN THE UNITED STATES OF AMERICA

1   3   5   7   9   10   8   6   4   2

First U.S. Edition

FOR JASON TSANG

(if there is . . . *go and get it*)

There's been a Death, in the Opposite House,

As lately as Today—

I know it, by the numb look

Such Houses have—alway—

EMILY DICKINSON
The Complete Poems of Emily Dickinson

Sometimes a child with wise eyes is born.

Then some people will call that child an old soul.

That is enough to make God laugh. For instance there is Yemaya Saramagua, who lives in the somewherehouse.

A somewherehouse is a brittle tower of worn brick and cedar wood, its roof cradled in a net of brushwood. Around it is a hush, the wrong quiet of woods when the birds are afraid. The somewhere-house is four floors tall. The attic is a friendly crawl of linked rooms, aglister with brilliant mirrors propped against walls and window ledges. On the second floor, rooms and rooms and rooms, some so tiny, pale and clean that they are no more than fancies, sugar-cubed afterthoughts stacked behind doorways. Below is a basement pillared with stone. Spiders zigzag their gluey webs all over the chairs. The basement's back wall holds two doors. One door takes Yemaya straight out into London and the ragged hum of a city after dark. The other door opens out onto the striped flag and cooking-smell cheer of that tattered jester, Lagos—always, this door leads to a place that is floridly day.

The Kayodes live on the third floor, in three large rooms criss-crossed with melancholic skipping ropes of gauze. All day and all night they mutter, only to one another, and only in Yoruba. The smallest of the Kayodes is a boy with eyes like silver coins. For hair he wears a fuzzy cap of skull-shaped film. He is so old that he walks about on tiptoes, his ragged heels doubtful of bearing his weight un-shattered.

The second Kayode is asleep most of the time. Her braids are woven into a downy coronet. From the arms of a rocking chair by the furthermost window, the sleeping woman traces out her dreams on vellum. Kayode allows the sheets of paper to skate off her lap and meet the floor as she finishes each drawing; the figures in her dreams are dressed in witch-light. The third Kayode is tall, thickset and bushy-headed; his silhouette cuts the shape of a round-headed meat cleaver. His eyes, black disks cast with a rising glitter, unsettle with a glance.

When Yemaya, or Aya, came to the somewherehouse, her bat-tered trunk full of beads and clothes came too. Her bottleful of vanilla essence was wrapped up soft in the centre. And the Kayodes were already there. They had called to one another, harsh-tongued, Kayode, Kayode, Kayode, from room to room. But when Aya set-tled, they took flight and clustered together in their rooms.

If you were to come in through the front door of the some-wherehouse, you would walk into the air born in Aya's pans, the condensed aroma of yams and plantains shallow-fried in palm oil, or home-smoked cod, its skin stiffened in salt and chilli. The smell clings to the rough blue carpet underfoot, drifts over the holes worn into it in the corner where the shoes are stacked. The smell ropes and rubs itself against your hair and skin. You turn, and you are only disturbing the motion of this holy smoke before it settles around you again. On Sundays, Aya cooks a feast for four and takes tray after tray upstairs to the Kayodes, plates piled high with yellow rice and beans, slivers of slow-roasted pork and *escabeche*. The Kayodes will not talk to her; the Kayodes don't eat, but Aya doesn't understand about waste.

Aya overflows with *ache*, or power. When the accent is taken off it, *ache* describes, in English, bone-deep pain. But otherwise *ache* is blood . . . fleeing and returning . . . red momentum. *Ache* is, *ache* is is is, kin to fear—a frayed pause near the end of a thread where the cloth matters too much to fail. The kind of need that takes you across water on nothing but bare feet. *Ache* is energy, damage, it is constant, in Aya's mind all the time. She was born that way— powerful, half mad, but quiet about it.

. . . .

His last name shall be his father's name.

His second name shall be his grandfather's name.

His first name shall be a name for his ownself, but unknown to him, all those fathers before his grandfather live in this name. That is something a mother has the power to do to her son. Anyhow I am going to be a terrible mother; my son has raised the alarm. He is desperately pushing my stomach away from him.

On Monday I wake up and spend about an hour in alternation between vomiting and breathless whimpering; with tap water I rinse away far more food than I could have eaten. I am afraid to open my mouth and taste air. Air tastes like grease; air tilts my stomach until it spills yet more. I prop up my legs on the closed toilet seat and lean my head against the sink so that the bathroom is holding me. At some point Aaron comes and ties my hair up in a high knot, rinses my face, gentle, with warm water. For some reason he checks the whites of my eyes. Then he wraps himself around me and hugs me, hugs me. He goes away when I mutter "Go away" and vomit over his shoulder.

On Tuesday I buy a pregnancy test, and two blue windows have me wincing; they tell me my son is coming.

He is coming, yes, out of my inconsistency, my irregular approach to pill popping, which bores me.

He is coming, my son, from an inaccurately remembered chat about the rhythm method in sex education lessons at my Catholic school. The Church doesn't want the rhythm method to work, of course it doesn't. Babies, hurray, and so on.

My son. I don't even know where I got the idea of him from. When I was five I discussed him with Mami, and because I was years away from having a period, she laughed and humoured me, suggested names, until I seemed to forget about it. I didn't forget about it, I just didn't talk about it. I realised quickly that people would think I was crazy if I seemed too convinced that I was due a son. But I just knew. I fast-forwarded over the process of getting a son (I had vague ideas about one day having to do something large and bloody, put my eye out, or split my forehead open) and instead I just had my boy, warm, alive, walking beside me, gaining strength from me. He was full of laughter and he wanted me to be happy and so I was.

My brother Tomás was born when I was nine, and I loved him straightaway, curiously and wholly in my imagination, with the kind of affection that one doesn't touch for fear of breakage. Because he was a quiet baby and gave my parents less night trouble than I had given them, I watched Tomás for cot death when my parents were asleep. Sometimes Tomás saw me. I wonder what he saw—a big face flitting over him, mouth open for suction, searchlight eyes picking out his breath. I wonder if it seemed I had come to kill him. Babies are not trusting. Tomás mewed at me the first few times I broke sleep to visit him, then he just watched me back, or slept.

Tomás was in no way my son. He designated himself Papi's son—I think the real reason why Tomás learned to walk was because of his need to keep track of our papi. There are photographs of

Tomás determinedly weaving along behind Papi, Papi slowing down and looking back, rapt, at this tiny beauty who places a firm hand on the back of Papi's knee, gathering the trouser material into a peak in his fingers, not as a restriction but as a reminder. Papi would say to him jocularly, "Tomás, Tomás, T-boy," but my brother wouldn't respond to that kind of talk.

They thought Tomás might be autistic, but he wasn't autistic.

He was just serious. Already he was serious.

Sometimes Papi and Chabella call Tomás "the London baby."

But before Tomás, when Papi, Chabella and I were in our Hamburg house, I was a sleepwalker. I went to bed with everyone else, fell asleep, tottered in circles around the house and woke up to the sound of early-morning bicycle bells and wheels soft-shooting over paved stone. I woke wherever I had dropped in exhaustion—curled in a ball under the kitchen table with my long nightie dragged down longer and wound around my numb feet.

Mami took the opportunity to ask me if we had rats; she thinks that a house at night is a kingdom of rats. I wasn't in any position to notice rats. But when I started sleeping normally, I remembered that two silent girls had been there with me when I sleepwalked. They never let me go outside, never let me take down the bolts Chabella so fastidiously fastened every night. The girls detained me with their small, fuzzy selves, embraces, smiles, their scent; we played hide-and-seek, but they were always easy to find because they smelled of Chabella. They were completely bald, heads smooth and deep brown, small-boned faces with eye sockets like vast copper settings for their frozen amber eyes. They saw me and their pupils dilated as if darkness had just fallen, as if I was their endarkenment.

Often the girls were wet, their clothes soaked through even when the weather outside was dry. I communicated to them about my son. I can't remember who told what to whom. But I never said anything to my mami about the girls—she would have had me exorcised or something. She keeps saying that when it came to being born, I was a difficult one to persuade. She miscarried twice, early in each pregnancy. When she told me about her miscarriages, I felt accused.

I said, "It's not my fault," and Chabella shrugged.

I don't know how long my son has been around, but I have been eating crap. Now the boy needs seeds and fresh fruit and oily fish and folic acid and carefulness and stuff. So I am disturbed when Chabella, my mami, brings me a plastic bucketful of pineapples and half-ripe mangoes and unripe papaya. I don't want to tell Chabella anything, but I think she Knows something, and I sit as far away from her as possible so she can't smell me. Chabella asks after Aaron, whom she loves and calls her *moquenquen*, her *pikin*, her heart child. Of Aaron Chabella says, "So handsome! And, praise God, he doesn't know it."

Aaron knows that one of Mami's favourite singers is Melanie Safka. He bothers with Woodstock singing more than Papi or I or Tomás do; he gets the way that the singing never moves beyond the conversational, the way the music escapes through a percussion-tiled back door into a cry of care that is meant to find a softer sigh as answer. Like Mami, who listened before she knew what the words meant, he knows exactly when the lift in voice is going to happen and breathes out, ah, when it does.

To Chabella Aaron never forgets to murmur, *"You're beautiful people. . . . you look like a friend of mine. . . ."*

Chabella says, "You." She smiles like a sun brought down.

He tells her, "Don't let it get to your head."

But on this visit, Chabella just sits there and eyes me and drowns seven tablespoons of sweetener in milky tea. And she critically discusses my hair, which is now inexplicably seeping oil from beneath the bands and clips I've held it up with.

I have such a head of hair that Chabella had to put aside twice the time she needed for her own hair to sit down and grapple with mine. In Chabella's hands, my hair seemed tall, thick and mysterious; her fingers got lost in it as she struggled to relocate partings she'd made seconds before. I know that my friends from my sleepwalking days have something to do with all the hair I have.

And it was my hair that told me on Monday evening that something different was happening in my body. As I sectioned my hair and seized strands from the root to wrap them in cotton thread, my hair told me, No. It came away in my hands in soupspoon curls. My hair has never had anything come between it and my system before. Mami never let me have my hair relaxed—the smell of hair chemicals makes her ill. While this is probably true, her reasons are also political.

Sugar makes Chabella sick, too; she doesn't even want to have a look at it. It has to do with the year Castro called for Cubans to harvest ten million tons of sugarcane to pay off Cuba's debt to Russia. Papi's memories of that time are brief because they are bright— Papi, who knew just as little as Chabella does about sugarcane farming, cheerfully tried to fulfil his quota, whistling, his tongue shifting coca leaves around his mouth while he worked.

Chabella is much younger than him, so she wasn't there in the fields. But she has stories from her aunts who struggled amongst the leaves and cut themselves on sharp stubs left from poorly harvested cane. Sugar makes Chabella cry. She hints at other memories, other sugar horrors, ancestral. Since Chabella only bakes with sweeteners, Papi sometimes complains that the texture of her *cucuruchos* is different from that of the ones his mother used to make. But he doesn't complain too loudly or persistently.

From Chabella I've learnt how to fight anyone, man or woman, whilst sitting down completely still. It's all in the quality, not the quantity, of the tears; the soundless shudder as if the water comes from a deep place lined with rocks. When Mami gets sick, she cries like that, and the threat of that was enough for me not to bother with hair relaxers.

Chabella tried to teach me *Gelassenheit*—the longing to let go and collapse under holy madness—long before I read anything by Hans Denck. I drank *Gelassenheit* in by the litre at the kitchen table, where I sat on Mami's lap and watched her twist rice paper into graceful shapes whose petals were melded together with fine honey. The prayer flowers were ships built to sail nowhere—set aflame they unreeled a bitter scent and carried the tiny pleas scribbled on their petals only as far as the limits of the glass bowl before they died.

Mami recited letters to me; they were from friends she had grown up with, friends who had spread out to Granma, Camagüey and Holguín. There were letters from her cousins in Villa Clara and

Pinar del Río, photographs and notes from her sister in Matanzas reminding her how lucky she was to be abroad, how lucky, *querida*, beloved, not to have to constantly pit yourself against *la lucha*, that struggle for life! The tone of the letters wasn't envious, only kind. There news was that people were getting married, being born, people eloping with lovers to Santiago de Cuba and getting caught and told off and given family blessings. People were winning street-wide cooking contests for the best *ropa vieja*, people were ripping off hapless tourists. As Mami spoke her alien litany to me, she depressed the centres of each flower with a deft thumb so that each one could host a fire in its heart. Each petal read:

Ayude

She was asking for help.

But love gets in the way of her paper flowers, love keeps them secret from Papi. Chabella and Papi have ways of looking at each other, ways of touching that are full of stunned caution. They trip over each other constantly, marvel each time. When Mami sits down at the table, wiping her hands on her cooking skirt after she's set dishes before us, Papi takes her hand, strokes her fingers, says her name as if he's asking it. Mami nods at him; her lips smile, her eyes smile. I grew up doubting that anyone would ever look at me in the same way. My doubt contains no great trauma; it's casual, the way people doubt they can jump off a bridge and fly.

Papi taught at the university where Chabella was a student. He is twenty years older than Mami. And rare, they were rare, black academics in Cuba, black academics in a lot of places. I only know young-man Papi from photographs. Young-man Papi with his un-kempt Afro and tortoiseshell spectacles. Once he had finally, achingly understood that Castro's Revolution was not his, Papi es-chewed America—rather, after stints at the University of Hamburg and the Sorbonne, he brought Mami and I to London. Papi says he was "sent abroad by Castro," as if Castro, having singled out the aca-demics and bourgeoisie that he didn't want in his revolution, had first restricted their research possibilities, then leant over and lifted them all airborne with a single puff.

I was seven years old when we came here. I've come to think that there's an age beyond which it is impossible to lift a child from the pervading marinade of an original country, pat them down with a paper napkin and then deep-fry them in another country, another language like hot oil scalding the first language away. I arrived here just before that age.

One time I needed to know an A-level essay's worth of Kantian ethics, but the very layout of the book I was reading took the words away from me. Papi leaned over my chair. My papi put warmth be-tween me and the ceiling with his stubbly chin and his kind eyes and a hand on my shoulder. He explained to me some things about Kant and duty. He couldn't make me understand what he was talking about. Mami sat with me then and told me again, with long pauses as she moved the ideas she remembered from German to English. When she prays to the saints for intercession, her Spanish is dam-aged and slow because she is moving her thoughts from Africa to Cuba and back again.

———————

St. Teresa of Ávila was the one who brought me to St. Catherine's for the first time. In her autobiography, St. Teresa of Ávila tells of a meeting with the devil, and it seemed to her that the devil was a short Negro. Of course it's funny about the devil being black; I thought it was funny, but at the same time . . .

I needed to do something after I put down the Ávila book; I needed to do the worst thing I could do in the world, something to call down hellfire and justice. I took my fifteen-year-old self to Chabella's room. I took a pair of scissors to the most beautiful dress in the world, Chabella's hoop-skirted wedding dress, so full-skirted a dress that it can stand up all by itself. I took the scissors to it, but I stopped before I could cut. I went to my best friend Amy Eleni's house instead. When I briefly described what was going on, she took me to her parents' loft, opened up a wooden chest and tossed her mother's wedding dress at me.

"Go on then," she said. She was laughing. But I couldn't do anything to the dress. Despina's dress was the second most beautiful in the world—this dress was satin, with a mist of silver mesh, the kind of dress that makes its wearer look newly wept. In the chest the dress had looked very narrow, narrower even than I thought Despina could be, but Amy Eleni wasn't scared of getting stuck in it. Amy Eleni didn't even care about the dress; she just put it on to show me. She flicked up the zip of Despina's tear-dress as if it were all just jeans.

She turned to the dusty mirror sideways on, struck a pose, hands on her hips, her elbows crooked governess-style. She kicked back at the air to loosen her pose, and the dress seams creaked at her thigh. I couldn't breathe, but Amy Eleni breathed. I looked at Amy Eleni in the mirror, but she didn't see me looking. She struck another pose on tiptoe, arms held high, neck swaying as if something heavy was on her head. The skylights caught an accusing flash of sun that by-passed stacked sea-grass boxes to illuminate the dress.

The poor dress, it was too much. I stopped Amy Eleni with my hands, kept her waist straight under my palms to let her know that she shouldn't bend anymore, and I turned her in a swish of cold white as I examined the dress for damage. She drooped and jiggled her wrists, pretending to be a puppet. But before my eyes the dress's shoulder was turning to sad, shredded cloth. Before I could even open my mouth, Amy Eleni said, "It'll survive, wedding dresses survive anything. People have sex in wedding dresses. I mean, Jesus. Once I put this dress on and I climbed a tree in it! I fell, though . . ."

I screamed small and checked the satin for grass stains, but Amy Eleni sniggered, batted my hand away, named a book and said I really needed to read it.

Books. I am attracted and repelled; books are conversations that are not addressed to me and I want to sneak up and listen but I also want to be invited in. If I was invited in the conversation would not be what it was.

After reading that Avila book, I scared Chabella badly. She decided that I was having a "moral, religious and mental breakdown!" I was only saying what was on my mind. The conversation that made Chabella decide that we were going to take a weekend retreat went exactly like this:

ME: Chabella, is it true that the Church refuses to confirm the presence of a single soul in Hell?

CHABELLA (*with an enormous, proud smile*): Ai, *querida*.

ME: Not even Hitler or Stalin or It the Clown?

CHABELLA: Not even them. Forgiveness—

ME (*interrupting*): What about Teresa of Ávila?

CHABELLA: —is always an option. Mm, St. Teresa, what?

ME: Well Teresa of Ávila is a bitch, after all, so I expect she's in Hell.

CHABELLA: (*screams for three or four long seconds, while I just sit and look at her. Gasps. Holds her head with tears pouring down her face, shrinks and shakes as if I am punching her.*)

Chabella said it wasn't so much the words, but the way my face went when I said them—she said my face "twisted" and she couldn't recognise me. Chabella knows the rites of exorcism by heart. She is prone to exaggeration.

When Papi heard that Chabella and I were going on a retreat, he gave six-year-old Tomás a high five and said, "Just you and me, London baby. Show me some of those London ways." Papi had to give Tomás the high five very gently, it was in fact a matter of pressing his palm against Tomás's fingers, or Tomás would have fallen down. Tomás was happy with the idea of us going away, too. He cackled, "Bye."

When we actually left the following week, he said "Wait for me" and ran upstairs to throw some toys into his rucksack. Mami closed the front door and he cried out: "No! No!"

The way Tomás said "no," the way he said it.

He didn't know what two days would feel like; he didn't understand that he would only have to go to sleep and get up twice, and then we'd be back.

That first weekend at St. Catherine's, Chabella and I slept in the same room on low, neat white beds with scratchy blankets. We didn't talk about Catholicism or Teresa; we were already in the Church, high up with a sweet vanilla smell and the softest hush all around. We laughed together in the night for no reason at all. We tried to be quiet because you were supposed to be quiet, and anyway, everyone was sleeping. But Mami would just look at me with her nostrils quivering and that was enough to set me off. At Mass, when I looked at my mami she glittered. When she sang, the song came from the wound on her tongue. While Mami slept at night, and I lay with my eyes closed,

a shadow fell, fast and from a great height it fell

it put me inside

it put me inside

the weight of it. Dark came to rest on my eyelids; strange and painful pennies. What if, what if I had opened my eyes and tried to look at what was there in that room . . .

. . . with sleepy awe I felt it: *I am loved.* And outside there were tall trees that had other people's sleep caught in their branches, dreams like white lights, that first time Mami took me away to save my soul.

Now it's 4 a.m., and I'm still awake with my fingers splayed over my neck and its old loop of pain

(and I am at St. Catherine's again,

at the window again

amazed again

at the way a steep hill holds growing green on its swerve when it will support nothing else).

On the wall is St. Catherine of Siena, sheets of chestnut hair floating in heaven-driven winds, Catherine who I always fail to love when I remember that she is not the Catherine of spiked-wheel martyrdom. Catherine of Siena looks at me with all of her soul in her soft smile; she looks at me, glad that I will not be staying. I think about the mothers I know or have seen or have heard of. My mother, Amy Eleni's mother, mothers in books, mothers in Chabella's *apataki*, her stories about the gods. Twenty-four not being old enough, I want to tell my son, *not now, please*.

For six days I have been praying, really praying, a state of angry joy that I fell into through a crack in the bottom of my heart. I have not been able to close my eyes for longer than it takes to blink. I am back to childish bargaining with God for explicit support of my son, as if my son is special, or for advance pardon for the swift ending of my son, as if I am special. Or anything, anything, God give me anything.

Food. Everything I eat, my mouth lets it go, my stomach heaves painful, sour streams. My breasts are rotten lumps hooked into my rib cage, and I can't touch my body at all, I can't. I keep holding my hands away from myself, or holding my hands together. But the afternoons ripen here in radiant languor as forty women draw a little more breath into their black-and-white cassocks so as to continue dying slowly from love. When it rains the sisters, capes heavy with water, rotate in fragrant clusters through the slate walkways of the chapel.

At the door, Sister Perpetua takes both my hands and looks at me from beneath the clean borders of her cowl. Her "hello" smile is the same as her "goodbye" smile. She lets me come, lets me go my way, looks at me now the same way that she did when I arrived a week ago. I tottered in on six-inch wedges with the meekest look that I could give her over the top of a pair of oversize sunglasses, the crown of my floppy brown hat settled around my ears and Aaron's discarded khaki jacket, longer and looser than the black dress I wore beneath it, flapping open despite my best efforts to belt it in several places. She brusquely tells me that this time I came on retreat from a joyous heart, that I was here with her at St. Catherine's because I am being slain by the Holy Spirit.

"Jesus is in your life," Sister Perpetua says again, while I look at her and do not think of Jesus at all because Sister Perpetua's beauty is bewitched: her lips are a frozen red that thaws out into pink at the corners; her eyebrows climb to tapered peaks above dark chocolate eyes. Sister Perpetua has the face that Snow White's mother had wished upon her. But it isn't that something is keeping her young, just that something is keeping her beautiful. I love Sister Perpetua for stupid reasons: she does not whisper in chapel but talks for God to hear; she has seen me crying and she just lets me cry; when she wants me to pray with her she covers my hands with her soft ones.

The first time I came she found me in the chapel and told me about an African priest who the Church had confirmed was in heaven. She did not tell Chabella, she only told me, as if she knew that I needed it. I told her about the shadow at night, and she talked about the Cloud of Unknowing, how when God is near, you are driven into the darkness outside of reason and it is a good, sweet rest. I tried to explain that it wasn't *un*knowing. But mystics are difficult to argue with.

———————

I'm still not used to Aaron's flat, even though I moved in four months ago, even though he calls it "ours." The house is in the middle of a semidetached row; always at attention, jutting straight up with a windowed stare that holds sleepy intelligence near its base, as if the right command could send it leaping sideways. I approach it with caution. I feel like an interview candidate arriving in order to be considered for tenancy by the house itself. I lose myself to the extent that I raise a hand to knock at the door though the keys are already dangling on their ring from the index finger of my other hand. We live in the bottom half of the converted two-floor house that Aaron's dad, a man made thin by nerves and neatness and ownership of a real estate agency, gave him for his twenty-first birthday.

The streets around the house are misted with trees and re-edged with cut-out-and-colour delis and small, glass-fronted restaurants whose clientele don't seem to do lunch, or dinner, or anything other than beautifully hued cocktails.

Inside the house is a middle floor forced between the green-carpeted staircase that leads up to Miss Lassiter's flat and the peeling wooden steps that lead down to Aaron's. I am wary here; I remember that Miss Lassiter's envelope is due today. Miss Lassiter is now Aaron's tenant, though she used to be his father's. She leaves monthly envelopes outside Aaron's door without knocking. Aaron doggedly maintains that she's shy, but I don't enjoy Miss Lassiter. When I meet her on the stairs, she thrusts her walking stick out before her like a probe. The outlines of her face are buried in clasped whorls of wool; she wears stiff black gloves, and holds her fingers together so that her thumb is a loner. The gloves make her hands look like blunted hooks.

I tiptoe downstairs and open the front door of the flat. Immediately Aaron is filming me. Kente cloth is threaded into a vivid print belt for his jeans, his socked feet slip on the floorboards. I make a face at him; he lifts his eye away from the viewfinder and, smiling, directs me with his hand, showing me which slats of space I can walk in without damaging his angle.

"So, Maja," he intones, and I know that he's making a close-up of my face. "Who wins? Aaron or . . . GOD?"

I hang up my coat and spread my hands in the shade; he frantically indicates that I should come forward and turn a little more to the right. I do.

"What are you talking about?"

"What am I *talking* about?" He walks backward, ignoring my attempt to try and get the camera off him. "My girlfriend goes off to a nunnery four times in as many months, and I'm not supposed to worry that she's about to marry Jesus . . ."

I stop at the kitchen door; Aaron is inside now, shored up against a crumbling wharf of green tile, stacked plates and opened jars. I look into the camera for what feels like forever—I look until I forget that I am seeing anything and my eyes spill over with tension water, and he is abashed and nervously shifts the camera.

When he puts the camera down on the kitchen table I see how tired he is, see the caved-in yawn lines around his mouth and the panda patches around his eyes. He comes to me and rests his forehead against mine. I only really notice the notations that exhaustion leaves on his face when I've been separated from the reasons for it: the broken braying of his pager; the fifty-six-hour cover shift at the hospital that upends us into a fraught airless rectangle of calling each other at the wrong time, not answering calls from each other when it's most important, me wondering what it means when he forgets to say "I love you" before saying goodbye. His hair is getting too long. He is beginning a beard, and it's in an awkward adolescent phase, bristling in patches despite itself.

I don't want dinner, but he starts pounding steaming boiled yams for fresh *fufu* at the kitchen counter. The only help he lets me give is simple; heating up a chicken stew he's already made. I like watching Aaron burn like this, his body clock hopelessly awry, forehead wrinkled as he revolves around the steel cog of his own nervous energy. I think he likes it when I try to sing him to sleep, although he doesn't fall for it—he just looks at me with the covers wadded under his chin, wearing a smile of melting gold like a child's. Sometimes he wakes up in the night asking what time it is and asking whether someone else finished the tourniquet job he started because he's forgotten to go back, or asking who collected the X-rays. When he sees that it's only me, he laughs and curls up against me and falls asleep again.

He eats dinner; I watch him skimming balls of doughlike *fufu* into a rich, dense stew. He asks if I want to talk about the retreat. With the question put as formally as that, I say I don't. He's relieved—almost immediately he changes tack and asks whether I'm singing tonight. I'm not, and he's not on call tonight, so he says, "We should go and see a play or a film or something."

"Okay," I say, pretending to leaf through *Time Out*, knowing that he'll fall asleep before he even finds his shoes.

On the sofa he begins to drowse with his head on my lap, mumbling, "Sorry I'm so crap," into the fabric of my jeans. I draw my fingers through his hair and tell him to shut up. He sleeps with his grey eyes half open and intent on some object at floor level.

Aaron knows Amy Eleni from a church choir they both used to sing in before Amy Eleni dropped out. I think they must have recognised something in each other, some poorly concealed intensity that other people find nerve-racking. The first time I met him, when he joined me on a tinsel-strewn sofa at Amy Eleni's birthday party, Aaron drifted into sleep the way he is drifting now. Then it was because he trusted the swell of skin longing that drew us together in a searching curve, had us asking each other with our eyes and our small, ironic smiles, *Can I touch you?* His head sought my lap as if he had every right to claim me for his pillow. And I, I drew my knees up a little higher, feeling his soft hair slipping as he moved with me, feeling his eyes on my lips, drinking in his face; in that way we kissed before we kissed.

Aaron has a strange accent, unevenly crammed with tonality. Some words he sings, others he says so flatly that they're lost. I thought at first that he might be one of the more outlandish white South Africans until he told me that he had been born and raised in Ghana. When I remember, my accent is as firm and clean as I can make it; it bears unabbreviated sentences with all their rich vowels gutted out by a sharp tip of mindfulness. I speak like this because my parents, their voices smoothed to calm, placeless melody through academia, speak English like this. And I speak like this because it is important that I'm understood. In a country where ears are attuned to courteous, clipped white noise, being asked to repeat myself batters down the words in me, makes my tongue fall down my throat.

At the party, Aaron seemed to be listening to more than just my words; when he dropped his gaze I heard our breathing—his breath absorbed mine and took wings and fluttered shallow, weak, confused at its suddenly expanded span. I was so obviously talking about nothing that I stopped to ask him a question, and it was only when he answered thickly and after a long pause that I realised he had been snoring lightly.

His mouth is maddeningly soft and full; I draw my thumb lightly over his lips and he nips at me.

I hear feet dragging on the steps outside, and the sound has my heartbeat jumping in the palm of my hand, even though I know it's only Miss Lassiter. It's only Miss Lassiter, and her envelope is due today. But it holds me still when she takes so long to put the envelope down, waits so long silent outside the door before she shuffles away. (it's just that she's old, it's just that she's old, she can't move so quickly)

I have to wait. I have to wait until I feel that Miss Lassiter has gone. It takes a long time to feel that Miss Lassiter has gone. She is only really gone when Mami calls.

Mami is in the pay phone down the road from her and Papi's house.

"I'm never going back in there again," Chabella whispers. I imagine her in the phone box, her fingers holding on to the receiver around one of the disposable handkerchiefs that she reserves for public toilets and public telephones. I close the sitting-room door and sandwich the phone between my ear and my shoulder as I pull my coat on. That pang around my throat comes back, it comes like a guillotine.

"Do you want to stay here?" I ask, automatically. "Shall I come and get you? What happened?"

Mami's sob. One sound, arrested because it is so rageful. The words that follow can only tread softly over that sound.

"He's broken it."

"What?"

"My altar."

Mami is a Santero. She constantly tells me that I don't know what that means. I soon outgrew Mami's evening flower ceremonies. After a while, the flowers that seemed to answer Chabella's questions in raptures of hush and smoke revealed themselves to be limp rice paper. What is it that's holy about those flowers? Is it that they burn? Or that they burn so readily? But you can burn a cross, a witch, a piece of toast . . .

Chabella's papi was not a believer in anything much, and believers in Habana were suspicious that Chabella wanted to be one of them. They did not know her or her father, and they had to be careful, so Mami had to make her own Santeria. When I think of her Santeria initiation I see her surrounded by her Orishas, her guardian Yoruba gods. I see my mami kneeling with her eyes turned ecstatically upward into the wet curtains of her eyelids as her priest cuts two bars, each one as thick as a slug's trail, into the flesh of her tongue. Her altar is a series of four interlinked shrines, grooved pentagons of painted wood and brass threaded with flowers and rosaries and shells and stones and candles and saucers, all of fidelity's sparse jewellery.

The Orishas came into Cuba on the ships of 1500, which were built as temporary coffers for black gold. The Yoruba gods discovered their Cuba in the dark, hidden in bigger emergencies and cries of warning as patrol ships tried to intercept the cargo. The gods were hidden in the fear of being drowned. They were hidden in the unseen smack, smack, smack of the next man's head on the ship's boards as he tried to damage his brain and decrease his market value. The gods were not afraid, but they wept.

On arrival, the Orishas became beloved in secret. Slaves had to be Catholic and obedient or they'd be killed, or worse. The word "slave" is a big deal to Chabella and Papi; neither of them can get out from under it. It is blackness in Cuba. It is sometimes bittersweet, for such is the song of the *morena*; it is two fingers placed on a wrist when a white Cuban is trying to describe you. Papi tries to systematise it and talk about the destruction of identity and the fragility of personality, but he is scared of the Word. Mami hides inside the Word, finds reveries in it, tries to locate a power that she is owed.

The slaves in Cuba learnt to recognise their gods when they saw ripped white bedsheets, forked scraps of wood, overturned tin buckets. These things marked places where mass could be celebrated. If you still knew who you were, you had to keep it a secret. The gods hid among the saints and apostles and nobody perceived them unless they wanted to; it didn't take as much as people had thought for Catholicism and Yoruba to fuse together. The saints intercede for us with God, who must despise us to let us suffer so. The Orishas intercede for us with Olorun who, being a darker side of God, possibly despises us more. A painting of a saint welling holy tears and the story of an Orisha teach you the same thing—if you cry for someone, it counts as a prayer.

T W O

....

MAMA PROSERPINE AND HER ASPECTS

In the Cuba house, before before, Aya and her mama loved so fiercely. For noonday naps they lay entangled in the centre of the bed, fingers tearing tracks in each other's hair. When awake, Aya followed where her mama went, shoes clacking on bamboo tiles. Perched on an outcrop of their greeny-gold garden, Aya and her mama were so close together that they heard the water slewing down the rocks with the same ear.

And Aya's mama warned: Beware Proserpine, since she is the murder that walked from my heart.

Before Aya was born, Proserpine came and caught Aya's mama unawares. Proserpine came when Aya's mama was still carrying baby Aya in her stomach, ripe, ripe, and feeling it. Every step Mama took she felt in her stomach, through Aya. Steps became sharp teeth, they bit. They tried to pull baby and mother asunder. Temper was the only way to be higher. One day, because she had raised her voice against him

(with Mama's full voice comes fear, oh, fear to split you open and make you pour out good gold like yolk)

Papa caused Mama to fall to the ground. Mama fell hard and, as Papa had wanted, as he had needed, she fell quiet. She lay. She lay under minutes like fingers, and after a handful Aya did not move in her mother's stomach.

The stillness brought the thought: *I've lost this baby.*

Then transparency.

Mama became as a season is; she felt weather in her, she felt empty heat. Slowly she came to understand that she wasn't alone, that she had some secret help inside her. They got up, Aya's mama and her help, and they took a bone-handled cutlass, and they went to the next room to kill Aya's papa.

When they came, Aya's papa saw two women and one face—the face was small and faraway, and it looked on him with laughter.

Aya's papa said, "Who is that? Who's there?"

Mama and her helper didn't answer—they cut Mama's fingertip to make sure the knife was sharp enough. The blood rushed well, and quickly. They accused him. They said to him, "You've made her lose her son."

Aya's papa said, "Not a son, a daughter. You haven't lost her, you couldn't have."

But still these two accused him and turned their tiny eyes on him as if his death was already a lens that they looked through.

"Who is that? What's there?" Papa called. "Name it, name her."

Mama said later: It was too much temptation for my help; he was giving her a chance to be. So she broke away from me to name herself—Proserpine—and a name was all he needed to take her from me.

....

Like every girl, I only need to look up and a little to the right of me to see the hysteria that belongs to me, the one that hangs on a hook like an empty jacket and flutters with disappointment that I cannot wear her all the time. I call her my hysteric, and this personal hysteric of mine is designer made (though I'm not sure who made her), flattering and comfortable, attractive even, if you're around people who like that sort of thing. She is not anyone, my hysteric; she is blank, electricity dancing around a filament, singing to kill. It's not that there are two Majas; there is only one, but she can disappear into her own tension and may one day never come back.

My second ever boyfriend—frizzy-blond-haired and built like a rugby player—was a postgraduate student five years older than me when I was in my first year. Luke seemed to prefer my personal hysteric to me. He told me over and over that I was beautiful, sweet, so clever.

In his mouth, on his tongue, those words were not safe.

And he said these terrible things earnestly enough to make me sit on my hands when I was across from him at dinner. In his mouth, on his tongue, those words cast a spell which conjured me into the things he kept insisting I was.

Luke was always pleading with me to calm down before I even realised that I was unsettled. I stopped daring to raise my voice at him, or smile too much, even. Luke filled bedtime mugs for me, brimful with creamy white, warm Kahlúa and milk. When I sipped them sleepily from the enfoldment of his arms, I became convinced that I was ill, and that it was terminal. There was no other reason for such care, for the way he laid hands on me so lightly that it seemed I was already disappearing. One night, drunk, drunk, drunk, I dropped my empty shot glass and a full one for Luke, sat down beside the pieces and arranged them in my skin, twisting clear flowers planted to grow from my soles, my arms. It hurt. But wearing my hysteric, it became a matter of art and pain and so on. It was extreme, it was because of tension. Luke took me to the emergency room and spoke to me, richly, quietly, held me for as long as he could while I cried and put my sight away from my torn skin.

We went to a girls' school, Amy Eleni and I. We know about subtle, slow murder, the ways that glances and silences and unnecessarily kind words can have a girl running into traffic trying to get hit so that she doesn't have to turn up the next day. When Amy Eleni arrived at the hospital she was in no mood for pleasantries. She took Luke aside and told him to "Fuck *right* off. Immediately."

Luke became typical; he called her a man-hating dyke, and she made some movement toward him, some movement that scared him. It was as if she was going to pincer his testicles and he thought she'd do it, so he shrank. When she told me about it her voice rose and fell, bitter and sad. Amy Eleni told me gossip about Luke as I waited to be allowed to go home. One girl had said to her, "Luke only goes out with nutters. But he's never been out with a black girl before, so she must be extra psychotic."

My hysteric smells foreign, like perfumed sand, but maybe that's how she's supposed to smell. She is not part of me, but part of my store. In times of need she converts into my emergency image of

Chabella, a poorly done portrait that I can show people when I need to ask, "Have you seen this woman?"

I have no natural sensitivity; I am forced to it.

For a boyfriend from the Ivory Coast, handsome and strong like a mined mineral, I cut off all my hair. Because he said he preferred me like that, all long neck, bare ears and hopeful eyes. I hated my hair like that, hated it almost too much to live. When I wasn't with him I spent a lot of time crying. Chabella, who sometimes is my mind outside of me, said, musingly, "You look like a boy with that haircut. Your nose . . . it takes over the middle of your face when there's no hair to look at. It's strange, because in actuality your nose isn't that big."

Amy Eleni only said, "It'll grow. Your hair always grows really fast."

But I had to keep cutting away new growth with scissors. When he broke up with me, he said he was unhappy that I didn't seem to love my hair in its natural state. I asked him, Is its natural state short? He just said he had to go. I ran a bath; the hysteric came and I was persuaded to try and drown myself. But Amy Eleni phoned and I realised I wanted to answer the phone just a little bit more than I wanted to die.

Amy Eleni gets it. When I first tried to describe the hysteric to her, she snorted and said, "You can't speak for everyone. *My* personal hysteric walks three paces behind me at all times, and when things get a bit much, I kind of hang back and she kind of hurries forward, and she jumps on my back and takes me down. Then she stands up in my place." I said I didn't like that idea, I said it sounded like a denial of responsibility, a denial that Amy Eleni was underneath her hysteric.

"I am underneath her," Amy Eleni said. "She has her fucking stilettos digging into my spine."

When Amy Eleni isn't doing well her thoughts ignore her and come out exactly the way they want to. One summer her mother went to Cyprus without her. Even though Amy Eleni wanted to go, so much. But Despina was punishing her because of a bad school report. We were in her bedroom at her parents' house, and she was sitting on the broad window ledge with her curls squashed against the glass, her hands clawing the window as if she was trying to hold her house upright. She said insistently, through gritted teeth, "Do you aid me with my pulse which is gone away." She said it a few times before I heard the words. I can't remember her expression; instead I think of redness. But if she had punched the window she would only have hurt herself.

When we were fourteen Amy Eleni decided that she and I should be friends. Before that, she wouldn't talk to anyone she didn't want to talk to. She was a bit dangerous. She ate lunch by herself—as if lunchtime for the packed-lunch students wasn't all about setting up a circle of chairs in the school hall for your group, as if lunchtime wasn't about showing that you had a group. She placed her chair near the centre of the hall so that she faced outward, looking toward the door, and she sat cross-legged on it, eating interesting-looking food that didn't match her precise, English features; flat pita sandwiches filled with grilled chicken, cold stuffed vine leaves, squares of honeyed pastry, pomegranates. She ate daintily and with a calm that said she couldn't be bothered with the likes of us.

At lunchtime I always struggled with Chabella's sandwiches. Like all her food, Mami's sandwiches are works of slow-cooked love. They're ostentatious and difficult to eat in public—by the time you curl your fingers around one and take a bite, the marinated pork or chicken has already spilled out from atop the onion-and-tomato-stuffed cocoon of wheat-rich bread, and a shower of sandwich and salsa spatters your hands and your lap. You can't even lick your fingers as you would leaning on the table at home because you feel guilty, you feel embarrassed, you feel mad to have brought in such a luxury bed of a sandwich when everyone else is making do with the equivalent of string hammocks.

Amy Eleni was probably equal to the challenge of a Chabella sandwich—I had never seen her blush. She made no attempt to customise her uniform; she just let it hang off her in limp monochrome. Her hair was longer, then. She let it all curl into a big, burnt-yellow shock, thick enough for me to pile up on her head later in a crown of Senegalese twists. But at that time everyone, including me, ignored her insistence on being addressed at all times as "Amy Eleni." We just kept calling her "Amy," which sometimes forced her to shout "Die before your parents do!" and slap her rump in the direction of the person who was disregarding her wishes. The rumours about her were numerous, but the predominant one was that Amy had three boyfriends and was having sex with all of them on a timetable basis.

One day Amy Eleni, her most devastating smile in place, beckoned me away from the centre of my lunch circle, where I had been sitting with one foot up on the edge of another girl's chair laboriously washing pink varnish over her fingernails. I went over to Amy Eleni with the nail varnish still in my hand, and she took it from me and screwed the lid back on. The first thing she told me, with breathtaking serenity, was that we should be best friends because we were both pretty, and pretty girls always found it difficult to make real girlfriends who wouldn't turn Judas on them. The second thing she told me was that I absolutely had to call her Amy Eleni; Eleni was her middle name but she took her Cypriot heritage seriously and found it hard enough to keep it up when she looked like a common- or garden-variety English kid and had a surname like Lang. Then she mentioned that at her Holy Communion she had spat out the Host into her hand because she didn't believe in all that Jesus crap, and that the following Saturday she had snuck back into the church while the priest was taking confession and had tried to make the fig- urine of the baby Jesus beat upon a drum to prove his reality. She'd then broken the figurine because it hadn't. I stared at her and smiled, timid, aghast. She burst out laughing. She named a book and said I really needed to read it.

Our favourite film is *Vertigo*. Amy Eleni and I must watch it sev- enteen or eighteen times a year, and with each viewing our raptness grows looser and looser; we don't need the visuals anymore—one or the other of us can go into the kitchen halfway through and call out the dialogue while making up two cups of Horlicks. From the minute you see empty, beautiful, blond Madeleine Elster, you know she is doomed because she exists in a way that Scottie, the male lead, just doesn't. You know that Madeleine is in big trouble because she's a vast wound in a landscape where wounds aren't allowed to stay open—people have to shut up and heal up. She's in trouble because the film works to a plan that makes trauma speak itself out, speak it- self to excess until it dies; this film at the peak of its slyness, when people sweat and lick their lips excessively and pound their chests and grab their hair and twist their heads from side to side, performing this unspeakable torment.

When things are serious and either Amy Eleni or I need to beat our personal hysteric, the informal code is to seize your head and twist coils of your hair around your fingers and groan, "I'm not mad! I'm not mad! I don't want to die!" And if you have a friend who knows, then the friend grabs her head too and replies, "There's someone inside of me, and she says I must die!" That way it is stupid, and funny, and serious.

Our hysteric is the revelation that we refuse to be consoled for all this noise, for all this noise and for the attacks on our softnesses, the loss of sensitivity to my scalp with every batch of box braids. Sometimes we cannot see or hear or breathe because of our fright that this is all our bodies will know. We're scared by the happy, hollow discipline that lines our brains and stomachs if we manage to stop after one biscuit. We need some kind of answer. We need to know what that biscuit-tin discipline is, where it comes from. We need to know whether it's a sign that our bones are turning against the rest of us, whether anyone will help us if our bones win out, or whether the people who should help us will say "You look wonderful!" instead.

Why can't we kill this panic, or do the other thing and make it mute?

My heart bounces on the end of a string whenever I hear the names of Chabella's Orishas. Those gods who trip us up, then haul us up, then string us up, who understand that it hurts but also understand that it needs to. They're deadly friends from stories, their

names braided into explanations for the heavy nights edged with uncertain light like dull pearls, the nights when Chabella would wake
me up at hourly intervals, pleading with me to sip a little, just a little, of one herbal tincture or another. Nights when I protested with
all my soul to be allowed to sleep instead. That is how the Orishas
are real to me: Olorun, the father god, greatest of gods, god without
a face; Ochun the beautiful, fertile dancer; wise man Orumbila;
Yemaya of the ocean; fiery Chango; wily Echun-Elegua; reaper Iku;
Ogun, the man of iron.

They make Papi impatient. "Those are Yoruba gods," he tells
Mami. "And you are not Yoruba. You are a black Cuban. There is a
difference. For an intelligent person, you really surprise me. To us,
these gods are historical artefacts."

Papi rubs his head bemusedly with both hands and tries not to
laugh during the midnight Masses and Easter vigils Mami drags us
to. He's not entirely in the wrong; it's easy to laugh at Mass in a
Catholic Church where everyone is so straight-faced and ceremoni-
ous, even if they're just shaking a stick or something. Once when
Mami, overcome with tears as a sung *Gloria* confirmed that Christ
has risen, asked Papi in a whisper whether he felt anything, he
squeezed her hand with both of his. He muttered to me, instead of
to her, "I'm seventy-four, yes, but I'm still lucid."

Papi's irritation must begin as soon as he steps inside the house.
Where there would usually stand a lump of shaped brass, Mami and
Papi's coat stand has a host grinning from its top—a concrete skull,
eye sockets filled with dull shells. The shells are eyes for Elegua to
look through, Echun-Elegua is the trickster god who protects us
from the works of other, inferior tricksters. He hides behind the

door of his ramshackle, crazy-beamed house, watching the people who hurry up and down his crossroads like so many dusty-backed beetles. Some people are speeding past so quickly, so intent on their maps that they don't even notice Elegua's house rocking nonchalantly on the heels of its stilt feet like Baba Yaga's hut getting ready to run.

Mami says of Elegua, "If you know anything about him, you fear his kindness."

When Chabella first became a Santero, Elegua chose her for his own—unusual that he should have chosen a woman. But then perhaps my mother's family is favoured. My great-grandmother, Bisabuela Carmen, was a female *babalawo*, a Santeria priest.

My middle name is Carmen.

I like to sleep with the washed-out, monochrome, passport-size photo of Bisabuela Carmen under my pillow—the only other copy of it is slotted into Chabella's altar. In the pictures, Bisabuela Carmen's skin doubles in on itself in a river of wrinkles; her mouth and nose are washed away. Her gaze is bright, tough; she looks as if she doesn't care and not caring is a statement—really, I don't *care!*

Abuela Laline told Mami that once, when a child had been struck dead by lightning, Carmen called up the personification of lightning, Iya, for a fight—but Iya wouldn't come. Chango came, amused, to see what the fuss was about, and so Carmen wrestled Chango, the storm god at the bottom of St. Barbara's stare. When Chabella says that Chango "came," she means that at a Santeria mass Chango stepped down from heaven. He slid into the space left between song and drumbeat, he pierced veils of spiced smoke, and he possessed the body of a burly, full-grown man. Then he seized my *bisabuela* Carmen by the neck. Carmen must have been terrified but, as Mami says, "anyhow she tried." She lost, of course she lost.

Chango broke both of Carmen's arms and a leg, sparing her life because she surprised him—her boldness surpassed humanity. But Chango was wary ever afterward of Carmen's sharp nails and deep bite. Mami's *apataki* tales aren't only about the gods; they flow and cover her family too, her memories place a mantle around Bisabuela Carmen, whose namesake I am.

Carmen was born in Camagüey six years before slavery was officially abolished in Cuba. My *bisabuela* lived her last years in her other son-in-law's house because she could not sleep under the same roof as my grandfather, Abuelo Damason the Unbeliever. Abuela Laline was unhappy; Consuelo was only her half sister but seemed always to have been the smiled-upon one—Carmen had forgotten to halve her love. Also, Bisabuela Carmen predicted lunacy for my *abuelo* Damason. Abuela Laline hissed, "How could you wish lunacy on the father of my children, Mami?"

Carmen replied, "I don't wish it. But if you forget your ancestors you forget yourself. Isn't that what it is to run mad, to forget yourself?"

Laline reported Carmen's words back to Mami decades later, in tones of triumph, because Abuelo Damason had remained lucid and sardonic about everything going on around him right up until the day his heart muscle wound tight and flung him into the next life with the force of its uncoiling. But at the time of her prediction, my *bisabuela* Carmen was adamant in her decision to live with Consuelo. Bisabuela Carmen ignored Consuelo's children, Chabella's boy cousins. She insisted on having Chabella by her on weekends. At mealtimes, Chabella brought food to Bisabuela Carmen's room, knelt by the old woman's rocking chair and hand-fed her. Carmen's teeth were worn stumps. She sucked at her teeth and she looked out of the window and she said, "Jesus bless you," between mouthfuls of mashed cassava and *ajiaco*.

Carmen smelt of sour wine. Chabella took an interest in her *abuela* because her *abuela* called her "Carmen" too. Nobody in that house dared to contradict the old woman and remind her of her granddaughter's real name. Carmen told Chabella stories about the Orishas as if she were telling about a place that she had just left and was impatient to get back to—without breaking the flow of her words she shook and rocked in her chair, she rose and lifted her voice, and clapped her hands.

On Carmen's mantelpiece, amongst her tall candles was a statuette of a black Madonna. One afternoon, in the middle of her taletelling, Carmen lifted her head and stared at the statuette. She strode across the dim room with her African-print gown beating the air around her like wings, and she took the black Madonna in her hand and crushed its head against the wall. Dust fell out, and then a white flower. It was not a flower that Chabella could name. Chabella touched the flower and fresh dew rolled off the fringed petals, petals closed like a mouth around a spiky green stamen. There was blood on some of the petals, but it was not the Madonna's blood, it was Carmen's—she'd cut her finger on a piece of the porcelain.

Carmen got to know that Chabella couldn't eat pork chops because she was troubled by the problem of the bone beneath the meat. Carmen took a pork chop and tore the meat off the bone and divided it with her teeth. Chabella watched her *abuela* struggle with the meat against the suction of her gums and she understood that this was love. Bisabuela Carmen spat the brown mess into Chabella's bowl and panted, "There, no bones. Don't be afraid of it anymore."

Chabella discovered that meat eaten from the bone was not so bad after all.

Bisabuela Carmen put cracked lips to Chabella's ear and said, "Carmen, we are one. Carmen, you are born again, but you are born without your tongue. Find it. Be who you were before before."

Mami's Elegua collar came to her long before she became a Santero or understood what Santeria was. It came to her from Bisabuela Carmen's hand. In Chabella's first moment of ownership, the collar was of such weight that when she looked down at the double cup she'd made of her hands, the collar was in the centre of it and her fingertips were filled with the blood that had drained away from her palms.

Chabella wanted to know if this collar was the tongue that Carmen had said was missing from her.

Yes, no, perhaps, Bisabuela Carmen said.

Chabella was twelve when Carmen died. Carmen did not warn Chabella of her intentions, but one morning she made a hand gesture of submission, lowering her palms with a resigned flick, turned over onto her stomach in bed
(for that was how she liked to sleep)
and let her breath leave her.

Because she is venerated and loved to distraction, because Chabella will not let her fade, my *bisabuela* is a friend who is locked inside her own face.

———————

The cold has driven Mami back into the house; she is perched woodenly on the arm of a sitting-room chair. From the next room Papi wonders aloud why some women need to act like madwomen and give old men trouble. Mami is directly beneath the benign gaze of Elegua's double, the paint-swaddled Holy Child of Atocha. Tomás and I call him the Holy Kid. He is happy today. Before him on a small mahogany wall bracket is a shallow dish full of pallid *aguardiente*, Elegua's favourite alcoholic offering.

When Mami sees me, she scrambles up from her seat. I pick up her overnight bag—its canvas corners are collapsing; the last time she used it, Tomás was being born. Tomás, the most fastened fifteen-year-old I have ever known, is probably lying on his bed right now, plugged into his Walkman; Fela Kuti's hoarse euphony, or N.W.A.

Before we can leave, Papi carefully emerges from the kitchen (hobbling is beneath him, but he is unable to disguise his arthritis) his close-cut grey hair gleaming in the light that ricochets from his glasses. He says, "Maja, help me talk to this woman. You'd better help me talk to her. She tried to poison me . . ."

Mami puts her hand in mine and tugs me away.

"I will come back when you have fixed my altar," Chabella tells Papi, coldly. "And when you've put it back where it was."

Papi groans, *"Isabella."* Nobody calls my mami that except in desperation.

Once Mami and I are safely outside. She says "Look at you in those jeans!" and taps my thigh with forced gaiety. "Just look at you in those jeans. They fit too close, they'll do some kind of damage. *M'hija*, you will not be able to have children if you're not careful."

Aaron sleeps amongst toppled blankets on the sitting-room floor. Mami and I tiptoe past him. I make her a late dinner and pretend not to hear her tutting loudly over the mess in the kitchen. Chabella eats enormous amounts of food with consummate delicacy; she gives the impression of eating sparely and denying herself, lining shredded pieces of fried plantain around the edge of her bowl of stew, mashing *fufu* into the stew with her spoon. But she eats it all, slowly and in small mouthfuls. With her other hand, she serenely marks practice A-level German coursework. Fifty-two, still dewy-skinned, with a serious, slow-burning bonfire stare and a head of coal-black hair, Chabella looks better and stronger than she ever did in her thirties and forties. I sit opposite her, chin in hand, watching her, smiling stupidly because she is so beautiful.

"Listen to this," she says, pausing and looking at me. "This boy is absurd. His mother is wasting money paying me to help him pass. He will never pass; his head is a coconut. Here I see that he has sat down and thought to himself 'I need to write another paragraph, but I am too stupid to use any more German.' So what does he do? He writes an entire paragraph in English and puts *die*, *der* and *das* where he feels it is appropriate. *Sonntag abend bin ich ins Kino gegangen*, and then he puts a *dash*—not even a connective sentence—and a list of films: *Austin Powers*, *Das Fifth Element*, *Face/Off*, *Der Full Monty*—"

"When are you going to make up with Papi?" I ask.

Mami says, "When he puts my altar back."

Her face is drawn.

"Chabella," I say.

"I can stand anything but that. There is so much of me that hasn't survived with all this moving around. Paris. And Hamburg—"

I put a hand to Chabella's cheek, and she puts her hand over mine.
"Do you wish you'd stayed there? You can speak the language . . ."
"No, of course not. Germans are racist."
I laugh. "All of them?"
She doesn't smile. "All of them," she says, firmly. "Every single one."
"What about Brigitte?" I ask.
Mami says, "Brigitte doesn't count as German. Brigitte was trying to get away."
I ask her why Papi moved her altar, and she raises her hands defensively, as if I'm going to hit her.
"I asked my *babalawo* for something for your father's pain—you know it kills him to walk around with his ankles like wood, but he will never say anything. I knew that he'd refuse the remedy because it's herbal and because it's 'religious,' and he wanted me to make him coffee, so—"
"Mami!"
"Maja, I know. I know! And then I think I put in too much, because he vomited. My God, yes, he vomited, violently, so violently, and kept on stopping and starting like that for something like half an hour; I was praying. I thought maybe he'd vomit out the arthritis or something, either that or die. But then he stopped and he was fine. But straightaway he was shouting at me, calling me stupid woman, what had I done, because he said he knew I had done something, and he was saying all kinds of things to me—'You think you're powerful,' he said, and then he said that I think I am a witch—"
"Chabella, it's okay, I know. It's Papi. You know he'll calm down."
She knows.

"But when will *I* calm down?" Chabella asks. She flounces into mine and Aaron's bedroom and slams the door. Beneath his covers in the sitting room, Aaron convulses at the sound and asks "Whaaaa?" then subsides.

I tidy up Mami's papers and wait.

I do not wait long. Dressed in her pajamas now, Chabella opens the door a little way and murmurs, "Sing for me please?"

I start to hum, and to speak tunefully to myself, the way I do when I'm climbing into song. I am nervous because it's been a few days and the most terrifying thing for someone whose vocal cords are strung for both song and speech would be to reach into the dark between one and the other for melody and find nothing. I find it.

It's the five-year-old Maja that brings jazz into me, blocking my chest so that I have to sing it out. I turn my Cuba over in my mind: a myriad of saltwater noons whirring around the inside of Vedado; a drinking glass stained camel-colour. I remember paper plates fuzzed with fruitcake crumbs, livid seizures of multicoloured ribbon and being swung, squealing, dizzy, from arm to arm along a line of much older boys at someone's *quinceañera*. I struggled away when people cried on me as we were leaving from José Martí.

At the height of the Cuban summer, the heat came down from the sky differently from anywhere else I've been, came down with a passion for me, for every pore of my uncovered skin. I carefully extract my only complete memory that is longer than my life somehow
(God gave a loaf to every bird
But just a Crumb to me
I dare not eat it——though I starve)

I remember a tiny, veiled woman appeared beneath the palm trees at the bottom of the garden of a house in Vedado. Our going-away party. It was full moon, white paper moon; the glass lanterns on the tables cast shadowed orange crescents onto the grass. I peered out from beneath the high table, an earthy hinterland where I and another girl with a soft, ruddy face were sitting and eating papaya in the centre of a polished starfish of adult feet. There was a stir as someone else noticed that woman at the end of the garden, the woman who was not one of us. People began asking who she was. And then she began to sing to us out of the falling night. We couldn't understand her words—she mixed Spanish with another language that no one there knew—but the first notes felled me the way lightning brings down trees without explanation or permission.

The girl who was under the table with me began to suffer a fit— her eyes whirled blind, she slurped and dribbled and winced as she bit her tongue over and over. One of her hands drummed at the side of her head as if trying desperately to dislodge something. I noticed her only distantly. To avoid her slapping me by accident, I moved away, closer to the warm grass outside and the song. I didn't think to tell anyone about the other girl's fit. It was only when the woman had finished singing and slipped away under cover of the grown-ups' applause that the girl's mother discovered her under the table and carried her away.

My Cuba is a hut with a tabletop for a roof, wall-less and un-moored by strange music and feet and fruit juice. So of course my singing is nothing like Billie's speech from amidst the pieces of her heart, and it doesn't imitate Ella's pure tone; my noise doesn't sound anywhere near as good as they do because I am not really singing. No one knows that but me. Peace. When I rework my Cuba I allow myself to notice that, just to the right of me, Papi's tuxedoed knees are shaking. I understand what I didn't understand then, that he didn't see a path beyond leaving forever, that the country had been ripped up from under him and handed to an "everyone" far above. And that it was scary, scary to free-fall the way that he knew he was about to, with all chains cut, no land behind him and no solid ground before him.

"Mami, I was thinking of becoming a postulant, you know," I say, after a silence. But I say it in a joking way, as if Chabella is supposed to laugh. She does.

"Well, if Aaron isn't making you happy, there are other men, you know . . . you don't have to become a nun . . . anyway, what's wrong with Aaron?"

She yawns, and goes to bed.

If I'd begun in the right way I might have been able to tell her why I ran away to St. Catherine's. But I think about the two tiny, jewel-eyed girls who used to walk with me in my sleep, and I feel nauseated. It's like telling Mami about my son will bring bad luck. If I say anything it'll bring back the potions and the night vigils.

Miss Lassiter's telephone is ringing—she has it on a loud setting so that it soaks through the separating floors like a tremulous wave.

THREE

UNTO THE LITTLE

Aaron holds tube and lift doors open for people if he's nearest, crumpling his newspaper against the hard edges as if he can stop gravity with paper. While waiting at bus stops he pulls faces at children in front of their parents. His smile has corners and a slant that no one else's has. With no way of knowing whether I can trust him, I go on what I have to go on in the dark—when he touches me, there's no describing the snow-blister craziness, seething quiet but large, waiting. When he whispers in my ear, I buckle under him. When we are walking, he reaches for me carelessly, holds me carefully, dips his hand into my pocket and holds it there so that I end up pulling him along. Or, his fingers hover over the nape of my neck, absentmindedly tapping me to the pattern of my pulse, rubbing circles that make me dizzy. The whole time he talks, describes things as if we are on a clock face

("Ugly baby in pram at twelve o'clock . . . Maja . . . I didn't know a baby could be so ugly . . . you have to look . . . but don't be blatant . . .")

as if he doesn't feel his effect on me, as if I have no effect on him, or my effect on him is spent. I think he lives by Lewis Carroll rules: his foremost to yelp before a needle pricks him, just to get the yelping over with.

I don't know why I can't tell him about my son, our son.

Aaron was the "hang king" at his school, which means that he has a bizarre strength that seems to live chiefly in his upper arms. One afternoon we went to the jungle gym and he hung, long body perfectly vertical, from the second-highest bar on the climbing frame, dreamily sweeping the ground with his trainers, while I sat with his camera on my lap and let it watch while we talked. He hung, muscles crackling in knotty forks throughout his arms, for a full ten minutes. He talked the entire time. I kept asking him if he was okay; he said—gravely, calmly, kissably—yes. He asked me which of the X-Men I'd be. I said "Rogue," and he groaned and said, "Too, too obvious."

I asked him what it had been like going to school in Ghana; he said, "It was okay."

I tilted the camera upward; sun burst off the lens and into his eyes.

"Ouch."

"Sorry. So. Aaron—what was it like going to school in Ghana, being white and everything?" I said it formally, in what I hoped was documentary style.

He said, "In Accra it was okay. People didn't really fuck with each other the way I've heard about over here; initiations and ganging up and stuff. I mean, people would wrestle or whatever, but . . ."

He faltered, but I didn't prompt him. From the angle at which the camera caught him, he was harsh—his face was formed from sharp, variant planes.

"What's weird is that it took another white guy to bring some crap in. He started in on me a week after he transferred, as if he had some kind of chip on his shoulder. I think his parents were colonial throwbacks who couldn't bear to leave Ghana or something, and he couldn't believe that my mum had set up the school. He kept talking about it and it wasn't relevant. My mum didn't teach. She owned the place, but she just ran administration. She could probably have stopped me from getting expelled, but that was it. Anyway one time I was sitting in the library with this screen between me and Geoffrey, and I was doing some maths or something, and this boy comes in and sits with Geoffrey and starts joshing with him in a fake hearty way that he must have picked up from his old school, and this boy was like, 'Aaron, yeah, he's all right; a bit Jewish, though.' I swear, English people—the way some of them can be sometimes. A certain type of English twat is a certain type of English twat even if he grew up somewhere else—the kind that pretends he doesn't notice differences when really he notices, and he does care, and he does think about it.

"Geoffrey didn't even know what this boy was talking about, so he looked at me; this whole thing was so blatant that anyone sitting where Geoffrey and this boy were sitting could see the top of my head. Geoffrey laughed because he's polite that way and he has this thing where he never lets a person know that he's not interested in what they're saying, and Geoffrey said, 'So?' And the guy says, in this incredibly joking way, 'Oh, he's a bit stingy, a bit of a hoarder, isn't it, Levy?' and he laughed this booming hearty laugh, which Geoffrey didn't get. Because he hadn't made that connection between Jewish and stingy yet. I was the only Jewish guy he knew and I don't even talk about it and I'm not even . . . I mean, it's just my dad who's Jewish, and not even religiously. I don't even . . . anyway so when the guy involved me in his crappy joke it was like, either I fight this guy or I laugh. I laughed."

"Oh."

I let out my breath, disappointed, but trying not to let Aaron see. He saw. He grimaced, dropped off the bars, stretched, then came and sat beside me on the bench, turning the camera off with an easy click.

He said, "Yeah, but . . ." and he draped himself over the other end of the bench, miles away from me. "The thing is I was so pissed off; so pissed off I can't explain, and it got worse because I had to act like I didn't even remember what he said. And after a month it was so bad I couldn't look this boy in the face without feeling myself slipping, like maybe I'd head-butt him or something. So one night he went swimming with some of the others and I went through his things and took all his money. I took, I mean, literally everything, including his small change. Then I went into town and flushed some of the money down various café toilets, and I kept some of it.

"Then . . . well, he was desperate for some money and he wouldn't be seeing his parents for another two weeks, and none of the teachers could find out who'd jacked him, and blah blah. So I lent him his own money and charged him thirty percent interest. Just to take some of that bitterness out of me. And when he tried to argue with me about the interest, I laughed, and I wanted him to know about me, so I said, 'Well, it's money. And I'm just too fucking Jewish about money, you know.' He couldn't prove a thing. He didn't say anything anyway, so maybe he didn't get it. He probably didn't even remember that he'd been talking crap about me. I don't know why I was so pissed off. It was excessive; that reaction was excessive. I should have just punched him in the face instead of creeping around plotting."

(Like some kind of girl.)

"Stop analysing yourself," I said. "It was a prank. You did what you had to do in order to calm down."

Aaron didn't answer me. Stealing from someone as a substitution for laying their head open with a hammer does not count as a prank.

I switched the camera on again, and we watched Aaron, the camera and I, until he loosened his palms and let his hands lie on the bench between us.

I'm to pick up Tomás from sports-day practice, so I cross the road to wait for a bus. Cars thread past the traffic lights like an outpour of lost buttons.

Concealed beneath yards of dilapidated denim, my brother has hard-muscled calves, near-elastic knees that can hew a scissor bend, heels that are separated from his toes by a lofty arch that is never firm on the ground. It is easy to forget the Tomás who howls and throws punches at the air as soon as his quicksilver sprint releases him. Because almost everywhere else, careful thought creases his face like a dark orchid opening its petals.

When he was six, I was fourteen, and I wanted to be thin, so I learnt to live for a while on the smells of things—orange zest, wheat-bobbled crusts of bread. I licked ice and the cold lay on my tongue the same way that food might. When Chabella showed me recent pictures of my dimpled, glossy-haired cousins in Habana Vieja who were the same age as me, I rejoiced. Because, yes, they might have lighter skin than me and be hailed *"Chica caliente!"* and they might always have boys hanging around on the stretch of street outside the houses they lived in, but I was really more beautiful (thinner)

than them.

I became expert at guiding Tomás, who muttered weak protestations in his rumbling baby-bear voice, away from his colouring books and upstairs so that I could dress him in my old clothes. He was small for his age. Papi still calls him *el enano*, the dwarf, even though he stands taller than all of us now. But back then my brother was swamped in my clothes—the bottoms of my jeans dragged after him like double wedding trains.

One day I poured my Holy Communion dress over him and cajoled him to take a few steps, and he tried, tottered and was catapulted to the ground in a felled tarpaulin of white beads and satin. I laughed myself dizzy. I went to help him up; he lay completely still, his face buried beneath the dress's sequinned sweetheart collar. He was so lean I could hardly find his body to pick him up and set him aright; he didn't even have a little child's potbelly. Tomás's body was drawn together, hunched, as if the holding space allotted by his skin was too cramped and bones and breath couldn't coexist. I thought, my god, to be so narrow, to be nothing more than a thought. He had no contour; it was straight down with him, sculpted bone that made muffled clatter against the fingertips, straight down from shoulders to thighs. I didn't believe that this boy would ever grow. I wished that this was my body, my simple cage. I pushed the dress three-quarters of the way up and clasped both hands around his thigh with a ring of room to spare, and I stared and stared. Material rustled, and Tomás's head emerged from out of the dress's neck. He lay still, encased in my dress and my hands. In his gaze I came to know that something was not right in this kind of play.

Through the park's trees a race has begun, and I squint short-sightedly, trying to differentiate Tomás from the other two tall, short-haired black boys lashing the ground with trainer-clad feet. I spot him as I wend my way through the rows of low metal benches, stepping over seats. On the track, Tomás is second, arms pumping, neck muscles straining as he tries to get near the boy ahead of him. But the boy in front, his face laced on one side with a frothy comma of white paint, is leaping far, far ahead like a blank signal, so un-reachable that only Tomás and he actually finish—near the finish line, the third boy curses, kicks off his shoes so that they fly wide, and jogs disconsolately off the track.

Two girls are sitting near me; their hair is in ponytails and they're wearing the claret-coloured uniform of my old school. One is a West African girl, the other vaguely Jamaican-looking with that chill cast of the lips. They cheer and smile and wave their school scarves. They call out, "Tomás! Tomás!" and I smile at them.

"Do you know him?" the shorter of the two calls to me. She's the West African girl, pretty, snub-nosed, and wide-eyed, and I hope that if she has a crush on Tomás he is paying her some kind of attention. I nod encouragingly at her, tell her that he's my brother, and check the track where Tomás and the white-faced boy are standing with their hands on their hips, puffing and stretching and listening to their PE teacher. Then the white-faced boy vaults over the barrier between the benches and the track and jogs toward us—he is Tomás, and I should wear my glasses more often. With the face paint, though, Tomás is different. The eye set in the white is cold and black and bright to excess, as if it contains him. He sits down between me and the girl, grins at the questions I'm wearing on my face, kisses my cheek. He licks his finger and draws it down his own cheek. Paint peels off like icing chipped with a knife. "It's edible paint," he says. "Vanilla."

"And why is it on your face?"

He shrugs. The girl beside him wraps her scarf around his neck and unconvincingly garottes him. He has taken to shaving a forward slash into his eyebrow, and I think I would like that in any male but my younger brother. Under his vest, the skin around his shoulder blade is swollen with a shiny purplish tinge. I touch it; it's still tender. Tomás pulls away and gets up to leave. Once we're out of the girls' sight he swerves and asks me what I'm doing here.

"Chabella wants you—"

"I know. I heard her fussing last night."

"She asked me to come and pick you up—"

"Just in case I got lost on the way to your flat, isn't it?"

"Was that sarcasm?"

"Nooooo," he says, pulling his rucksack straps tighter on his shoulders. His stance tells me nothing.

I follow behind him and ask, "Was *that* sarcasm?"

Nothing, so I say, "You were so fast today. I didn't even know you could run that fast. What's up, Speedy Gonzales?"

He doesn't look around, but he takes a handkerchief from his pocket, wets it with his tongue and starts wiping off the face paint with even, practiced dabs.

"So, that short girl's pretty," I try. "Is she your girlfriend?"

"No, man!"

"Ex-girlfriend?"

"No, man!"

I see the problem. "Why don't you just ask her out? I think she likes you."

He doesn't say anything until we get to the bus stop. He looks blankly at the bus timetable, then at me. "Do you think so?"

I try to keep a straight face. "Think what?"

He looks hopelessly circumspect. Girls are wearying him already.

"That she, you know, likes me or whatever."

"Yes, man."

On the top deck of the bus, he sits beside me and leans on me so that his elbow digs slightly into my side; he corners me with thermal weight.

"What happened to your shoulder?" I ask.

Tomás clears his throat, squeaks unintentionally, pulls a face because his voice is breaking and he can no longer trust it.

I say again, "Your arm?"

"There's this boy in my class whose dad is Colombian or something. He's such a dickhead. Truly. If you met him, you would straightaway think 'What a dickhead.' It's something about the way he talks, the way he walks, his big walnut-shaped head—"

"You hate him," I say. I am laughing.

"No, he's a good goalie. I just think he's a dickhead. His name is Jorge Ruiz-Cole."

"Jorge Ruiz-Cole," I repeat, obediently. "What did Jorge Ruiz-Cole do?"

He replies on a long, low whistle, trying to strain his voice deep.

"Well, he thinks he knows everything about Cubans, right, because his dad's from Colombia or whatever, so he keeps asking me things, like about food and our family in Cuba and stuff like that, and I usually don't answer him, so yesterday he asks me how come my surname doesn't come in two parts, like why don't I have two parts to my surname instead of just having my father's surname. And I didn't answer him. But he started pushing me and saying come on, come on, why are you so quiet, what, are you a bastard, is it your mother's name? So I said, okay, it's because we're black Cubans, and it's not the same as white Cubans you know, because at first in my mother's family and my father's family kids had the same surname because both their parents were slaves in the same household and had the same surname, their owners' surname. You can't have the children called Luis Fernandez-Fernandez or Luis Carrera-Carrera, so they had to work it out so that only the fathers' surname got passed down, right? That's what I told him. And when I said it, all the others started booing Jorge Ruiz-Cole and telling him to leave it and saying 'Picking on a slave's son! You knew that, you fat bastard!' Because this guy Jorge is actually quite fat."

I put a finger over the hairless stroke in Tomás's eyebrow, filling in his gap.

"Then what happened?"

Tomás pinches me, not to hurt, just as a reflex to my touching him. "He got angry," he says, slowly. "Really angry. Because I think he was trying to make them laugh, but they were all on my side, because we'd watched *Roots* in history last week. So he was all pissed off, and he punched me in the face."

"Your face looks fine."

"I know. He's shit at punching. So I punched him in the face, and then it was a fight." He sighed.

"And?"

"And then some of his friends came in."

"Came in where?"

"Into the fight. It wasn't personal, it was just, like, they were getting into the whole fighting thing."

I stare at him. "And *your* friends?"

Tomás stretches, looks around me and out of the window.

"*¡Esos bastardos pequeños!* No one stuck up for you? Not one of them?"

"It's . . . just school," he says.

"It's meant to be a Catholic school!"

We both think about that. We both dismiss it as a redundant factor.

He says, "Don't tell Papi or Chabella."

Tomás came home after his first day at secondary school and said he wasn't going back. He said it standing up very straight by the kitchen table, as if he were making a formal report. Tomás was talking fact. Mami and Papi looked at each other; they had been prepared for the boy to say this.

(I had said the same kind of thing after my first day at secondary school: "Please don't make me go anymore, please, please, please or I promise you I will die of school! *¡Moriré!* And then you'll see.")

Papi went to a boys' school too. He told Tomás to approach school using game theory; identify an aim (to survive) and two key strategies to minimise losses. He had to work out who were the strongest players and count himself as a weak player until he could make enough alliances to consider himself safe.

Mami bit her lip. She had a pupil to tutor in half an hour, but she promised Tomás that afterward she would make him the best *pasteles* he'd ever had and they would talk. Tomás stood there with the strap of his schoolbag unravelling around his hand and he shook his head, meaning no, there would be no debate on the matter.

Chabella said, "Tomás, come now. Is it the other boys?"

Tomás said something, but we couldn't understand him because his teeth were clattering so loudly against each other. Papi sat and looked at Tomás; he looked and looked, his gaze became abstracted somehow. Tomás put his hand to his forehead, hid his eyes, but he stayed where he was until Papi told him, "Say that again?"

Tomás managed, "It's so cold there." Papi got up and checked Tomás's face, held Tomás to him in a rough bear hug that Tomás struggled against. Contact was gaylord.

Mami said again, "Is it the other boys?"

Papi said, "Don't you hear him? He's cold."

He ran Tomás a hot bath, made him undress and get into it.

Tomás sat in the bath with steam rising off him in blinding waves. He shivered and said, "Can't get warm."

He kept his school scarf on, looped around his neck like a boa constrictor. He wrapped his arms around himself and jolted in silence; with each shiver he almost fell out of the bath. It was like the cold had jammed itself deep into his bones and was climbing back up atop a pneumatic drill. It was only September. In the bathroom we debated Tomás's sanity, even though there wasn't really room for all of us in there. Chabella cradled his head and chanted prayers and wondered aloud, "Has someone cursed the London baby? Someone is sending him strong memories of Cuban weather so that he cannot bear it here."

Papi said, "How is it that neither of these children have inherited my excellent nervous system?"

I shouted Papi down, "What, what?" and Chabella said, "Your nervous system, your nervous system indeed." She cupped her hands around Tomás's ear and blew gently, gently, warm air into his mind. Tomás's eyes fluttered closed and he sighed, but he still trembled.

Papi shook his head impatiently and said, "Chabella, that's enough. It's obvious that he's in some kind of shock. Though why school should send him into shock and none of the other boys, God only knows. What the boy needs is to restart his circulation."

His voice was so fierce it made Chabella stand away to let him by. Papi sat on the edge of the bath, reached into the water and closed his fingers around Tomás's ankle. Tomás flinched, panicked and yelled, "No, get off!"

Papi said, "Nonsense. I'm your father." He ran his palm along

Tomás's right foot, then his left, over and over, circle shapes, star shapes. Papi tickled Tomás's soles, pinched his calves, rubbed the muscles there. He watched Tomás relax and lie back in the water, shoulders pillowed on soapy bubbles. Chabella closed the door then, and she didn't ask Tomás about the other boys anymore. She sent him back to school with sweet tea and extra scarves. My brother came home with an empty flask and a report: the day had been warmer.

....

In Aya's Cuba, before before, a trick of silence rippled over the bleached façade of La Regla house as soon as a stranger's voice was heard. The house teetered amongst sun-frayed baobab branches, a spoilt child proudly cradled in a multitude of arms, oblivious to danger. Yemaya, much younger then, played the way that she preferred to, hiding-and-seeking another pretend Yemaya amongst hill-size tree roots.

But a red-eyed visitor, he caught Aya. He had scars on both cheeks; they hissed the name of his tribe. He seized Aya by the arm and shook her. He was so much bigger than her that his long finger and thumb encircled her wrist and left room. Under the crisp sweep of his hat brim, he snarled his face away until it was gone into a puckered muzzle.

Aya

(thought, he wants to kill me)

didn't know how to appease such hate—it wasn't that she was too young; it was that there was too much.

"At first I thought you were one of them," he said. "But you're just a child."

Around the man's neck hung a locket of size, it clunked against his chest with its mouth open and a glossy white woman smiled out. Brown hair, pink cheeks. This visitor thought the glossy woman was something to do with Mama. Aya stared; was it true?

"Anyway," the red-eyed visitor said, "I must have something for my pains."

He had been drinking palm wine; she smelt it. It was his drunkenness that made him try to steal her from her home, it was folly that made him lift her and throw her over his shoulder. Aya did not struggle—she was surprised. She just thought about herself, pinned over this man's shoulder like a sash on a costume. Her face lay against the man's sweaty back, her knees grazed his stomach. The man stank. He clamped a hand around each of her ankles to hold her still, and he began to run. He ran fast, and Aya's breath was almost tipped out of her.

Winded, she gasped, "So you like wine?"

She said, "You are lucky. I am for the thirsty ones."

She spoke faintly, but she spoke plainly. She told the man, fine, keep running, keep holding on to my legs like that. Kidnap me and you shall have all your dreams. She told this visitor that if he didn't leave go of her, he would have all the palm wine in the world to drink. Yes, she said, this I can do for you and more, but all the palm wine in the world will never be enough to kill the thirst that will draw your stomach to your throat, tight, tight and tight. How you will drink for that thirst? You will drink so much that you'll drown inside your own body, and your last breath will slide out over a dark bubble of bloodied wine.

Finally the man set her down and he shambled away, crying out.

Aya walked home. The visitor had not brought her far; they had not left the forest. The sun was setting, and creatures that she could only feel made their paths through the trees.

After him Aya waited for others who had been turned away and tried to do them the favours they had come to ask of Mama and the other elders. As long as the favours were small, Aya could do them.

One day, Mama caught Aya carefully peeling away a kneeling grandmother's cloudy-milk cataracts. She brought Aya to her bedroom, where rows and rows of her plainly cut wooden masks watched with thick smiles. The masks hung on brackets that slid through their eyeholes with lighted candles balanced on their flattened planes. The masks bled red-and-purple silk linings that made puddles where they touched the floor, but Mama stepped over them with graceful economy, drawing her wrapper up over her ankle in the same motion that she used to raise her foot. Mama sat on her tied-cane chair and put Yemaya on her knee; she smilingly accepted sticky showers of guava kisses on both cheeks, but she was not diverted. She said, "Aya. I suggest you don't do as these visitors ask. I think it is like telling lies."

But Yemaya Saramagua, she wants the visitors.

On the utmost tiptoe with leaf-strewn balcony stone, a pain burnt into each overstretched arch, Aya tells the trees, "It's not that I'm lonely." The trees stoop over the somewherehouse with their heads fused together and they do not listen and they cannot be reached. "Not that."

And the visitors come. They come with beaded collars in her favourite colours layered on their necks like second skins. They come chewing on her name; confident like teeth cracking kola nuts; sure as sure, bitterness bursts and loses its way under the sallow pinch of salt.

Once, a bad woman came.

She came in through the London door and found her way up the basement stairs with so little noise that Aya was startled. The woman was deep yellow and slightly built. An ivory comb with a whorled oval head crawled up her frizzy heap of hair. Someone had made this bad woman come here. She was not willing and she wore no beads; she had broken them because she was afraid. Her shoulders were a bad fit; the tops of them stood higher than was correct, and they gave her the appearance of constantly trying to achieve flight. For healing she had brought her poorly only son, a wan stick-boy of twelve who she was slowly sickening with pinches of ground glass because she hated him, because she loved him, and he would not obey her or stay by her side when he was well. The woman, on her knees beside her son,

(who met the floor of the somewherehouse without question or effort—it was only then that Aya realized that the previous acts of standing and walking had made no sense to him)
murmured meek pleas.

The boy, slumped at the other end of his mother's arm, did not understand what was happening to him, now or before. When Aya lifted her veil and the boy saw her face, he mewled in panic, coughed. Then, to the stirring of a great tenderness in Aya, the boy mastered himself in ashen silence the way he thought a brave somebody should.

Aya healed him.

She led the boy toward the bath, down the wayward third-floor hallway, which threw itself off into a triangular corner after a few narrow and uncertain yards. Aya took the sick boy past the closed door beyond which the Kayodes sang. She held her arms around the boy's shoulders to keep him from stumbling and bent close to him to ask his name, but the boy's eyelids slammed shut at the sound of the Kayodes' singing. His face suffered an unconsciously repeated twitch.

Aya pitied the boy less.

She sent a drop of her vanilla essence to the bottom of the deep bath, then rocked back, easy, easy on her heels; the bath steam knotted as her vanilla stung it, the bath steam drank weight and was left tangible.

She stroked a wisp of it and it stayed intact, moved with her, curled under and around her hand. Air had to be taken in the tiniest sniffs.

The sick boy sat and watched her. The sick boy blinked and said nothing. Aya left him to undress and wash. Then she went downstairs and stared at the mother until the woman bent low with her fingers welded into pincers to support her head. When the son came down alone, there was life in his eyes again. He trembled in his clothes and reached for his mother, who clawed him up into her arms.

And Aya didn't warn the son about the mother's food.

FOUR

HENRY S. FOOTE

Amy Eleni's hands. At first I was scared to let her wash my hair because I thought it would be too difficult for her. But really my hair is simple—once it is washed and fed with coconut oil, it sighs and falls asleep. And nobody washes my hair like Amy Eleni used to. Aaron is too gentle; he gets scared the minute he touches my scalp. But Amy Eleni puts one soft hand on my forehead and, with her other hand, rakes slippery fingers through my hair, comes back down with more air on the ends of her fingertips like seaweed fronds to breathe through underwater. But when she started seeing Sara, Sara insisted that she and Amy Eleni wash each other's hair exclusively.

Sara was an art history student and she looked like a storybook pixie. She had a pointed nose and quirky eyebrows and there was always the slightest hint of glitter near her mouth. She would take half a lace curtain and a ribbon and tie it around herself over jeans and say, "Yeah, it's a top." Apparently that was charming. Either way, the glass bottle of foamy aloe in Amy Eleni's cabinet disappeared and was replaced with some shampoo with fruit and silk extracts, stuff that would break my simple curls in half.

The shampoo was the first thing to go when Sara broke up with Amy Eleni. But I couldn't rejoice; the breakup was too bad for that. Sara had decided to do her postgraduate degree outside London ("----------Uni," Sara carefully drew dashes instead of a place-name, as if worried that Amy Eleni might stalk her down there) and it was over in a note.

We found the note just as we were about to watch *Vertigo* again. The viewing was a celebration; Amy Eleni had been living in her new flat for only a week. She sighed and chewed her thumbnail when she read it. She looked as if she was at the counter in a café, trying to decide what to have.

To me, she said, "Don't worry; I'm not going to cry all over you."

The Sara-shampoo went out in a black binbag; we watched *Vertigo*, ate baklava and sneered at Sara's glitter-mole. Amy Eleni was fine.

But later in the evening she couldn't mark the essays she had to mark, because her right hand felt broken. Amy Eleni laid her hand on her notebook and we both looked at the hand very carefully. I straightened out her fingers and let them curl them up again; they were limp but strangely tough, like peeled prawns. Amy Eleni didn't say anything while I stretched her fingers, but her whole body said "Don't."

I asked, "Where exactly does it hurt?"

Amy Eleni looked at me with eyes so honest that I couldn't look back and found a spot on her temple to look at instead. She laid her head against my arm and said, "It's the whole hand. I smell the broken bone. Can't you? The smell, like potted beef. Get a knife and cut out the broken bone, cut it right out—this you can do. I don't mind as I have another hand."

That note. Sara shouldn't have done it. If she knew Amy Eleni at all she would know that Amy Eleni's hysteric punches walls inside. I told Amy Eleni I'd mark the essays. She just had to come back together enough to tell me what marks she wanted me to give. Amy Eleni sat up straight and frowned and said, with dangerous civility, "I told you a knife please; a rotten egg spoils the world."

I got her aspirin, bandaged her hand, and put her to bed with the weak promise of a knife later. She didn't believe me. She turned her back on me. She lay there as quiet as church.

I stayed up for a long time, marking essays on Amy Eleni's sofa, trying to work out what Amy Eleni would have thought of each pupil's answer to the question "Why did Hamlet delay his revenge?"

I let Tomás into the flat, and we find Chabella trying to make Aaron's video camera work—she is pressing and wrenching at the boxed slot that holds the camera battery, and that makes me nervous, so I take it away from her. She says, "You know I looked in the cupboard. All that ground cassava, all that rice. I bet you eat it plain. You eat too much colourless food, do you know that? If you're not careful, when you have a child it will be an albino; yes, laugh, go on, but I don't babysit albinos . . ."

I give her Tomás; he allows himself to be enveloped in Chabella and her patchouli and ylang-ylang scent. He answers all her questions and lets her sit on his lap and be his tiny Mami. He agrees to be cooked for. I know that Chabella finds Tomás easier. The Tomás Project has a clearer direction: Bring the boy out of himself! Make sure he's not hungry! Make sure he understands that he is handsome! But don't let him think he's too handsome! And Chabella must also make sure that Tomás does his homework. Papi is too trusting with Tomás's homework; he waves his hand and says, "The dwarf will get it done sooner or later."

Tomás starts his maths at the kitchen table, clearing away my song sheets and gummy food wrappers without comment. Chabella, dicing yellow squash on the chopping board, announces that she wants to spring-clean the flat.

"Mami, no, we like it like this," I tell her.

"I will ask Aaron," Mami replies, hacking steadfastly at an old carrot. I wince; it looks as if she's slicing up a knobbly orange finger. "He will agree with me."

He probably will.

"He'll go straight to sleep when he gets back anyway," I say, jangling my keys in my hand.

"Is that what happens? He goes to work, comes back, goes to sleep? Last night you didn't even let him get into the bed. *He-ye-ye*, the way these young women are caring for their men . . ."

Tomás gets up from the table and disappears into the sitting room. From inside the sound system, Prince Nico Mbargo's electric guitarist lets loose a miracle riff and the Prince shouts his mother's name. *"Ah! SUSAN! Presenting you with . . . Sweet Mother!"* Tomás one-two-steps into the kitchen and to Chabella's delight, into her outstretched arms. He mouths, *"Sweet mother I no go forget you."*

Chabella, laughing and beautiful, cradles Tomás's head and kisses the tip of his nose and opens her arms a little wider for me, and even though I am supposed to be on my way to see Papi, I throw my arms around them both.

I didn't know how many cycles of egg donation Amy Eleni had gone through before she told me. At some point I noticed that she was wearing her sleeves excessively long. And I feared the hysteric, (of course I forever fear the hysteric)
she who no longer manifests herself in screaming and fainting and clinging to walls but gets modern and hides herself in a numbness of the skin that demands cutting. There was no way to find out without making a fuss, so I just watched Amy Eleni. We went for manicures together; I reached out and snatched up her sleeve, quickly, let it fall back quickly. She was amused, but I had seen yellowing puncture marks, fastidiously spaced bruises fading back into her skin tone. The manicurist asked me if I could just keep my hands still for a minute.

I mouthed, "What are you shooting up on?" I tried to put on an expression that said I knew something about shooting up on drugs.

Amy Eleni said, "For heaven's sake."

Afterward we went walking through Regent's Park, through sunlight and sprays of raw green. Amy Eleni handed me information sheet after information sheet from her bag. They were crumpled, studded with thumbprints, as paper gets when you carry it everywhere. Even a passport must get like that if you take it out to look at it often enough. Lots of thank-yous, lots of details, lots of drug names, advice: *Expect bloating as you produce more than one egg per cycle; make sure you have comfortable clothes with elastic waistbands.*

All I could say, all I could think, was, "You're selling your *eggs?*"

Amy Eleni turned very white; either I was making her angry or she was about to throw up. "I'm not selling them, all right? The clinic pays expenses, but they're not allowed to pay donors for the eggs."

I nodded. I said, "That's . . . wow. I could never do something like that. Giving infertile couples a baby and stuff. That's . . ."

(You're giving your eggs away, just right out from inside you like that?)

"I don't mind clinics."

I tried to make Amy Eleni sit down on a bench with me, but she kept walking, fast, almost at a jog. I barely managed to keep up with her.

"You remember when I was going out with Sara? Well, when I told my mum about her, my mum just gave me this look, like . . . ugh. I don't know. That look. It was kind of disgusted and kind of resigned. As if she'd eaten something that she knew she wasn't going to like and she was thinking, 'Yeah, nasty, but I knew it.' Then the first thing she said was, 'So you think you're a lesbian. But what are you going to do with your fertility? You're just going to waste your fertility like that?' And I didn't have an answer for her. I had answers for almost everything else, like if she started crying and saying she raised me wrong, then I could have given her a stupid hug or something. Or if she tried to send me to church, we could have had it out. But she didn't even seem to give a shit. It was like, Oh, my daughter, the lesbian, the waste of time."

I put my hand on Amy Eleni's arm, to make her slow down, and, also, to be touching her.

———

The Elegua head on the coat stand is pitching forward a little.
Papi must have tried to take it down. I set it aright,
(something rattles inside its hollow)
I am careful and lift my hands away as soon as it is safe. The Elegua
head has a clammy feel, like wet clay, or skin beginning to perspire.

I find Papi on the sitting-room sofa, crumpled and bemused in
the same white shirt and brown trousers Chabella and I left him in,
and I know that he has slept the night there facing the pale bubble of
wallpaper left in the wake of Mami's altar. The bedrooms are upstairs, and with no one around to pretend full health to, Papi has not
bothered to attempt the stairs. He blinks at me sadly. "Maja," he says.
"*No es justo.*"

I throw myself down beside him and put an arm around his neck
to nuzzle him just beneath his earlobe, where his jawbone begins;
that's a part of him that has never changed, and with my eyes closed
I imagine him as a much younger man, surprised, thinking, *Who is
this girl near me, older than me and younger?* I imagine him unable to understand what it is to have a grown daughter.

"I know it's not fair. But just think, Mami hasn't given you
trouble like this before."

"So what?" Papi retorts. "When trouble comes, you don't sit
around thinking, Oh, but at least I haven't had trouble before. The
point is that you forget all other times. That's what's so bad about
trouble, that's what makes it trouble—you can't see your way
around it.

"When I met her, *Dios mío*, such a woman. You could see . . .
good, just good, all soul—she was studying German but she also
went to lectures that had nothing to do with German. Like my lec-

tures. If you knew someone like that you'd call them a boffin or nerd or geek or neek or something, wouldn't you? You think it's so wonderful not to know anything. But your mami, she came up to me with a copy of my book on the Cuban conquistadors and a list of questions. And she just listened to me with her face like someone who has not lived and is trying to begin.

"You, Maja, you wonder why the people who have to teach you never like you; it's because you sit there looking at them as if you don't believe a word they're saying. That parents' evening when you sat beside me and yawned while your history teacher was praising your mock exam results. If I had been your teacher, at that moment I would have taken a big red pen and drawn a line through the results and said, 'My mistake, she failed. Her problem is a lack of interest.' You are lucky that you have been educated in a country where you're supposed to act uninterested. You're very lucky that you've been educated in a country where it is not necessary to get out. Imagine if the only way you could have a good life was to learn your books! Would you yawn then? No, indeed, you would grin and say, Thank you Mr. Englishman, please tell me how I may continue to improve."

"I yawned because I was tired! I have manners," I protest. "Anyway, Mami—"

"Chabella," said Papi, "would never in a million years have yawned. In fact she was too focussed. She looked at me and I spoke rubbish. She was . . . I mean . . . all of those years I spent building my intellect and here comes this woman and throws it all away. Why did she have to wait until I'm retired and settled and, and . . . *satisfecho de mi mismo* before poisoning me?"

We study each other. I know that he forgave Chabella approximately two seconds after he realised what had happened.

"How is your body now?" I ask.

Papi nods, waves me off, fumbles down the back of the sofa and pulls out a pouch of Cohiba cigars. He lights one with a match. Chabella is desperate to know where Papi hides his cigars so that she can throw them away and save his life, but he changes his hiding place every week or so.

Papi used to smoke pipes. Ages ago Amy Eleni and I smoked his pipes too, when he and Chabella were out; we stuck our heads out of my bedroom window to send away the clotted scent of apple tobacco. We wore chequered flat caps and grumbled about immigrants while we smoked. "Bloody Africans, Pakis, bloody Cubans, soap dodgers," Amy Eleni muttered in a maniacally off-kilter Cockney accent. "Send 'em away, or they'll have the whip hand over us, mate. There'll be rivers of mud. Yeah, that's right, that's what I said, rivers of mud. You cut one of those darkies and you'll see; they bleed stinkin' river water."

For my part, I puffed out smoke spirals and said in sly reference, "Damned Cypriots. Dark as sin, what. Wrong colour, aren't they. Taking our jobs and marrying our gentlemen. They didn't fight any of our battles, what." It was 1987—in Poplar, people were still calling out things like "Soap dodger!" in the streets.

"Are you hungry?" I ask Papi. I have brought some leftovers in plastic tubs, and I point to the bag of them at my feet, but Papi shakes his head.

"I could cook something else," I tell him, standing. With a simple touch to my forearm, Papi brings me back down beside him.

"So she's really serious about this altar," he says.

"*Pero por supuesto*—but of course, Papi."

"Because you know how you Cuban women can be sometimes. *Dramático, siempre el drama*." He gingerly flexes his hands, examines his inflamed finger joints.

I say, "No, she's . . . it's real."

"But I need to think about this. If I have that thing moved back here, it is like saying that it's okay that she is going to consult with these people, these poor, ill people who are looking for something that has meaning and don't know what it is they're looking for and call it Santeria. As for my wife being one of them, it makes me think, *What is it that she wants that I haven't given her?*"

Papi wouldn't be asking me this if I were Tomás. I am slow to reply because if I am to be Mami's voice in this argument I need to think of what she'd say, and I don't know.

Papi shifts the cigar to the other side of his mouth and says, "Santeria is a garbled religion. So it draws on Catholicism, and it draws on Yoruba religion. It's like throwing a rosary in the air and saying it's magic because it fell from a slave's hand. Suffering isn't transformative."

I say, "True, but that doesn't mean that suffering can't be religious."

He doesn't hear me.

"I mean, Maja, these gods or whatever, these beliefs don't transcend time and space; they stretch them unnecessarily, stretch the geography of the world like an elastic band. And you can't do that. You can't erase borders and stride over Spanish into Yoruba like that. You can only pretend that you have."

I would hate to be in a lecture of his and ask him a question. He just doesn't hear you. He closes his eyes, sucks in smoke, streams it out, just breathes and breathes. The Holy Child of Atocha is looking him full in the face; the *aguardiente* dish has evaporated. The Holy Child of Atocha is staring at Papi and Papi does not care.

"I'm going to bring the altar back downstairs," I tell him. "And then we can fix whatever parts of it are broken."

Papi reaches for his ashtray, knocks ash off his Cohiba without opening his eyes.

"Papi?"

"Yes, Maja, let's do that," he says finally, in quiet, good-humoured obedience. As I go upstairs, he calls, "Please bring some air freshener down."

I stop in the doorway of Tomás's bedroom, unwilling to test the borders of his wild order of Cuban flags and Union Jacks and WWF relics. They jostle with collaged images of Rogue and Wolverine from Marvel's X-Men.

Tomás has a teddy bear now; it sits on his pillow, by his head. The bear has one clubfoot and one normal foot. He is a production line reject; his fur is too black, as dark as despair must be. The bear's name is Henry S. Foote. Amy Eleni found him in a charity shop last month. A few days before her discovery, she, Tomás and I had watched a TV programme about the American Civil War.

The presenter mentioned, very briefly, a Mississippi senator called Henry S. Foote who got so het up about the question of the South's secession from the North that, right in the middle of the Congress building, he threatened the Congressman next to him with a loaded revolver. The presenter was just talking about how feelings were running high in the mid-nineteenth century, and Henry S. Foote only came up for a second, Henry S. Foote was only an example he was using. But because of Tomás, we ended up talking about Henry S. Foote for the rest of the programme.

Tomás was upset by him. He kept saying, "What was Henry S. Foote carrying that gun around for?"

I said, "Maybe he just really wanted to keep his slaves or whatever."

Amy Eleni offered the opinion that politics were different in those days. Or that Henry S. Foote was toying with the idea of killing himself. I suggested that Henry S. Foote had gout and was irritable. Together Amy Eleni and I proffered a theory that Henry S. Foote suffered from undiagnosed paranoid schizophrenia and had this compulsion to protect himself with terminal intensity. Or that Henry S. Foote was so rabidly anti-abolition because he had black ancestors and was terrified that someone might find out.

Tomás didn't accept anything we said. He said, "No, Henry S. Foote was fucked up."

Chabella popped out of nowhere and nearly chewed Tomás's ear off about his language. Then, while clothes shopping, Amy Eleni saw the bear. She brought the ugly thing over to the house, pointed at the clubfoot and raised her eyebrows at Tomás, who immediately remembered and said, "Henry S. Foote." Then they both nodded, as if something was confirmed.

Tubes of face paint form a deliberate circle on Tomás's dresser. His paintbrushes are gelled stiff and white.

Next door is my old room, where Mami's altar stands concertinaed on unsteady legs against my wardrobe. I touch the altar and rickety bells ring from somewhere inside. My room is exactly the same as it was when I was still at university; completely and obsessively black and white. Mami has not allowed any changes, and she has not allowed any of Tomás's friends to sleep in my bed for fear of bad luck. The black ceiling was laboriously painted, with Amy Eleni's unquestioning help, over a long weekend. The floorboards are white, but the rug is black and so are the bedcovers. The wardrobe is white, the bookshelves are white, and every book on them is covered in black paper and laminate.

I did all of this at the end of my first year of an English literature degree, when note-taking had worn me down and I realised how I hated books and would kill the spirit of all novels if that power was mine. I believed that God must and would in his mercy kill me rather than let me survive the summer and start the next term. I didn't think about switching courses; I didn't want to. Papi is not so badly wrong when he says of Cuban women, "*Siempre el dramático.*"

Papi and Tomás were at the library when I took out a pot of black paint and started for my bedroom windows. But Mami had been lurking and watching me and had decided, Not in my house. She ran into the room to wrestle me for the paintpot, shouting, "*¡Loca, tu está loca!*"

At the foot of the altar, Papi has set down debris removed from his and Mami's bedroom—a framed picture of the Holy Child of Atocha, smaller than the one on the sitting-room wall, and Mami's silk-lined, gold-painted incense box. I open the box to make sure that her Santeria beads—devotional chains in Elegua's colours—are still there; they lie intact at the bottom of the case, beneath a bed of folded rice-paper flowers. The collar is a rope of heavy black and red, strands of beads coiled like a sated snake. I close the box and catch Brigitte's photo in the act of fluttering from altar to floor, return it to its place beside the photo of my *bisabuela*.

Brigitte, expert escapee. Brigitte got out of East Germany, got out of Cuba, left Chabella behind. Brigitte is a white-gold blaze, and it's not just that the photo of her was developed badly. Her platinum-blond bob flicks over her face and half hides her sharp smile. A brown hand is on Brigitte's shoulder, but Chabella has cut the rest of herself out of that picture because it is the only one that she has of Brigitte. Mami remembers that maybe it was a problem with her Spanish, or maybe it was the thin drama of her red-lipsticked mouth, but Brigitte spoke and smiled with a great deal of tension. She measured out her murmur as if she didn't have much time to say what she needed to say, but understood the importance of clarity. When she said, "Please . . . I need some more soap," it was an event.

Abuela Laline didn't understand or trust Brigitte's knife-edge stability. But Chabella did. Of Brigitte, Chabella has said, "People like Brigitte are made for guarding the world from harm. They stay in a room with whatever is bad and they hold the door closed from the inside."

Laline spoke stiffly to Brigitte, always formal. Laline had to tolerate Brigitte because Brigitte was her husband's guest. I suggested that maybe Abuela Laline didn't like Brigitte because she thought that Abuelo Damason was carrying on another affair right under her nose. Chabella shook her head. She said, "No, everyone could see it wasn't like that with them. Brigitte was . . . I mean, the way she looked at my papi, the way she spoke to him it was man-to-man. Yes, she was clever, but my mami was very clever too, and yet when she met eyes with my papi her cleverness didn't stop her will from sort of stepping back. So I don't know what it was with Brigitte. When I say 'man-to-man' I don't mean that Papi and Brigitte sat up smoking and drinking together or anything. Because she was . . . I mean you never saw her without lipstick, you never smelt her, you only smelt perfume. She re-dyed her hair as soon as a little darkness came through at the roots. When she arrived, she couldn't even lift her own suitcase out of Papi's car; I had to do it because your aunts and your *abuela* had gone into hiding upstairs so that they could watch Brigitte from the windows. But my papi kept saying to her, 'When you came toward me at the train station, more than anything else I wondered whether I would be able to beat you in a fight.' "

Brigitte didn't laugh or seem annoyed when Chabella kept asking her her age; she just calmly gave my mami variations on the theme of: "As you can see, I'm much older than you, *nicht wahr?*"

To fifteen-year-old Mami, Brigitte maintained—in "take it or leave it" tones—that she had been shot by a jealous boyfriend while at university.

"I don't want you to make any generalisations about German men," she said, "but every single German man that I have been involved with has been too . . . obvious. This boyfriend, I knew he was a very jealous man, and I knew that he thought you have rights to something as long as you want it more than anyone else. On top of all this he believed that the largest acts speak in a new and transcendent tongue. And so yes, very boringly, when I wanted to leave him he did try something—a large and wilful act."

Chabella rebuked her, "*Ai* Brigitte, he shot you, you know! How can you say 'boringly'?"

Abuelo Damason brought Brigitte home because he was good friends with someone in Santa Clara who cared about her. The someone was a man who knew she needed to get across into America before he could breathe out and believe that all was well with her. But Brigitte needed some time before she would try to leave from José Martí Airport; she shared Chabella's bedroom for five months. Brigitte swished around in tweed skirts with flipped hems, nylons with black diamond seams, and open-toed pumps, and she let Chabella use her makeup without asking. Without saying a word, Brigitte managed to convince Chabella and her papi that Chabella should have stopped wearing kneesocks and strapped shoes at thirteen. Brigitte needed it to be completely dark when she slept. She didn't like to wake up all at once, so she wore a black eye-mask at night and had grown expert at finding her way around without taking it off. Chabella grew used to seeing her flitting about the house with only the light pressure of her right hand on the wall to show her uncertainty.

Brigitte called Chabella *moquenquen*, made her the universal child just as their housemaid Maria did. *Moquenquen* said in Brigitte's accent sounded cold at first, almost sarcastic. When Chabella tied on her white headscarf to go to Santeria mass, Brigitte didn't ask her where she was going but said, "Please, say a prayer for me. I, too, like to fight on every level. I am also the type to throw coins into wishing wells."

Brigitte and Chabella would lie wounded by the heat on their bedroom floor some noontimes listening to Elvis Presley, then to The Platters with the volume turned low. Brigitte's understanding of English was far better than Chabella's, but she still refused to divulge which of the songs told the truth about love. She gave Chabella copies of *Das Kapital* and *The Communist Manifesto*. Chabella still has the books; they are in German and were cherished, but not by Chabella. The books' pages sprout hairlike shreds, rubbed bald by a finger running underneath each line again and again.

Brigitte said of the books, "Isabella, such thoughts! But . . . what had been made of them . . . ah. *Zerrissen*. I am . . . *estoy en el conflicto*."

Often in her first month at my *abuelo* Damason's house, when Brigitte couldn't find the Spanish for what she was thinking, she would fall to repeating the German word instead and very seriously miming its meaning with her long, smooth arms, which she shaved so that the dark hairs wouldn't show. Mami squeaked "What, what?" and made desperate guesses. But the more Brigitte mimed, the less Chabella understood, and they made their own comedies. Brigitte's would constantly try to reach for those words most difficult for a foreigner to remember.

Brigitte was afraid that every place in the world was the site of a murder. She was afraid of Fidel because, above all, he asked for the people's affection, and she didn't see how justice could live alongside affection. She tried to describe a regime of love: lovers get jealous; they are petty and impetuous; they give you stupid gifts that you cannot use. When things become desperate, lovers may stalk you, and ultimately, if they saw a way to, they would tap your phone. So, love into hate.

Brigitte refused to show Chabella the bullet wound she'd been given by her jealous boyfriend. Instead she narrowed her eyes, hovered a finger above the soft bend of Chabella's elbow and said, "There." She stabbed down into the air just above the spot and clicked her tongue against the roof of her mouth. The pain of it crashed through all Chabella's joints.

Brigitte was a *Republiksflüchtling*. She came to Chabella and Habana at the same time as there was a feeling of imminent change, a sense that the world had set an alarm and the trees and buildings and sky would tell the time before the people could. Nobody could give a date, but people gossiped and did not trust the stoic face of Habana, the mud-glued potholes and dull, scrolled balconies. Things would change completely—but when?

Chabella imagined that roof tiling would slip westward like birds chasing warm weather do, the clouds would let down a white drinking straw and someone above would suck up all the harbour water like it was *ron*. The trees would shake down a new kind of water, leaves as liquid sacrifice.

Brigitte's escape circumstances were privileged, but for Chabella and my grandparents, Brigitte was evidence of a hushed statistic of the time. She presented herself to the Montoyas as one of those East German citizens—one in every six—who managed to flee the country before the Wall went up. Brigitte was both lucky and clever; her parents had been longtime members of the Communist Party and had kept on believing even when Hitler and National Socialism had put them in danger. But when Germany was divided between the power blocs, police and Soviet tanks crushed the grass roots, the workers who demonstrated and raided food factories because they had already given of themselves according to their ability but were still hungry.

Brigitte heard about it on the radio but she had already known it in her head and the knowledge translated into a great silence inside. In her views she was careful to toe the party line, and she took her well-chosen degree in political philosophy with its emphasis on Marxism. And she used that degree to disappear with permission. Brigitte took Spanish classes and bent her thoughts toward Cuba, since Cuba was close to America and America was not Communist or Fascist or anything too strongly other than rich.

The temporary teaching post that Brigitte obtained at the University of Santa Clara was justified by the "rising levels of interest in political philosophy amongst students," but really it was small-scale antagonism against the fading Batista dictatorship. Brigitte's post was intended by the faculty to help foster links between one nation on the path to Utopia and another. After a week's classes, she finally did what her heart was telling her to do and disappeared.

Then, when Brigitte needed money, my *abuelo* Damason said to her, "I'll pay you to teach my daughters German. The German language is poetic—that is to say it is both vague and precise. Perhaps once my girls have learnt German they will all become men and go and fight for freedom and frustrated dreams."

Apparently this grandfather of mine had a way of talking that made him sound as if he was never entirely sincere. Brigitte's lips thinned.

Even after Abuelo Damason had managed to convince her that he had not been mocking her country's role in the war, Brigitte still refused to teach his daughters German. My *tía* Dayame refused to learn German. Tía Pilar refused to learn German, and so did my *tía* Caridad. They all said the same thing, "What's the point of learning German?" but each of them had different reasons. The sisters were not close.

"German is the language of ideas," my *abuelo* repeated, in an attempt to persuade Brigitte and his daughters.

"But not of reality," Brigitte said, and she was sad. Chabella took up Brigitte's copy of *Der Struwwelpeter* and started reading aloud Heinrich Hoffmann's dire warning to bad children. Her beginner's accent was jaw-dropping—Chabella can still muster that accent now. When she puts it on she sounds like an adenoidal man might if he were morphing into a frog. Brigitte looked at her blankly. Brigitte said, "Do you have any idea of the meaning of those words?"

Chabella looked at an illustration; a giant in yellow trousers was dipping two squirming boys headfirst into a cauldron of ink. She said, "Not exactly."

Brigitte said calmly, "You'll sound better if you elongate your vowels when you see those two little dots—they're called umlauts." And so Chabella's first German lesson began.

That is the collection of things Chabella and I have decided about Brigitte. She is the only nonsaintly white face in Chabella's candlelit display. Brigitte bought her place in Chabella's altar with the gold-dust scarcity in Habana of red leather pumps. Brigitte put a pair under Chabella's pillow the morning she finally left for America. And Chabella didn't even find the pumps until she hid her face in the pillow to cry because she missed Brigitte. Brigitte had known that she would do that. When she left Chabella at the front door, Brigitte didn't hug my mami, but she touched her fingers to her own red lips and said, "This is a kiss." Chabella felt it the same as the gunshot. *"Esto es un beso, moquenquen, dies ist ein Kuss,"* and then no word from Brigitte again.

Not long after she left, Batista left too—he fled Cuba. The change that everyone had promised and threatened came, and it came in the form of a military junta, which meant that uniformed men toted guns and smiled celebratory peace and did not fire in places where they could be heard. Chabella didn't break her routine of stumbling into the one pothole on her street that was her particular bane.

When Mami speaks German she becomes wise. Glad crinkles frame her lips and eyes. *Weltschmerzen, Dasein, Sitz im Leben,* and so, and so, from web of thought to web of thought she departs from images and describes things unseen.

I walk back to Aaron's with my Walkman switched on. My favourite song is sung slowly, blues about a woman who is alone and still and doesn't understand that she doesn't like it that way. But because the woman is patient and because she has perfect hair and because she enchants her clothes with French perfume, she sometimes gets a visit from her man, and then, oh. Then the song is poison in your ear, music to seal you in. Because when her visitor comes, the shadow song begins. Nobody should have reason to cry the way someone is crying inside this song, not alone. Nobody should have it inside them to climb just that note and keep ascending, they couldn't, not even if they were crazy.

The song woman who curls her hair, she is white, I think. The singing woman, the one who makes me know that the song woman curls her hair, she is black, her voice is whiskey dark. The scream in this song is bigger than either of them and it's both of them doing it, both of them telling on each other until it seems that they fuse into one face and the piano player and his gentle backing notes are playing themselves out from a dangerous position on the screamer's nose. But the piano player doesn't fall into the mouth, of course. Screaming doesn't do anything.

I rewind and replay as I walk down streets and into walls of cloth and skin and people and "excuse me"s and late-afternoon confusions of pavement and sky.

Once, when I was listening to this song at the bus stop, out of the corner of my eye I saw a woman staring at me, I saw a woman lift her hand to touch me, and when I looked at her properly, it was Chabella. I pushed the headphones down and she smiled uncertainly and said, "I almost didn't recognise you. But after all I thought, No, that girl looks like me."

Another time when I arrived at band rehearsal listening to this favourite song of mine, I lifted off my earphones gingerly and cupped my hands to my ears, expecting blood.

One day in Habana, the day that would end in Nochebuena,
(the good night, Christmas Eve)
Yemaya, in love with Cuba, went walking in La Regla, repeating
after the Columbus in her mind's eye, "This is the most beautiful
land I have ever seen."

The day was hot but gentle; beneath its healing steam lay granite,
decrepit wood, rocks gloved in blanched sand. The harbour water
caught sunlight in layered hoops of petrol-coloured dirt and tried to
keep its clarity secret, but the divers told. Small, earth-brown boys
kept bobbing up, their backbones hacking out of their skin, hair
plastered to their heads, coin pouches around their waists rattling as
they added new handfuls of slick bronze to their store.

Aya gathered up her seven skirts—blue lacing silver lacing more
blue—and raced herself. She ran past irregularly spaced palm trees
looming with their tops drying out. She ran past a woman clothed in a
swarm of toddlers; the woman cooked corncobs on a charcoal-heated
griddle with her skirt hitched up around her knees. With her other
hand, she kept her children from cooking themselves on her pan.

Yemaya didn't even stop
(though she felt a pull and a fuzzy, bite-sized happiness like a kiss on
the nape of her neck)
at the small household shrine, strung and nailed to a house's doorway, that was meant for her. Ignored, Our Lady of Regla pouted
sweet and pink from a ribboned cage of sea lavender and long-
funnelled trout lilies, and cowrie shells with fluted mouths.

Aya stopped at the watchmaker's parlour—here, a man with
hair dreadlocked like a powerful man, like a *babalawo*, made watches
and clocks, squinted over tiny, intricate mechanisms with pincers
and thin magnets and hammers the size of Aya's little finger. His
clocks were not ordinary, but he sold them, at carelessly cheap
prices, out of his living room. This watchmaker, he spoke exactly
like a Cuban—but he said he was not Cuban.

Yemaya saw that, amongst old, knotted mahogany clocks with
glazed faces, new clocks peeped out. Their faces were plain,
mounted on blocklike bases with hands of beaten brass that drove
the minutes forward on their glint. Anyone who stood too close to
see the time on one of these clocks felt a wafer-thin breeze from
elsewhere, a colder place, a higher place. The watchmaker, a scatter-
ing of sawdust in his hair, waited for her at the counter with his fingers folded over some secret in his palm.

"Hold out your hand," he said, smiling. He looked at her as if he
thought her beautiful, and this was rare, and this made Yemaya trust
him. She held out both her hands, cupping them to carry away
sweetness, and he chided her, "Greedy. One hand is enough."

His gift was a loose knot of seeds. They looked like oval wood
chips, but something green slept inside them. She wondered what

a drop of her vanilla would do to them, and stowed them thoughtfully in the pocket of her top skirt before she remembered to say thank you.

Her watchmaker said, "One day, not now, they'll grow for you, and show you what it is that you most desire. Remember, won't you?"

She nodded, and he told her then that he was going home. "But you must keep those seeds safe. Another time, many years ago, I gave some seeds such as these to a woman as a gift. What this woman most wanted was children, but she was barren. When she spoke of children, I saw how much of her life these dream children had already taken. She knew so much about them, and so little about anything else. She had decided she wanted two boys and a gentle girl, the two boys to take care of the girl and keep each other company. And they would all love one another. I had some of these seeds, and—"

"Where did you get them from?" Aya asked, eagerly.

With a wounded stare, the watchmaker said simply, "They are mine."

She raised her hand in apology. He continued: "I told her to plant and water them, and to wait and see. She came back to me one month later, shaking. 'Those seeds,' the woman said, 'are growing.'

"I said, 'Of course.' Her face—

"She said, 'Children. Children are growing from the seeds.'

"I said, 'Of course.' Then I asked her—because she wanted me to ask—what kind of children? But she shook her head. She just shook her head. She couldn't explain. How many are there? Three. Just as many as she'd wanted. I saw such fear in her . . . she asked me what to do, then answered herself. She would leave them buried, her children; maybe that way they would die before they could properly draw breath. A cruel thing—I told her so. But she kept saying, 'It is better this way. It is better this way.' "

The watchmaker stopped speaking—Aya saw that he was lost. She pressed his hand.

"What kind of children are better left buried?" he asked her.

She tried to guess the end of his tale, the moral of it. "Did you dig the children up?"

He did not.

"Did she take pity?"

"She dug them up in their ninth month, and they fled her. They must have known that she never wanted them to draw breath. Children know, and when they know . . . it is terrible."

"They fled her? How do you know?"

The watchmaker gagged, gaped, put his hand over his mouth, then seemed to recover himself and pretended to wipe dust from his face. "I saw them."

Aya's vanilla didn't make the watchmaker's seeds grow, and neither did plain water. When she dug up the seeds and pocketed them, she wondered whether it was because she didn't yet know what she wanted.

....

Dominique and I were good friends until we lost interest in each other. We had only really been friends because she lived two doors away. Then she moved, and nothing. Chabella was disappointed in us both: "You're black girls, as good as sisters!"

Chabella made me phone Dominique a couple of times. I wasn't allowed to mention that I had phoned against my will. Dominique phoned me a couple of times as well. It was excruciating for us both, and then we were allowed to stop. Even after I stopped, it was awkward for a little bit.

Dominique was in my class from primary school right up until we left sixth form for university. Either I had never looked at her properly, or her face receded beneath the swathes of her hair until I forgot it. Dominique is from Trinidad, and she had beautiful hair, soft and thick, which her mother, like mine, banned her from straightening and helped her comb out into a fan. People teased her about it all the time and called her "picky head." Dominique took the name calmly, without offering any insults of her own, which I couldn't understand. But then some people give off a strange sense of preoccupation, as if there is something in their lives so important to them that they have to keep it silent, and close. And to keep this thing close, they make sacrifices.

Of course, Mami loved Dominique's hair. And she loved Dominique, who ate everything Mami served at dinner with genuine relish. Dominique tried to teach me some of her sunny, rolling patois. I couldn't pick it up, but I offered to teach her Spanish. She said, "No thanks."

Dominique's mum, Cedelka, was a cleaner; she became good friends with Chabella, and her stories about the everyday filthiness of the people she cleaned for racked Mami with guilt. Their conversations always ended with Cedelka assuring Chabella that Chabella worked just as hard as she did, taking care of her family and doing "all that language stuff," and Chabella rhapsodising on Cedelka's natural wisdom.

Cedelka wore dreadlocks and she was all soulful eyes and beautiful lips. When I played or ate dinner at Dominique's, or when Cedelka came to collect Dominique from my house, she would reveal an instinct for freezing gracefully, a way of turning her face to the light when she stepped outside.

I always knew when Chabella had been talking to Dominique's mum because she would start to mutter, "I don't work hard enough, I'm not useful, all this paper and scribbling, making me soft." Chabella would take out her sponges and scrubbers and bleach and get on her hands and knees to clean the kitchen and bathroom from corner to corner. Papi didn't like that. He especially hated it if I helped her, which I did to stop her from crying. "I don't want to see my wife scrubbing away like that," he would say. "I write textbooks! Chabella, use a mop, or we'll get a cleaner. And please, my daughter is not your assistant. Maja, go and have a bath and read a book or something."

"Get a *cleaner*! And you just equated this hypothetical cleaning woman with a mop!" Chabella's eyes filled with tears.

Papi kissed her, sweat and soapsuds and all. "I was joking. Forget it."

He didn't know that mostly the cleaning was fun once we'd started; it was only the idea of it that made me sigh and drag my feet. We were never very thorough and it was more like play-acting, down on the floor with soapy rags and cleaner rags on our heads as we mimed to the Supremes and the Drifters and Melanie Safka's "Brand New Key."

Cedelka said to me, half jokingly, "Please don't try and teach my daughter Spanish! Black people ain't meant to speak Spanish!"

"Black people ain't meant to speak English, neither, then. Or French Creole," I said, using exactly the same tone.

Cedelka swatted at my head. "You must get that big brain from your big-brain parents."

I remembered what Cedelka said when I was in year nine, when the most popular girls in my and Amy Eleni's form were those with African parents; girls with perfectly straightened hair and mellow gospel voices that changed the sound of the sung school Mass; girls who had—or pretended to have—Igbo, Ewe, Yoruba, Chiga, Ganda, Swahili. They built a kind of slang that was composed of slightly anglicized words borrowed from their pool of languages. The code sounded impossibly cool if you had the right turn of the tongue for it, which I didn't, although some of the white girls did. Lucy, who started up the slang, was Ugandan; she had a pretty heart-shaped face and rabidly intent method of marking her netball opponent.

At school a lot of the other girls brought flags out on their countries' independence days. With permission from the teachers, they tied them around their upper arms or waists and tied their hair up with ribbons in their flags' colours. On Nigerian Independence Day, one girl did a special assembly on her country and passed around an overwhelming amount of fried Nigerian snacks. Amy Eleni and I were at the back. Amy Eleni put her hand up and said, "Can I just ask you what you think of this idea: if your parents taught you to be so proud of Nigeria, how come they're over here?"

The girl stammered and fiddled with her tie-dyed head wrap. People started hissing disagreement with Amy Eleni. Amy Eleni and I hissed back. Isn't living in your country the best way to show that you think it worthy of love? You choose to live in a country because there's something there that makes it better than anywhere else. You set your daily life down regardless of the restrictive conditions. It's the same sort of the thing Clarence talks about in *True Romance*—he says real love is remaining loyal when it's easier, even excusable, not to.

The talk about Nigerian independence continued. Amy Eleni sighed and wrote a long note in small letters on her hand. The note was so long that she had to take my hand to write on, too, and we could only read her note to me by placing our biro-splotched palms alongside each other. The note said:

> *You know what, if you want to talk about your original country, if you want to be serious about it, fine. But you don't need to pretend that you love the place. People need to stop using love of some country that they don't live in as an excuse for their inability to shut up about it.*

We kept the note on our hands all day, smiling enigmatically and turning our hands palms-down when other girls wheedled, "Let me see."

Dominique was at home sick the day Lucy came up to me at registration, peeped at me through heavy lashes and said, "You know, a lot of the others have been saying that out of you and Dominique, we like you better. You're all right. You're roots."

I must have seemed stupid to her. I said, "Huh?" I thought a black girl was a black girl. Why did it come down to a choice between me and Dominique and not any of the other girls? Then I got it; we were both black without coming from the right place. We were the slave girls from Trinidad and Cuba; not supposed to speak Spanish, not supposed to speak English either. I wanted to curse Lucy Cuban-style, but I was afraid she'd understand; she was predicted an A-star for GCSE Spanish.

Tonight I am singing a set at a café whose poetry-night theme is "Solitude." They've asked me to start with my three least-favourite songs: "In my Solitude," "Black Coffee" and "Misty Blue." When the band's leader, Michael, called to tell me about it last week, he anticipated my response, chanting "Oh, whine, whine, whine," along with me. "Don't worry about it—next week it's Ronnie Scott's, with our own songs . . ."

I hastily assemble my things so that they're in the general vicinity of the full-length bedroom mirror—makeup bag, a selection of black stiletto heels, armfuls of dresses on hangers, hair tongs tangled in their own plug lead, sheer tights that are to the best of my knowledge unladdered. Aaron's side of our dresser is analytically tidy: a small city of glass-bottled gift colognes and sable-backed hairbrushes, mostly unused, alongside a depleted bundle of the tough, dried-wood chewing sticks he swears by—my teeth ache just looking at them. The only things on his bedside table are a water glass and a photograph of him and his best friend at age ten. In the picture Geoffrey is cola dark, with astonishing, vinelike sideburns. Aaron is defiantly pale and chubby-cheeked; his hair is slicked into some attempt at a Jheri curl. They both have carelessly gappy smiles; they stand together in a heaving Accra side street swept with umber dust, against a battered blue backdrop that says PEPSICO.

I have yet to meet Geoffrey, who still lives in Accra. But the fact that Aaron always refers to him as "Geoffrey," never "Geoff" or "G," makes me think of him as diffident and kind and slightly stuffy. A boy who felt the pressure of being a cabinet minister's son and tried his best to behave himself, growing up into the kind of man who rolls his English around in his mouth as plummily as he can.

I strip to my underwear and I study myself in the mirror; it is a bronzed sorrel woman with a net of curly hair who looks back, and she does not look Jamaican or Ghanaian or Kenyan or Sudanese—the only firm thing that is sure is that she is black. Mami says only Cubans look like Cubans; put three Cuban girls together—white, black, Latina, whatever—and you just see it. It is as if you could take away my colouring and I would be a white Cubana—a white Cubana not being after all, particularly white.

My eyes are long rather than wide, meagrely lashed and slanted unhurriedly upward at their corners. In my blood is a bright chain of transfusion, Spaniards, West Africans, indigenous Cubans, even the

Turkos: the Cuban Lebanese. My shape is that of a slightly distorted heavy pear; slender, Chabella-like shoulders and a gently rising collarbone cast lines that soften and swell past a high waist to what Amy Eleni and I refer to as "loot in the boot"—hips that escape spread fingerspans—then the line returns.

I prod my thigh and, standing on one leg, run my hand down my calf. I sink to the floor, sink to the middle of this slew of things that are supposed to tease out, bejewel, enhance, improve on what I have. I coat my hands with cocoa butter and slowly, slowly start to reconcile myself with my skin, inch by inch. I am scared to touch my stomach, not because it is tender but because it has begun to swell beyond the point where it can be comfortably rubbed with one hand. If I cup it with both hands the bump might rise to the space I allow it.

When Amy Eleni calls I am fiddling, trying to adjust the V-neck of my black dress so that it falls away from my shoulders and skims the arms left bare by my sleeveless polo neck.

"Hey, Maja. I'm coming to hear you sing tonight after all," she says.

"Good. How's Jenny?"

"I don't know; we broke up."

"Oh?"

"That's all you're getting on the phone. What of Aaron?"

"He's . . . tired a lot, and out a lot."

"Can I place the first bet on when he's going to pack the trainee-doctor thing in?"

"Come on, Amy Eleni."

"No, *you* come on. It's not like him to work. His dad is like, *ker-ching.*"

Before I can tell her off, she asks, "What's tonight's theme?"

"Of makeup, or the café?"

"Both—"

I tell her: makeup, purple; café, solitude.

"*Solitude?*"

Amy Eleni teaches A-level English language and literature; she has nothing but murder in her heart for amateur poets. She keeps telling me that most of them don't read anyone's poetry but their own, and that's why they always think they're doing something new, and why it's always so appallingly not. I keep telling her that the people in her class are seventeen and eighteen and that she should give them a break. I remind her of her own amateur poetry at seventeen and eighteen and am told, "Shut up! My poetry was never amateur!"

I hold my tights up to the light. They are laddered after all, and I have to hang up and look for another pair. Mami slips into the room with good-luck kisses for me and an opalescent white gardenia on a coiled green stalk. Before I can thank her she starts jabbing at my polo neck.

"What is this? Why are you wearing this? That's such a lovely dress, and you're spoiling it—"

I am just trying to protect my throat. Before I realise what I'm doing I have taken her hands and pushed them back at her hard, too hard; she stumbles and laughs, astonished. I catch myself and take the flower from her.

"Chabella," I say. "I can't wear this . . ."

Mami throws up her hands in the air. "Your brother chose it. I *told* him it was ugly."

Tomás, a pencil behind his ear, comes to look at me. "What's wrong with it? Billie Holiday used to wear one, didn't she? I thought you liked her. Are you off her now?"

I try to put the corsage box back into Mami's hand, but she skips away, giggling.

"It's just that, you know, she's . . . I can't explain. She's . . . well, it's just not right to wear her flower. And this is not a big-deal occasion. Even if it was a big-deal occasion, it still wouldn't be right to wear her *flower*."

Tomás rolls his eyes and withdraws. Mami, stamps her foot. "Am I a bad mother?" she demands.

"Chabella."

"I said, am I a bad mother? Didn't I always tell you how beautiful you are and what a good singer you are? Who is Billie Holiday, anyway?"

"Mami! She's—"

"Yes, I know. Anyway you're better at singing than she is. She just growls. And you're better-looking too, even if you spoil your dresses with strange tops. So put that flower on."

I turn to the mirror and comb my hair into an upsweep so that I can clasp it, but Chabella dives at me with the gardenia and fixes it at the back of my head with a hair clip. She puts her hands on my shoulders, her face a little behind mine, and looks at us in the mirror. We smile.

"When are you going to make up with Papi?" I ask. I have to ask while her gaze is on me.

"Is my altar back yet?" she asks. It is not a rhetorical question; she is not being stubborn, she looks so hopeful. And that's worse. I close my eyes because I had not expected to be grasped by this feeling of steam and anger, like a new player in a game where someone has suddenly changed the rules.

The wood-panelled café is low-lit and arranged like a fifties speakeasy with tables ranged in concentric circles around a make-shift stage with a microphone stand. Chabella's pretty hair is driven back with minuscule black pins so that it tickles her shoulders from high up, like a long feather. She clasps her hands and looks around, enraptured.

"They'll have a spotlight on you, and you'll look like a princess, except for that purple lipstick," she tells me.

Having blown Amy Eleni kisses and pointed out to Chabella those seats that I consider safe for her to sit in, I am the last of our band to arrive in the box room behind the café. Michael is there, tense as ever, waiting with one arm curled around his propped-up saxophone, drinking water in tight swallows that don't even wet his lips. When he sees me, he nods and smiles, but I know he's pleased to see me only because now we can start our sound check. Maxwell, dreadlocks swaying in the rush of their own weight, body bumps me, and Sophie, our tall, prettily spoken cellist, gracefully offers her cheek to be kissed. She is from Senegal, and she is, just as Maxwell—who has been trying to ask her out for six months—says, sexy like chocolate.

When we go out to warm up on the stage, I am happier than I thought I'd be, my foot tapping as Maxwell's taps, but it's always that way when I allow the song to come to me without question. Maxwell's face is serene as he drums, never airless, never strained. He beats time for himself and Sophie—and for Michael, who sways as his fingers ride his saxophone's polished stops. They are letting me take my own time, letting me fall in after them, but they know that I'm with them.

Really it's Michael's band; he cares most, he's the one who calls for all-day rehearsals, he's the one who helps us to understand where we've gone wrong when we fail to move together. I joined the band mainly because, after graduating, everyone became anxious that I should find something to do. Papi handed me weekly sheaves of job listings and told me to "start my life." Tomás said, "It's cool that you're home, but you're disturbing my growth." I kept beating him at Nintendo; he didn't like it, I knew. Chabella found me a post as an assistant librarian—one of her friends ran the local library. That roused me in a way that Papi and Tomás had been unable to. I screamed at Mami, "A books job! Chabella are you mad?"

Amy Eleni came by with some cassettes for me; Billie Holiday and Sarah Vaughan. With no real interest in the answer, I asked her how her teacher training was going. With no real interest in answering, Amy Eleni shrugged and said, "It's going." I wanted to defer the future indefinitely, and I sort of wished that Amy Eleni would too. But I listened to the cassettes. And I started singing in a way that I hadn't before, a kind of singing that made Mami and Tomás say, "Waaah, didn't know you could do that!" though Papi said nothing.

I sang to Amy Eleni. She didn't say "Waaah," but she came back with a bunch of ads put out by instrumental groups who wanted singers. I auditioned for Michael's because his was the shortest and the least demanding. He wanted someone to do standards, no particular look or age, and he'd added, "No divas."

Michael didn't seem impressed at any point during the audition, but I thought maybe he'd taken me on because he did an internal "Waaah" at my voice. When we were better friends he told me I was the only one who'd showed up for his auditions. He said, "I suppose I offended all the divas."

Standing discreetly near the back, the café's owner watches us with her fingers in her mouth—her eyes are boiling-water blue and she looks as if she might snap if she's not hearing good sounds. But I'm not ready to try my voice yet; we just test the microphones for static, and I follow the pieced strands of song that Maxwell and Sophie and Michael carelessly let swirl.

Amy Eleni, now contemplatively smoking a cigarette in a silvered holder, has seized Mami and they're both sitting behind glasses of Bacardi and Coke,

(Mami smiles a small and unforgiving smile if I ever refer to the mixture as a "Cuba Libre")

their backs to the other seats, which are filling with sprawled legs and talk. They're sitting at the table that stands directly beneath my gaze. Amy Eleni is wearing purple-tinted shades. Chabella waves and smiles at me; I shake my head sorrowfully at Chabella because this is not one of the tables I told her she could sit at. Amy Eleni is wearing a black hat identical to mine over her smooth, shiny blond bob. She is swathed from top to toe in black but for her red stilettos; her feet jiggle with impatience under the table.

I am certain that Amy Eleni's students fear her. It's not just that her expression constantly suggests that she's about to say something extremely harsh. She wears mirrored sunglasses indoors as often as she can get away with it, walks with her shoulders, and snaps her fingers when things aren't happening fast enough for her. But she doesn't look like a woman at all; she has all the angular, callous, radiant and uncompromising beauty of a girl who has only just grown into her body and barely has an understanding of what has happened. Her eyes are bright and keen and worrying.

When we were seventeen, she told me that she was gay. I was nonplussed; I kept expecting her to say "jokes." I thought she hadn't had boyfriends and never confessed to crushes because she had yet to meet a boy brave enough to take her on. I asked her if she was sure, because I hadn't noticed any struggle inside her, any extra-special looks levelled at girls, or any of the things that lesbians were supposed to do. Amy Eleni was resolutely nontactile—in our school, friendship was intricately tied in with touch; girls pinged each other's bra straps and poked each other's bellies and crowed "puppy fat!" and flicked their skinnier friends in the taut bands between their ribs. That was affection. Amy Eleni dispensed winks and air kisses. That was distance.

I pointed out Amy Eleni's no-touching thing as one of the factors that made her not gay. She winced, laughed. "It just means that I don't feel like running around grabbing people. It just means I'm sane," she said.

When I told Chabella, she left her wooden spoon in the stew she was stirring, closed her eyes tight and asked me in a near-whisper, "Are you gay as well?"

"I don't think so, Chabella."

"All right, because don't think I don't know that you've been kissing as many boys as you can."

I halfheartedly denied that, but Mami waved me off.

"I am very sorry to hear that Amy Eleni is gay. Her life will be harder than yours, you know."

Chabella gave me a topsy-turvy stone amulet on a piece of clean rope and told me to give it to Amy Eleni. I did, and Amy Eleni said coldly, "What is this, something to make me straight?"

I told her no. That wasn't Mami's style.

"You're not going to ask me who my first crush was?" Amy Eleni asked me. She was playing with Chabella's amulet. I hastily said, "No, no." Amy Eleni looked at me then, with a soft, auroral reproach that made my heart flip over and made me ashamed of myself and my arrogance and made me want to promise her something that I couldn't and made me think that I'd gone down in her estimation—all these things at once.

Mami had not always liked Amy Eleni; when she became the second girl after Dominique that I bothered to bring home for dinner, Mami was tense that entire first evening. The table was quiet whenever Amy Eleni lifted her fork to her mouth, and Chabella leant forward a little, as if she wanted to snatch the food out of Amy Eleni's jaws, as if she didn't think Amy Eleni should ever know what a good Cuban stew tasted like. Amy Eleni suspected as much, and to me she seemed more polite than I had ever seen her. Throughout the meal she said "Delicious," in varying tones and volumes. With a grin that admitted that she would listen but not understand, Amy Eleni asked Papi about his work, and she told Tomás all that she could remember about the glory days of the WWF. But when Amy Eleni went home, Chabella stopped me as I was going to bed and said sorrowfully, "You'll learn that the white girl is never your friend. She works to a different system. She only pretends to understand."

I said, "And what about Brigitte?"

Mami said, "Brigitte was my teacher. You know that."

The café is full now; shadow-spotted faces encircle me. I close my eyes, and my Cuba comes, and the band is with me and then it lets me go and I am free.

One morning Mami came downstairs wrapped in nothing but a cloth of preternatural white, with strands of her hair swimming around her face, strands of her hair tied with little flags of white cloth. Strips of soft skin showed here and there, where the cloth gaped and made mouths around her shoulder blades, parted in protest at being trussed so tight around her breasts. Because she was pregnant with Tomás, Tomás became part of the outfit too: it was he that made the cloth coast out in front of her and around her; it was he that made the white flow. Papi got up and ran, actually ran, for a camera. Chabella watched him go, and as Papi passed her he caught her hand and twirled her like a giggling top.

Me, I looked up from my Saturday morning cartoons and I gaped. I was eight; if I had been older I would have been able to admire Mami. I would have been able to apprehend Mami's white-sheet thing as a "look," the way people assess high-fashion catwalks and shut down their instinct to flee so they don't feel anymore how terrifying and elemental the shapes and colours are, the fact that people are walking around with cones on their heads and jewellery like chain mail, rouged violently right up to their foreheads, looking like the devil.

Anyway, my mami looked wild, wilder than animals. She was not made to live in a house or even on the plains, but in the atmosphere. Chabella turned off the TV; I didn't object. "I used to take classes in folk dance," she said, slipping a cassette into the sound system. She rewound it, took it out, fiddled with it, turned it over.

"Your *abuelo* Damason used to complain because they were expensive. But then the dance classes stopped with the Revolution because they were un-Cuban, they were too African. And it's true; I suppose El Jefe was right to be nervous that something was going on with Santeria. Something *is* going on. Those West Africans brought another country in with them, a whole other country in their heads. After dance classes stopped, you could only get to see people dance out *apataki* if you knew the roots people, the ones who didn't have any money, like dockworkers. They wouldn't teach me anything. Maybe they knew something about me that I didn't. It is hard to learn how to be black when people don't let you."

Mami pressed "play."

A drumbeat jumped up, collided with another one, and the two chased each other around and around—rhythm. Chabella laughed, gasped, held her belly against Tomás's kick. "He likes that," she said, proud. Both of us were shaking our shoulders to the rhythm. Even Papi was stamping as he steadily caught Chabella on film— click, click, click. Inside my head a group of drummers played, swaying in unison with a flourish of hands. Their drums were in their laps, small but with tough heads. The drum talk was threaded through with fast, loud *bembe* singing, Yoruba patched up with Spanish. I couldn't understand a word, but I understood that it was a story, and that the way Mami began to dance, she knew which story. Chabella was awkward at first, watching her step, trying to make a pattern, pulling faces as she touched the ground flat-footed and clumsy under the weight of Tomás. But then I saw the song come through her. It came because she didn't give up. The drums came like

Kata-kata-ka
Kata-kata-ka
KA-TA
Kata-kata-ka
Kata-kata-ka
KA-TA

Mami became Yemaya Saramagua, a sure, slow swell in her arms and her hips like water after a long thirst, her arms calling down rain, her hands making secret signs, snatching hearts.

Kata-kata-ka
Kata-kata-ka
KA-TA

Water is an unhappy eye. Alone it lives, wishing it were blind. Look into water; it will look back at you, and it will tremble. Yemaya Saramagua is her father's eye; she watches the earth for him. Her own eyes, though, are shy. Orisha of water, she could drown the world in a flood if she wanted to, but she has never been in love.

Kata-kata-ka

Oh, *now* she's in love!

Kata-kata-ka

She's in love with Ogun Arere; iron Aguanilli, handsome, strong, so cold that even in the midst of the flame he shrugs his shoulders. She shouldn't love him, but she can't help it. Come, come, Ogun Arere, come to your true love. But Ogun rejects her. Still she comes back. He would have to build a mighty dam to keep her love away.

KA-TA

The story went on. Mami stopped knowing that we were even there. Very quietly, Papi sat down.

Once the story had danced itself out, I waited for the goddess to be gone. Then, behind her back, I clapped until my hands hurt. Papi wolf-whistled. I felt winded. It was infinitely better than cartoons.

Mami didn't dance out *apataki* again, which made me think that it must have been some kind of Tomás-related thing, like a craving.

....

Aya's family is large. Each member of Aya's family has aspects, and those aspects have aspects. That is why, with only a little pain, the family could afford to separate when there was great need for them to do so. They had to scatter. When it happened, it was not so bad for Aya, as she did not love her aspects: Yemaya Ataramagwa was never still for a minute; light jumped in her hair and chased her so that she was confusing to look at. And she loved the Ogun River too well, annoying Aya by insisting every day that they two go to play there.

Yemaya Achabba was as cold and limp and quiet as a fish-scale coat.

Yemaya Oqqutte made eyes at men, and swung her hips lazily; her walk was a trail of sleepy invitation. The men and boys who came to her were the ones who did not know that they wanted to die.

Aya said goodbye to her aspects cheerfully, though they wept and said, "Do not forget us, Yemaya Saramagua."

Besides, Aya's family is a wild family. They do not need to speak to one another or eat together to know that they are family. They strike each other, curse each other, take fifty-year holidays, but, always, they love.

When Aya's family came into Cuba on a ship, they brought along with them three young ones from a Dahomey branch of the family who got confused and thought they were invited. They weren't invited, but it was too late. The Dahomeians had to stick with Aya's family, and so they discovered their Cuba in the dark, hidden in bigger emergencies, cries of warning as patrol ships tried to intercept the cargo. On arrival, communications arrived from the others; word from Haiti, from Brazil, from Jamaica, from America. Even from England there were some whispers, and then all the talk stopped. The conversations had become too strange. The family's aspects abroad had changed. It was hard to know what the difference was, but it was there. There were secrets.

When Papa left the Cuba family, he left absentmindedly, shunting a toothpick around his gums, leaving a partly spoken sentence in the air behind him. When he shut the door on his way out that day, the house trembled from roof to basement. Aya knew that Papa wasn't coming back, not to that house. Aya's mama knew it and so did all of Aya's uncles and aunts.

Mama's friend Echun, with his matted hair and his red-and-yellow-striped cap, he was disgusted at being mistaken by the Spanish for a harmless baby. The Holy Child of Atocha was rosy-cheeked and dimpled and couldn't drink as much palm wine and *aguardiente* as Echun would have liked. Echun went to Mama in her room, and all the flames wavering in the eyeholes of her masks shrank for fear of mischief being made upon them. When Echun wanted to shout, he stood up very straight and half closed his eyes. The first thing he asked Aya's mama was: "Why am I now called Elegua?" Mama had no answer.

Echun asked, "And why have those three jokers from Dahomey started to speak Spanish? Are they Spanish? Are they Cuban? I don't want to see those chattering Dahomeians. Same faces, different talk—it smells bad to me. If I could I would kill them. At least that would be a change."

Mama said only, "Echun. You always say more than you mean."

Echun embraced her before he uncorked a bottle of palm wine and swaggered out of the door. He went down to meet his friend Anansi, a recent acquaintance, a stickman with a potbelly and a beady-eyed grin. Anansi kept forgetting and calling Echun "Elegua," but that was all right as long as they were leaving.

Aya's uncle Iku laughed and clapped his hands to hear that Echun was gone—he had little love for Echun. Once, for a joke, Echun had cut Iku up and scattered him all over the universe. When Mama told Aya about this, Aya said, "Mama are you lying?"

Her mama would only say, "Yeye, what followed was the most important treasure hunt ever."

Ochun was the most beautiful of Aya's family, the one with the gentlest voice. She suffered secret agonies over the drab garb that her counterpart, Our Lady of Mercy, wore in portraits. Strangenesses came to Ochun: it seemed to her that Our Lady of Mercy came into her bedroom as the night breeze flapped her muslin curtains, and tried to throttle her while she slept. Ochun told no one of this. But she left La Regla house soon after Echun did, taking nothing but the short *bubi* she stood up in and the five bright silk scarves that crisscrossed her waist.

And the three Dahomeians, finding that no one would speak to them and that everyone disdained them, spoke amongst themselves in Spanish until they painstakingly relearned Yoruba. They were two males and a female, and there were no more of their kind since they came from a small, proud land whose borders were smudged away by time's white thumb. The Dahomeians had no aspects abroad. They had learnt Spanish because they could not afford to forget or to stop speaking, but no one could see that. No one in Aya's family, not even gentle Mama, remembered to pity the Dahomey folk. This the Dahomeians could not forgive. Once they had relearned Yoruba to their satisfaction, they left the house too.

Nobody asked after the Dahomey folk, though the family searched high and low for Ochun who did not normally leave home just like that.

Then, one night, it happened to Aya too. She tried to lie down and sleep there, in her father's house, but she couldn't lie down.

Midnight boomeranged ten thousand times in the space of a second, and night slammed shut to stop day from even beginning to point out a path to the sky's rim.

Ensoulment is never imagined as the cold terror that it is.

Snuffling, Aya packed before she knew that she'd done it.

She fled to be born. She fled to be native, to start somewhere, to grow in that same somewhere, to die there. She didn't know just then that she wasn't quickening toward home, but trusting home to find her.

Only Aya was to find the three Dahomeians. Only Aya was to discover what had become of Ochun and Echun. She found Ochun with her waistful of silk scraps, Echun with a guarded smile and drawers full of stubborn prayers. But by the time Aya found the Dahomeians, and by the time she found Ochun and Echun, she could not recognise them, and she did not know them by name. That is what aspects are like; they change.

SIX

LET NO PEBBLE SMILE

Amy Eleni said dinner at her house was stressful. We hung around in her room and ate crap most of the time, but Amy Eleni only ever invited me to dinner once. Her parents' house smells of church incense and is full of things like jade vases and brushed suede. It's the sort of place where you periodically flinch, not because anyone's raised a hand to you but because you realise that you are surrounded by objects that some would consider worth more than you.

At the dinner table, Amy Eleni's parents sat opposite us and said little. The silence wasn't unfriendly, just the kind of silence that happens when there's nothing new to say. The food was dizzying: lamb cooked in three different ways and spices; cracked wheat; meatballs; hot flatbreads. But Amy Eleni's dad was the only one who dared to eat much. The problem was Despina, Amy Eleni's mother, who sat completely still with a brocade shawl draped around her sharp shoulders and let no food pass her lips. Amy Eleni's father sopped up the quiet with one arm around the back of Despina's chair, humming more appreciatively the deeper he got into his heaped bowl. How could he eat?

Despina is so thin that you stare helplessly at her. And she knows that you can't believe it, and she drops her heavy eyelids with a smile. Despina is thin like being naked in public—you can see the beginnings of her teeth stamped in her face; you can see them through her skin when her mouth is closed. Despina is like a star, of both the fifties film and the sky varieties—untouchable, but not beautiful. She is startling in a way that really doesn't exist anymore, only still around because she is preserved, delayed. Her eyes are Amy Eleni's, but brighter. Her hair is Amy Eleni's, but lighter, under better control, pulled back into a smooth wavy fringe and ponytail. Her skin is darker, dark gold.

From across the table Despina stapled our stomachs with a tranquil gaze.

"Do please have some more of that, I see you like it," and so on.

She had a small plate in front of her that stayed completely clean throughout dinner, though she watched Amy Eleni's plate and thoughtfully sipped at water.

Pudding was caramelised pears; golden, sticky, sweet agony to smell, greater agony to discard after a couple of nervous pokings with our spoons. Amy Eleni and I didn't look at each other. In some of Chabella's *apataki*, the Orishas intervene to stop a mother from "eating her child in spirit." I wanted an Orisha to come and smite Despina so that I could get on with any caramelised pears.

After dinner, as soon as was decent, Amy Eleni and I went down to Whitechapel and got chocolate rugelaches at Rinkoffs. We sat on railings and stuffed doughy biscuit and chocolate, talking and spraying each other with food, seeing who could be the most disgusting.

I asked her if dinner was always like that, or whether it was just because I was there. Amy Eleni clutched her hair and pulled at it. "Oh, truly. I'm not mad! I'm not mad! I don't want to die!"

"There's someone inside of me, and she says I must die! *Jesus!*" I said.

"Christmas dinner is always particularly jolly at the Lang household," she said, and laughed so hard that she accidentally pushed rugelach out of her nostrils.

Once my sets are over, Chabella, Amy Eleni and I stay at the café, relocating to the farthest circle from the stage. In the darkness Amy Eleni and I snigger at the latest style of bad recital. A lot of the poems are about willow trees, and Amy Eleni and I debate back and forth over a couple of them; they are so overwrought that they've got to be po-faced comedy. Unexpectedly, Chabella likes one of them, says that that particular poet's representation of the tree manages to both promise and conceal dark things. She compares the structure to a highly condensed version of the first simple but strong poem she ever learnt in German, Goethe's "The Erlking," a poem that neither Amy Eleni nor I can remember. We shut up and drink our Cuba Libres. Someone rests a hand on my shoulder; I turn and a sweet-faced, curly-haired girl—maybe a Hispanic Cuban, maybe a girl that I should know—leans across the table to kiss Chabella, nods apologetically at Amy Eleni and crouches down beside my chair to talk to me.

"I loved your singing," she says. Before I can thank her she continues: "And I saw your mami, and your name on the program. And I remembered you."

She smiles at me, shushes Mami, daring me to guess who she is. Her accent is strong, so she is recent, and I want to help her out; I try not to sound too English when I reply, but I can't help it—she isn't family.

"I remember your face, I think," I say, hesitantly.

"I know yours," she says. "We used to play together before you left Habana. Then when you left our mothers kept swapping photos of us. In your photos you were always in jeans. We sent you a photo of me on my *quinceañera*, but I remember we didn't get one back from you because you said you didn't want a *quinceañera*; you insisted that turning fifteen was no big deal, that you didn't ask to be born. That made me laugh a lot."

I keep looking at the girl, but I still have no idea who she is; Chabella has flashed me so many photos of Cuban girls that I doubt I could even individually identify my cousins by name. I smile to buy time, but she throws her hands up and tells me I've run out of time.

"It's Magalys Pereira-Velázquez," she says, and I smile open-mouthed to show that I am glad and to hide that I still don't have a memory to put her face and her name together with. "The last time we saw each other, your parents were having a leaving party," Magalys says, and then I do remember; I remember that she was the girl from Vedado. Magalys is the girl who was under the table with me when the woman came and sang to us. Suddenly I am frightened that she will somehow remember that I didn't help her. I hold my arms around myself to hold Magalys away.

Chabella is fretting to call Tomás and make sure that he's safe and snug and asleep. I point out that if he *is* asleep she'll have to awaken him, but she holds out her hand for my phone. Her lip quivers and I lose my nerve. Seconds later she is cooing down the line at Tomás.

The only people still sprinkled around the café tables are couples or prospective couples with their voices set to murmuring and their faces close together.

Amy Eleni has to teach tomorrow, but, late as it is, she stays and smokes and is unusually low on comments, and I know then that her breakup has been hard on her. I can't stop glancing at the phone number that Magalys soft-pencilled onto a napkin before she left, but I don't want to talk to her because the memory of the leaving party is mine and she doesn't belong in it. Magalys has so much more of Cuba than I do; she proves it by walking up with her easy smile and strong accent.

The hum around us peaks and dips, and I look up to see an old, grey-haired black man, with a long face divided by an anxious smile, arms bearing a blizzard of white roses. He is inching up to us, and he is Papi, and his eyes are on Chabella.

"Okay, good night, London baby, my little dwarf. Sleep well," Chabella tells Tomás, weakly, and pushes a number of wrong buttons before ending the call, smiling at Papi, drawing him on.

I look around at everyone else, and everyone is looking at us. I am happy and embarrassed and stressed and I want to get up and help Papi, take his arm, but I know that he would hate that. So I wait in agony until he is directly before Mami and bends to kiss her cheek and say he's sorry, and then Amy Eleni stomps the ground and whoops and starts the clapping. Out of the corner of her mouth, she says to me, "What's going on?"

I tell her it's an anniversary, or a long story—I tell her that she should take her pick.

When we leave the café, Amy Eleni comes to wait for my bus with me. She looks at me for a long time, her eyes a deep green, dryadic despite the cold.

"I'm not mad, I'm not mad," she tries, a smile touching her lips. "I don't want to die."

I should do what? I should smile, or I should respond.

There's someone inside of me, and she says I must die.

But something is happening here, something that doesn't fall into good, okay, or bad. The hysteric isn't appealing to me; there is no need to beat her. I keep thinking, maybe if I could just know what my son looks like, who my son is, then I will be all right. I have strangeness in my family, a woman who was a priest when she wasn't supposed to be. I have delicacy in my family. I think. I don't know, am I delicate? I know by now that I am not going to be one of those pregnant women who touches her stomach in public; even when I am heavily pregnant I will keep my hands by my sides and keep a circumspect eye on the situation.

I tell Amy Eleni I am pregnant. I just say it. She winces, and I need to know why she did that, but immediately afterward she says, "Maja, that's wonderful. Aaron must be . . . Maja, that's . . ."

We hug; her hands dig into my shoulder blades as our heads bump. "He doesn't know," I say into her ear.

Amy Eleni's frown is full of needles; to donate eggs you are screened for

HIV

cystic fibrosis

hepatitis B

hepatitis C

cytomegalovirus

and they do a chromosomal analysis too.

All this I saw underlined in her leaflets; Dr. Maxwell screened me for them when I saw her. Amy Eleni's frown is full of test results printed on thin crackly paper with hole-punched edges. It's bloated with daily hormone injections, her frown. It goes on forever.

"What, is it not his kid or something?"

That's not really a question, so I just stare at her.

"Then tell him. Duh," she says.

As I let myself back into the flat Aaron shouts, "My mum called; she wants to have lunch with you on Saturday . . ."

I scowl at the ceiling. Aaron's mother, Rebecca, keeps saying things like, "Where are the go-getters? Where are the people who are going to make a difference?"

She doesn't sound accusing, just encouraging; she wants me to look around, then look into myself and see that the go-getter is me. Under a thatch of grey-black hair, Rebecca has Aaron's misty eyes, and she uses them to far more oppressive effect than he does. Over lunch we will not have a conversation; she will be attempting to en-list me for some cause.

In the bedroom, Aaron is kneeling by the dresser with his cam-corder trained on his head. He is parting his hair with his fingers. I pull my dress over my head, change into one of his T-shirts, hang the dress up. I refuse to ask him what he's doing. He's bare-chested and his jeans are slung low to reveal the top of his boxer shorts. He says sadly, "I'm getting old."

I go to him then, wrap my arms around him, tuck my chin over his shoulder so that I'm peeping up into the camera as well, but he wants me to inspect his hair. Mixed in with the black are minute strands of grey. I am not certain that I know what form the fear of turning into an old man takes. In my memory Papi seems always to have been grey, but always strong, never winding down his inner speed. I don't think anything of Aaron's hair, but because I have to say something I tell him I think it looks distinguished, and he groans. "It's the hospital."

Aaron switches off the camcorder. He stands to show me a bowl he's placed on a damp patch of carpet beside the mirror. Fat, sluggish drops of water fall from a discoloured part of the ceiling.

"There's a leak as well, and I can't sleep, but I've got to get up fucking early tomorrow, and I'm getting old."

"And thin. Eat!" I say, crashing onto the bed and bringing him, laughing, down with me. His rib cage is gaining definition beneath his skin, but a small pad of fat, a downscale of a kwashiorkor belly, is sticking out over the top of his waistband. His arms tighten around me, and I close my eyes and pretend to draw his face anew; I draw what is already there, and it is exactly as I would have it.

"You smell good," he says in my ear. His fingers lightly trace letters on my inner arm with his thumb. I can't tell what they spell; I'm not following their curves and lines, but the way his voice starts a sweet hum at the base of me.

I keep waking up and thinking that it is raining. I keep waking up with my fingers spread to protect my hair, but every time it is only the leak in the ceiling, dripping in a pattern intrinsic to itself, a self-orchestrated, maddening musical score for after dark. Aaron isn't sleeping; it's like he's waiting to be able to drag me into his vortex. The first time I wake, Aaron says, "When we were still living in Accra, Geoffrey's mum told us what happened to a cousin who was living in London. I was . . . I couldn't even connect what she was telling me with what was around me right then, the way people were relaxed and warm and sat out in the street and minded each other's business. Geoffrey's mum kept telling us, 'Londoners! They are mad, o!'

"Her cousin Ama moved into this flat in Croydon, and everything was fine for a week or so; she got on well enough with the neighbours, settled in, made a few personal touches with the decoration—it was all fine. Then this leak started, ruining her carpets, making a cold winter wet and worse, and it went on and on and on for weeks. She talked to the council about it but the council wouldn't come and take a look because the council are shit. She asked all her neighbours about the leak, but nobody knew what was happening—"

He stops. Why has he stopped? Checking me. He is such a neurotic storyteller; he never trusts that I am still listening. I think he works on a model of the first stories he learnt to love; Ghanaian call-and-response stories, tales as an eager echo thrown back and forth amongst the same people. "Yeah?" I prompt him, muffled by my pillow. I am so tired I am drooling.

"Well, then Ama noticed something. She noticed that the leaks had an extremely regular starting and stopping time. On Monday mornings, for example, the leak would dry up completely, but on Tuesday afternoons, the leak would get going at 3 p.m. or thereabouts."

I giggle. "Say it again," I say. I love it when he says "thereabouts"—he can't avoid saying it with the grandiloquence a semi-Ghanaian accent bestows on mashed-together English vowels. Aaron refuses to indulge me.

"So Ama had a proper look at her ceiling, and she found that the leak was coming from a perfectly round, perfectly drilled hole, quite a large hole, like the biggest setting on a Black and Decker."

I stop laughing. "Oh my God," I say. "Is this a true story?"

"It was the guy who lived directly above her, the same guy who passed on letters which had been mistakenly delivered to him, the same guy who'd smiled at her and shaken his head in confusion when she mentioned her problems with the leak. He'd drilled a hole in his floor, then sat himself down and drawn up a little timetable. Then, in consultation with that timetable, he would pour a couple of jugfuls of water down the hole. Either Ama had offended him in some obscure way, or this guy was mad, or both.

"Geoffrey's mum told us 'If you take a hen's egg from under her and she just looks at you and doesn't do anything, put that egg back.' Peace and quiet is a sign that something's wrong. Peace and quiet is like a broken response, a sign of people in pieces."

I look at the dark, I look at the ceiling and at the bowl, the bowl that is filling, that is nearly full. I think of Miss Lassiter, shrouded face bent intently over a bare patch on her floor. I switch on my bedside lamp and hit Aaron, almost crying.

"Why did you tell me that? What's *wrong* with you? Why did you tell me that?"

Aaron laughs and restrains me with embarrassing ease; he turns off my lamp and holds me until I fall asleep again.

The second time I wake, I hear the television and the leak together. I get out of bed to empty the bowl and find that it's already
been emptied. Aaron is lolling on the sitting-room sofa, remote
control in hand, eating cold plantain. He's watching an old video; in
it I am moving in with him and am instantly unnerved by the camera. On-screen I look as if I just left school; my hair is in box braids
that flip over into fuzzy buds at their ends, and I'm wearing dungarees and a red jumper. I'm hauling a suitcase behind me on wheels.
When I see him I squeak, "Please turn that off," and from behind the
camera he laughs.

"You should go to sleep," I tell Aaron from where I stand. He
doesn't look around but keeps watching me on-screen as I go into
the bathroom, followed at a shaky angle, and triumphantly slam my
toothbrush into the cup on the rim of the sink that held only his.

I go and find Chabella's fruit bucket beneath the kitchen table
and pick out a papaya, turning it over in my hand, checking for ripe-
ness, feeling the slight slippage of fruit beneath its skin and knowing
that it's time to eat it. The smell topples me in. Rind, fruit and seed
mesh on my tongue, become as dense and sweet as cake. I'm not the
one who wants the papaya, but I need all of it. I fall into a chair.

Aaron leans on my shoulder and reaches for the rest of the papaya in my hand, but I say, "Don't."

Pulp spills down my chin. I'm not angry, but serious, and he feels
it. He backs away, exaggeratedly slow, his hands up to show he's not
going to take the fruit. He takes another papaya from the bucket and
methodically prepares it with a knife, evacuating whole clusters of
seeds with a single flick.

I let seeds slide down the inside of my cheeks to wait, pooled in sticky juice, under my tongue. I know that he does that too. We look at each other and smile, lips wet, faces bulging. "Come on, spit," he gurgles. "You can't win this." He needs to sleep. He needs to sleep. It comes to me the power that I have, that I can do something to Aaron that goes beyond us. I could make myself take a bad fall; I could drink something noxious. I could go to a clinic and have "it" taken away. Even if I never tell him, I would have proved that I can deny him, that I can make my son wait. Panicked, I choke. Panicked, I spit. Aaron spits too, and shouts, "Yes! I won!"

We laugh.

．．．．．．．．．．．．．．．．．．

In the somewherehouse, amidst the faded cloth of their rooms, the smallest Kayode plays the fierce-eyed one at chess.

"Here she is again," the fierce-eyed Kayode mutters to the small one when he sees Aya.

The chessboard is missing knights, so the Kayodes are attacking each other's squares with their thumbs. It makes for a game complicated both to play and to follow.

Next door the woman Kayode rocks with her sleeping eyes open, darting, scanning. She lets her hand fill pages with lines. Her knuckles crack. On top of the pile of that dreamings' sketches, Aya sees her mama's thickly lashed black eyes. Mama is behind the grille of a confessional. The black lattice is garlanded with blank, long-stemmed lilies. The beginnings of a shadow scrape the pale diamond spaces behind her.

Aya tries to shake the Kayode woman awake. But the other two Kayodes come and hold Aya's hands away from their kin. They mutter fearfully.

"A visit," they chant at their sleeping woman, "a visit, see? What is to be done?"

Aya is marched out of the Kayodes' rooms and deposited on the stairs to greet the visiting. She watches a woman wearing her mama's favourite green *bubi* step out of the basement.

She is not Mama.

Her dark eyes are like gracefully tinted glass, but her eyelashes aren't long enough to trail into her hair when she lies down.

This woman gives off an electrical shhhhhh. Without saying she says, *You may not touch me.*

She is not Mama. Aya has never seen her before.

"Yeye my own," the woman says, smiling a secret smile. Her voice is Mama's. She does not spread her arms.

"Go away," Aya says. "You were not sent for."

Her eyes travel the gown that is Mama's and the face that is not.

"You don't know your mama? Strange day."

The woman believes herself to be repeating the truth; her mouth is relaxed, her words gently brisk. She sets her foot on the step to come up. Angered, Aya shouts and marks her with a finger.

"Proserpine, I see you!"

But Proserpine does not stop; Proserpine keeps on coming.

The Kayodes are behind Aya, all three, arms linked; if she wants, she could take one step back and be in their midst.

But, "Welcome, Ma," the Kayodes call to Proserpine, who has come in through the London door with almost no luggage, her fingers threaded through the handle of a shopping bag, a patina of expensive sunshine.

Mama Proserpine settles in a first-floor bedroom, a room that Aya has never chosen to sleep in because it sticks out of the house's side. The male Kayodes move around her, careful not to spoil Proserpine's new clothes. They fold and pat lightweight flared skirts and crisp shirts, slipping them into drawers with haste, as if some divided sylph that lives in them will waken, regroup and fly out of the window. From the window seat, Mama Proserpine gazes out into the alleyway of trees and submits to the woman Kayode's hands, allows her hair to be pinned up into a ruffled stalk.

SEVEN

....

PLAYING AT PASTE
(TILL QUALIFIED FOR PEARL)

A while ago Aaron wanted us to swap books that we loved; he wanted to read with me, read me. I said, "I don't read."

He asked again, and on this asking he was so close to me that our eyelashes brushed each other; his lips struck mine but didn't stay. I agreed to swap some books.

He gave me Saki short stories with a cracked spine, Rudyard Kipling's *Kim*, *The Great Gatsby*. I didn't read the books; I didn't need to. I could have told him that these were the books he would give me. Instead of reading them I smelt them, let them fall open at random pages to look for forehead- or fist-shaped pressure. I walked around wearing a pair of his jeans and put *Gatsby* in the back pocket the way the teenaged Aaron did—Volume I of Freud's *The Interpretation of Dreams* in one pocket, *Gatsby* in the other so that his backside was rectangular and intense and learned. In his jeans, which I had to hold up with braces over a T-shirt, my backside became a saggy jigsaw puzzle. I worried that people who walked behind me were staring at my behind and trying to make the pieces fit together. But I didn't worry enough to stop my experiment. The books' pages smelt of Aaron and another low, nutty smell that Aaron said was Accra.

Aaron asked me what I thought of *Gatsby*. I said, "Yeah, it's really good." He waited for more, so I said, "It's short, though." Aaron kissed me and wanted to know what I'd been doing with his books since I hadn't been reading them.

When it came to my part of the swap, I hovered over my shelves at home. I panicked at the last minute and gave him books in Spanish: García Lorca's *La casa de Bernarda Alba*; Alejo Carpentier's sensational voodoo stories that make Chabella and me laugh; Gertrudis Gómez de Avellaneda's book *Sab* about the strong slave who falls in love with a white woman and learns that love makes him better than everyone. When Aaron saw that the books were in Spanish, his brow creased and he opened and closed his mouth, then simply said, with his eyebrows raised, "Thank you."

For a week they sat on his bedside table, the books, and Aaron didn't go near them. I checked them when I visited him; I had keys to his flat and twice I let myself in to see if the books had moved. They hadn't. We didn't talk about the books; they were just there, faded titles sneering quietly. I didn't know why I'd done it to him when he was fair with his choices, so the second time I'd let myself in, when I heard him coming back from the hospital, I collected up the books and went to him to say sorry.

He listened, nodded, shrugged and threw his satchel onto the sofa. The bag coughed up its contents in one abrupt jangle; mints, keys, pens, Post-it pads, English translations of the books I'd given him. He said, "Yeah, they're quite good. Light reading. You know, tube reading . . ."

I dropped the books, rushed at him, snapping my teeth to bite. He lifted me off the ground, high so I squealed, and we fell together in a tangle. With a startled laugh he let the wall hold him upright on one side and held me to him with one big, square hand fitted perfectly to the small of my back. I felt how gentle he wanted to be with me, and I realised then, my nose buried in his jumper, that we smelt the same. Not just that he smelt of my perfume, but that he smelt of me. Good perfume on a clean body is a diaphanous membrane that changes and glows and grows on the skin so that each person smells slightly but vitally different wearing it. So the perfume that smelt of spicy patchouli on Amy Eleni floated high, white musk into the air around me, and around him too. The smell of us scared me.

"What?" said Aaron. He knew that something was wrong, or right, or something. I closed my eyes to concentrate on smelling him—*does he really . . . ?*

He held still. My lips followed the musk along the length of his wrist, where familiarity—the exact same blank between acid and alkali—danced; where I knew my kingdom. I smiled, blind, pushed his sleeve away with my nose as I travelled up his arm.

He told me, without embarrassment but without ease, that he wore my perfume so that he could smell me sometimes. He tilted my face so that I met his eyes squarely, and he said, "Do you think that's creepy?"

I said, "Is it a habit, wearing girl's perfume?"

He said, "Shut up, it's not," and the way he said it and the way he looked at me then made me think that he was trying to get to me before I could get to him, as if it was some kind of race.

Later I examined myself from four different angles in the mirror and thought, *Why? Am I dangerous? Does the hysteric show?* I don't shine like my mother does. I am not a pretty princess. We went out for cocktails and at the bar he spun my stool under me. All I could think of was contact, the static inches between his hand and my thigh. It was like a Peggy Lee song, smoky joy; what to order—cyanide or champagne? Anyway he got to me first, he definitely got to me first.

Aaron is different when he's at the hospital; brittle, swift—the rare times that we actually get to talk while he's there, his words tumble over each other.

It is so late. He has Jung's *The Archetypes and the Collective Unconscious* on his lap, and once I've chosen another cassette and put it into the video player, I slide the book onto the arm of the sofa so that I can take its place.

"You've been reading this book for about two years," I tell him.

He shrugs and nuzzles my cheek. "You should see it as a pleasing example of fidelity," he says. "What you don't notice is that it's not that I'm getting through it slowly, but that I'm reading it over and over and not getting bored."

The tape flickers and stalls, flooding the television screen with fine-grained grey; I get up to try the tape again, which involves giving the video player a thump with my fist. The problem with living in the basement half of a thick-built house is that everything works slightly less well: the radio has a scratchy signal; the television—aerial or no aerial—is temperamental about which channels it will let us see clearly; and the light is poor—our only windows are high and emerge at street level.

The sitting room is lined with lanterns and glass bubble lamps that radiate purple ultraviolet light. They are gifts from Aaron's mother, who is certain that we'll get depressed because we don't have access to sunlight. She keeps telling us that we should swap with Miss Lassiter. Aaron doesn't say anything when she starts on that topic, and his silence is his papal stamp, his way of saying no-not-ever. He doesn't believe that Miss Lassiter would survive a lack of light.

I join Aaron on the sofa again; the tape stalls again. Aaron, his head lolling against the back of the sofa, tuts drowsily with his eyes hooded, and I lay my head on his chest and let the video whir and click.

I ask him why he won't just go to sleep—he says he doesn't know.

I know that I am going to tell him. I rehearse phrases in my head. I must not say "my son," I must say "the baby." When I say it he takes my face in his hands, drapes me in a believer's smile. He doesn't look at me the way Amy Eleni looked at me. His questions, his voice—so happy.

A tape recording of the St. Peter oratorio with Aaron's name listed on the box revealed that he sang tenor at his stiff-collared schola cantorum in Accra. After he found himself settled in London, but before he became a junior house officer and had to decide between hymns and extra sleep, he joined the choir of St. Meredith's, a small church with bobbled grey gables.

I couldn't get my head around Aaron's ability to sing because I never heard him sing alone—if, burrowed into the beanbag on the floor of his room, I started singing, he'd chime in. But when I slyly dropped out of the melody, he stopped dead and grinned, made false beginnings of notes to make me sing first. So in my final two terms at university, I made a regular point of going to his Saturday rehearsals. It was a big choir for a small space. Aaron was dwarfed week after week by two broad-shouldered bass singers in knitted jumpers. He looked childishly healthy, dark hair, pale skin, a warm flush over his cheekbones. And he maintained the pursed-lip style of singing of much younger choirboys—eyes wide, troubled by God, the Latin lyric, or both.

One Saturday, in a week when November died amidst wet weather and frosted leaves, I arrived ten minutes into the rehearsal. I was tracking mud into the church, trying to be as quiet as I could considering I had my arms wrapped around a forty-by-forty-inch piece of sandalwood that scraped the floor. Having accepted that, despite Amy Eleni's best efforts, I was almost certainly going to fail my degree, I'd decided to go out with belligerence and submit both of my dissertations on wood in tiny biro letters—the first dissertation on one side of the block and the second on the other.

My arms had shaken as I bought the wood; they juddered all the way to the church, and I believed that I would be trembling until I handed the thing in. Part of me thought I could still save my degree if I behaved myself and played to the system. One of my teachers at Sacré Coeur, upon being asked whether he thought exam passes could be obtained through diligent prayer, had looked as if he was thinking very hard and then said, "Yes."

I half sat, half fell into a pew. The choir and their director, a Sister in a blue-and-cream habit, ignored me. Aaron's voice soared, naked, clear, but unsure of its strength:

> *Veni, veni Emmanuel*
> *Captivum solve Israel!*

The others rose a beat later and clustered his tinsel call, and I felt December coming with footsteps that shook the pavements, and all Decembers before, and the way that, at midnight Mass, Christmas sometimes seems so sad to me, a giant bedecked with crosses and stars and berries and robins frozen to death.

> *Qui gemit in exsilio,*
> *Privatus Dei Filio.*

> *Gaude, gaude! Emmanuel*
> *Nascetur pro te, Israel.*

When the rehearsal had finished, Aaron came over, slightly shamefaced, and I hugged him until he wheezed because he was more beautiful to me for having raised his voice alone.

"I know why you don't like to sing in front of me," I said in his ear. He put his arms around my shoulders and drove me out into the street before him.

"Because I'm not very good?" he hazarded, as if the reason I was trying to guess was not his own.

"Nope."

"You tell me then."

"Because you look and sound exactly as if you really mean it, as if you believe in every word."

Aaron said politely, "Is that right?" and burped, and I screamed "Disgusting" and stamped in a puddle to splash his Windbreaker. We stood at the bus stop, looking out into brown slush and crawling traffic, and, because he knew that I was still shaking with cold, he opened his Windbreaker and drew me in against his chest and buttoned us both up into it. There was room for him, me and my sandalwood under that monster of a coat, and there was his heart. It was kicking in his chest, so strong and steady I felt it pushing me. By the time he said, "Stop it," I had been lulled into such confusion that I thought he was talking about his heartbeat. That wasn't it; he wanted me to stop standing on his feet. That was why I had been feeling so tall.

EIGHT

·················

PEACES

To escape Proserpine, Aya slips through the Lagos door of the somewherehouse and hurtles through faded green rooms, past speckled
electrical fans that wheeze dust; she bangs the mosquito-netted
screen door of the Lagos house open as she bursts out. It must be a
Sunday; she shoulders her way through throngs of church-dressed
women hastily swapping ornate hats for head wraps to balance trays
packed with fried and baked wares. They head for the motorways, to
swarm at the sandy sides. Lithe, chirpy boys with baskets of bread
and popcorn flock around cars stopped by other cars, tin beads in a
necklace of traffic.

Between the gates of a decrepit compound, a man in white rests
his arm on the rim of a well. He looks at the sun askance. Aya stops
by him and drinks some water. The empty main house collapses into
its own baked torpor and ignores her. The man nods at her. He is her
watchmaker from Habana. Aya wants to embrace her watchmaker
and make him tell about the seeds he gave her so long ago, the ones
that wouldn't grow.

She speaks first, in Yoruba, "Peace, Baba. Is all well?"

His wheeze is as jagged-soft as shaved coconut. "You find me in peace; my ancestors have not forgotten me."

Aya is suddenly unsure of him.

"Do you make clocks?" she whispers.

Aya's watchmaker takes her palm and hides it between his own for a moment. When he takes his hand from hers, there is a thick glass bottle on her palm, "Drink Me" size from Wonderland when Alice was too big.

"That is different water," he tells her. "If you have seeds that told you 'No' before, they will agree to this."

She nods, looks back as she walks away.

He has forgotten her already. He squints at the sun now, and raises hands dripping with well water to his mouth. Aya juggles the watchmaker's seeds in her palm, juggles them all the way back to the somewherehouse, where she paces, watched by Proserpine.

Aya thinks.

Proserpine is still; her delicate elbows rest on her knees.

Aya hesitates at the somewherehouse's side door and looks out at the trees, their tangled mass of leaves and fruit. She decides that the grass outside has plenty. She turns and runs tracks around bewildered Proserpine, sowing seeds that skip and bump across the somewherehouse's floorboards. She chases the seeds with long shots of water that smell of fusty spice.

....

All the way to Papi and Chabella's I watch my shadow, try to step on it, feed it into every hungry, unlucky crack in the pavement. Nobody looks at me strangely. In Mami and Papi's part of Peckham, jerk chicken, Obalende *suya* and shops stocking Supermalt and Maggi sauce are seconds away. Neighbours mind their own business, get their shopping done and fix their eyes on something safe until they're indoors and can bolt up against the evenings, against the rowdies and the graffitists who sit on low walls and smoke and call out smart comments.

When I still lived at home, Chabella—both alarmed and pleased that those boys never seemed to bother me—made me escort Tomás around the area as often as I could. Once she asked me, "Why don't they pick on you? Which one is your boyfriend?" She didn't believe me when I told her that it simply seemed to be a matter of smiling a lot and making sure not to ignore them whenever they asked me something.

At home, Mami sits at Papi's feet, dictaphone in hand, setting German listening exercises in a high voice while Papi watches a programme about the Pharaohs with the sound turned off. The reel of flame-haloed faces in the altar looks away from them and flickers at the ceiling.

Mami asks if I'm singing tonight; I am, and she is excited for me. But Papi, though he hears what we are talking about, says nothing, which is what he usually does when he is asked a challenging question that he needs to think about for a while. At dinner a month ago, Aaron asked Papi whether he missed Cuba, and Papi remained silent until Chabella turned it into a discussion of Che Cola versus Coca-Cola. Che Cola lost miserably—Papi summed it up as "tasting like shit. And not even shit that's good for you."

But days later, Papi phoned and asked to speak to Aaron; he answered the question belatedly, the way people do if they think too much. He told him, "No, I don't miss Cuba. I'm not sure that I knew what it was when I lived there. I know now from the outside."

Aaron was holding the phone between us, and he and I shook our heads at each other because that didn't sound honest to either of us. Aaron said to Papi, "I don't get it."

Papi said, "Of course you get it. A white man in Ghana? The entire time you lived there, you had one foot outside its borders."

Aaron said firmly, "I really think you are wrong to say that, Juan. I am Ghanaian. I was born there."

I wish that Papi could give me his response to my singing, something that I can say "No, you are wrong to say that" to. I wish he would give me something other than a gently bemused teasing: "Why do you like to sing so much? It is too much. Even your aunt Lucia, she was just crazy for singing, but she calmed down and became an engineer."

I go upstairs and tiptoe into Papi and Chabella's bedroom. Chabella's vanities are all to do with her heart. On top of her dresser, photos of me and Tomás and Papi and Aaron and her cousins and her favourite pupils and all the living that she prays for; all these photos jostle with small, mysterious tasks that she has begun and neglected to finish—a plastic half bottle of holy water from Lourdes stands beside a full crystal bottle of rose water; both stand on top of a rectangle of ruched silk with a threaded needle dangling from one corner. Handfuls of seeds are strewn amongst wooden beads. Scraps of rice paper, maybe the beginnings of paper chains, are stuck to the side of the desk.

In Mami's top drawer are her photo albums, and I open one at random, my fingers blunt on the stiff pages, finding her again and again. In all of the pictures, Papi looks at Mami with tender concern, as if he has forgotten that it's his wedding too.
I find Chabella not just in her tense, happy bride's face
(she told me that for the entire day she was so happy that she thought she must faint, or die—nothing happened except that her heart grew fuller)
but in the people she left behind her; the way they smile from beneath the impression of her thumb pressed painfully over their faces.

On the phone, Amy Eleni says, "You know what I read about rats? I read that if they lived uninterrupted lives, they never stop growing. Imagine! You could get a rat as big as a dustbin. As big as a house."

(*So what*, I think. I am painting my nails and thinking of boys' names.)

"I mean, what if foetuses were like rats? Say a foetus stays in the womb longer than nine months, what if it went on a growth bender? What if a baby got as big as its mother?"

"Amy Eleni," I say, "shut up."

Why is she saying this? She knows about the hysteric, how she beats me by making things seem funny when they're not, by finding pain in speculation. But she can't know how it gets when I think about my son, so when she says, "What?" I just ask her if she still has my purple nail varnish.

Amy Eleni says Despina is not anorexic. She doesn't say it defiantly; she just says it, because she is sure. According to Amy Eleni, her mother "doesn't give a shit about her weight." Emily Brontë probably didn't care that much about her weight either, but she died hungry, with food in the house. I can't forget Despina's mint-tea cupboard, from the times I went over to Amy Eleni's house to drink mint tea with all the lovely sugar that Chabella wouldn't let me have.

The first time, Amy Eleni opened a kitchen cupboard and said, "This is the mint-tea cupboard." She said it formally, as if the cupboard was a person she was introducing me to. Inside sat one tiny, thick-spouted silver teapot. Behind the teapot was an organic wall of sugar, forty to fifty kilo bags of it, all packed so tightly together that it looked as if a giant fist had punched them into the back wall; the packets had lost their edges and ran into one another.

I thought, maybe Despina likes her mint tea sweet, maybe she's a hoarder, maybe she's an anorexic. Amy Eleni looked at me and said, "I think it's more of an aesthetic thing than anything else." We were sixteen. Aesthetic was Amy Eleni's favourite word that week.

I recognized the sugar wall, its jigsawed threat. I know that in this world something really is trying to stop me from having a large milk shake with my large fries. This suspicion emerges like a spasm in my jaw whenever what's crammed in there tastes too good. I used to think that the only reason Chabella could weep copiously and at the same time eat slabs of steak in stewed tomato sauce was that she was not complex. Cubans are cheerful, Cubans are resilient, Cubans are collectivist. In my mother's country, I thought, *la lucha* is such that people are not equipped to understand when they are unhappy. It's a situation-specific kindness from God—Cubans are born lacking: they have no internal off switch and so it is that they go on and on and on.

But look at the British! Their government had to have some of the suffragists force-fed through tubes because each one of them had located her off switch and leant her entire weight against it. These women were pissed off. And not a word about it being hard to eat; they did not see the joke in being weak. They did not want to take their place in *el dramático* or the tender masquerade of scented handkerchiefs and faintness and tears.

When the hysteric saw what the suffragists had done—the way that en masse they'd turned starvation onto its side—she must have been surprised. Her shock must have brought her close to speech. Here, in grey climates, are people mocking the things that happen in places that the sun loves more, those places where hunger herds people ahead of her and into blindness, where hunger makes a person run their tongue along their bottom lip to claim the wilted wings shed by dead flies. Suddenly so clear, or clearer, that people will use all of their frailty to hold out for more, that people go into sickness as a signal test.

Two months ago a woman drove her car off the end of a pier in Blackpool and drowned. But first, cloaked in deepening water, she smoked two cigarettes whilst waiting for the people milling around on the mainland to realise that they weren't going to be able to get help to her in time. People tried to get the woman's attention; they tried to reassure her. She refused to look their way. She was from Cameroon, which is why at first there was some confusion over whether she had accidentally driven off the pier or whether this was a suicide attempt.

People who actually knew this "pier woman" might not have described her as sensitive. They would probably have said she was "tough" or "loud" or "pushy," all the while thinking: "black." One eyewitness maintained that the entire thing was an accident. With her thumb Amy Eleni jabbed the offending lines in the *Fortean Times*: "Yeah right, eyewitness! If it was an accident why wasn't she making eye contact or looking for help? Why wasn't she asking for reassurance that she wasn't going to die?"

The pier woman was in the kind of trouble that calls for a material defence. Two unhurried cigarettes, a reminder to her body that breath can be made visible. Trouble: a thing heard on the air and in my headphones when my favourite song plays. It climbs inside and puppeteers until I echo. Maybe the hysteric is my mystic signal test, a way of checking, asking:

Who's there?

Something old? Someone holy . . . ?

Amy Eleni longed for a knife to slit away the webbing between her stiff fingers. I chased my vein lines with glass. Maybe we were having conversations so intense we couldn't hear them. If we could have heard what we were saying, Amy Eleni and I, we'd have cringed the way we do when we think of someone using prayer to bargain, cramming extra requests in on the back of the usual one-request-per-rosary-bead transaction. But the hysteric, she makes us able to say without knowing. She makes us able to say to this trouble that comes: *Wait! Please don't go. Just in case you're holy after all. Really I'm like you. I can be strange and deep-flowing too. See?*

Despina frightens me with her cold eyes and her measured voice and the long, lost time she spends standing before the bright Orthodox icons in the hallway when she gets back from work. I don't know what I'd do if Despina was my mother. She is the tallest silence. Despina is no Jacob. Neither is she Bisabuela Carmen that she would lay hands on her god and try to break him and make him stay. It's the reason why she's still alive; religious people know their place. I wonder does Chabella fit that pattern.

NINE

....

CLANDESTINE SPIRITUAL WARFARE

One of the first things that really felt like a London episode happened when Papi was away at a conference. I was ten. Papi called at 3 a.m. and Mami spoke to him in a cute, bright chirrup and woke me up to speak to him. She pinched me to stop me from begging him to come home.

Chabella's English was still really bad then; it embarrassed me. The teachers at school always asked to speak to Papi instead of her. I couldn't understand why she was able to understand English but couldn't speak it the way that she spoke German. It was too embarrassing, standing in between Mami and someone else, translating words Mami threw at them in Spanish when they had questioned her in English.

After Papi's phone call, Mami made her paper flowers and cried over them for a long time—she wet her flowers so that they wouldn't catch fire, she cried until she couldn't talk. I hugged her and kissed her. I hugged her and kissed her, religiously, like a ritual; I kissed and hugged her, medically, like a lifesaving technique. The flowers drowned anyway.

Chabella was still, and I was still. Outside someone, a woman, was crying; she was asking for help, gave a muffled scream, gulped back louder tears, cried, *Rape*. I looked to Mami, and Mami put a finger over her lips and went to the sitting-room window; we looked out carefully, carefully from under the hem of the net curtain.

Neat and narrow; the street had broken itself off into a chunk of shadowed road and dustbin and diamond-shaped lamplight—it looked painted on the air. Watching the road and the man and the woman in the road, I knew we'd never be able to touch what we saw, even if we went down and stood there.

The woman was white. She cried, *Please*, and a white man yanked at her ponytail so that she teetered on her spiky heels. It wasn't playful tugging, but the man was straining to look amused, to look as if he were at play. He locked an arm around her throat and walked away; she came with him in degrees. He was so casual that it didn't look as if he intended to drag her away, but just to walk with her held against him like a suit he was trying on for size. If it hadn't been for the involuntary sounds she made. Her lungs convulsed and spoke loudly for her, over and over, *puh puh puh puh*.

Around the corner a group of people laughed in a hard, ragged burst, but it took a second to realise that there were other people out on the road; the laughter was somehow like traffic, a noise that was not really sound but city liquefied. Mami and I shrank up against each other, shrank into each other. Beneath the curtains there was a shadow-strained forever that fell from ceiling to floor and roped us round in its folds. Mami whispered,

Puedo no,

I can't

before I even told her that she had to call the police.

"Mami you're not going to call the police?" I asked loudly.

The man and the woman were gone. Nothing and no one moved on the street. I knew that you didn't call the police for just anything. I was not sure what rape was then, but if it made a woman cry out like she was dying, and made me feel, *me too*, anything like that was serious enough for the police.

"*Mi inglés, mi inglés es tan malo, ellos no me entenderán,*" Mami said, and there were so many tears from her that I couldn't dry them with my hands. She wanted me to understand why she wasn't going to help, but I couldn't understand.

"So what if your English is bad?" I said. "I'll talk to them."

Mami kissed my forehead, her arms dropped down around me; I stiffened because she was laughing and crying at once and I didn't know what it meant. Her hands clasped around my throat, and when I looked into her eyes I couldn't find her. Instead I saw something inky and strange rising. I said, "Mami?"

She was hurting me.

"*Usted es una hija mala,*" she said. She sounded angry, but her eyes were shiny with hurt. "*¿Cómo atrévasele me contradice?*"

"Mami," I said, and I tried but my fingers couldn't unlock her iron ones. My vision took on black edges, and I began to believe that she was going to kill me; she was saying that I was a bad daughter and I didn't know why.

She let go of me; I fell down, and that was when I first learnt that I needed to protect my throat, my voice, because that was where my hands went first, to the circling pain. I croaked, and I vomited hard.

Chabella said she was sorry. She said it just once, she said it very softly, and then she got up and walked halfway across the room and came back to me with her eyes swimming and glowing so that I cowered and thought she was so sad because I was going to have to die. But then she walked away again, came back, walked away from me with her face pulled mask-tight until finally she came back for good and snatched me up into her arms and kissed me and hugged me. It wasn't enough; I was still afraid.

I need words from Chabella. It has maybe been that way since the first time I understood that she didn't already know what I was thinking. I was three; a friend had made me cry. Mami picked me up and asked me, "What's the matter, what?" Papi had rushed to pick me up too, but Mami got there first. Papi says I was so surprised she should have to ask that I knocked my forehead against hers in my haste to look properly into her eyes. I don't remember, but apparently I said, "I have to *tell* you?"

Miss Lassiter's telephone rings and rings, on and off, all afternoon long.

Kneeling by the sitting-room table, I write cheques for bills with my eyes three-quarters closed so I don't see how I'm decimating my bank account. Then I sit in the kitchen with my rosary wrapped around the hand that isn't trying to finish fitting lyrics to a song, beating the rosary hand against the table in abbreviated rhythms that aren't helping.

Magalys calls to ask me if I want to have coffee with her. I want her to have forgotten my Cuba, or at least dimmed it amidst the train of other memories. I wonder if she'll show me what I would have been like had we stayed in a Habana. She and her brother teach dance classes near Bond Street, and I can meet her at the studio because she'll be finished with her last class by the time I get there. It sounds as if at least ten million people are tap-dancing behind her, but her voice is very calm.

Tomás has got awkward digestion. His condition is called reflux. What happens is he eats something, waits half an hour, and, no matter how carefully he has chewed his food, he vomits. Even when he was nursing, he used to dribble milk hours after having fed. I observed all this with deep interest, the return of Tomás's food without invitation. Mami took him to the doctor, but the doctor said that as long as the reflux didn't happen while he was sleeping, it was okay. And it never did happen while he was sleeping. When he was smaller Tomás didn't used to think about it; he'd just go and vomit and then get on with whatever he was doing. He ate extra at meals in anticipation of the amount that he was going to lose. At fourteen I knew about bulimia; I'd read books with titles like *When It's Hard to Eat*. Tomás's vomiting like that wasn't good, but it couldn't be that bad because he didn't do it on purpose.

One day Papi noticed what Tomás was doing.

Papi put down his newspaper, put on his slippers and followed Tomás upstairs. I followed Papi. The two of us watched Tomás lean over the sink and spit up his lunch, then thoroughly and unselfconsciously rinse out his mouth and dab his face with a face towel, the way Mami had taught him. Tomás was five. I looked at Papi to see what he thought; Papi's mouth was wide open, his eyes were narrowed behind his reading glasses. Tomás turned, said, "What is it?" to both of us, and he tried to get past, but Papi clamped his hands down on Tomás's shoulders and knelt down so as to be small with him.

"You do that every day?"

Tomás said, incredulous, "What?"

"It happens two or three times a day," I interjected, surprised.

Papi didn't look at me. "Stop that, Tomás. Do you hear me? Do you see me doing that kind of thing? It's unheard of. Boys don't do that."

"Papi, girls don't do it either, though. Mami doesn't do it. Maja doesn't do it. Just me does it," Tomás argued.

Papi straightened up and looked down at Tomás. All he said was, "Don't test me." He went downstairs, back to his newspaper. Tomás came and took my hand, and gave me a look full of surprise. "It's okay?" he said. He meant everything. Papi, vomiting, everything.

"It's okay," I said, gently putting his other hand back down to his side—Mami didn't want him sucking his thumb because that was how people got buckteeth.

After that, Chabella and I watched Papi watching Tomás.

We all got to know the signs of Tomás's regurgitation, the way his cheeks expanded, the way he'd get a dizzy, gassed look from trying to hold it in. Then, when we couldn't bear to sit around watching Tomás hold sour food in his mouth anymore, Papi let Tomás scramble up the stairs to the bathroom. To Mami, Papi said, "Why is this happening to my son?"

Chabella said, "*El crecerá fuera de ello*, Juan, he'll grow out of it. He's so small now. And he's the London baby."

There was a thing that happened that I didn't tell Papi. My Spanish teacher wrote lots of letters for Amnesty International and thought that I should take more of an interest in Cuba. Miss Roberts was no more Spanish than I was, but we always had to call her Señora Roberts, to sustain the mood of the language lesson. After one lesson she leant on the edge of my desk and asked me, "You know what *gusano* means, don't you?"

I glanced at the door to make my intentions clear and I said, "Yeah, it means 'worm.' "

She said, "That's what they call antirevolutionaries and other dissidents in Cuba. It's actually a key term in Fidel's political vocabulary. *Gusano*. Or if not that then you're the son of a *gusano*. It's a terrible thing, isn't it, using language to take away the humanity of someone who opposes you?"

I said, "Yeah." I fidgeted with my bag strap; I didn't like the way Señora Roberts had said "Cuba," so softly as if she were trying to rein in the towering force of it, as if she expected me to gasp or something. I didn't like the way she was looking at me, eyebrows raised, lips quirked; she was looking at me as if we shared something, as if she knew me much better than she did.

I knew that Señora Roberts was thinking that my father must have told me all about being *gusano*, what it was like to have your colleagues begin to denounce you to avoid the label themselves. She thought that as she spoke a painful reel was playing behind my eyes, a sequence in which someone wearing a Cuban flag for a bandana spits in my father's face and shouts, "*¡Gusano!*" Then, perhaps, the same man kicks Papi's legs out from under him and stamps on his rib cage. But that is not the story. If Papi says "*gusano*," he doesn't let the word or its meaning come near him. Papi sits silent and bespectacled behind Cuban broadsheets, then he throws them away and says little about them.

What Papi *did* say about having to leave the country was something that Señora Roberts wouldn't have found exciting. He said that the process that ends with you fearing for your life is gradual and actually quite congenial. It begins in a warm daze as the sun lays you bare in corner-room meetings. Paper falls apart under your sweaty fingers as you read and reread directives and statements that you know it is essential for you to understand. If you don't teach certain things, or if you forget to praise certain people and initiatives, you are called to account and at first you think that you are defective— then you realise that you're becoming unreasonable because no one else is being reasonable.

Papi says, "If not reason, then what else can it be that separates us from animals, what is it that makes us fail to be innocent before God?"

I said, "I suppose by God, you mean reason undiluted."

Papi ignored me and said, "There is something else. Unless the nature programs are hiding something interesting from us, you never see a wolf struggling in a trap while a full pack of its own stand around it in a formal square, waiting for it to escape or to die. I don't know what to call it, this other thing that makes us different from the wolves."

"Papi, I think that's called malice."

"But that's not what it is. It's functional, it's a process, it's what must happen to ensure that a group remains a group. It's what happens when something inside you cancels out your outer appearance and you show yourself not to belong. That's what makes us different from the wolves; a body may appear as one of us and not be treated as one of us. Three categories of treatment instead of one. Person, God, and beast. And no *term* for what's at the heart of it. Well, German's the language of ideas. I'll ask Chabella," Papi said, and I knew that he wouldn't.

When Papi looks at Tomás trying to fight his reflux, I can see how darkly simple his pain is. My brother did not get his coordination from Papi. Papi was a bad dishwasher and bad at keeping stacked crockery close to his body—he would forget his limits, place his hands higher and let the bottom of the stack go to pieces on the floor. Or if it was cutlery he had to wash them all over again. He didn't think of money as money, he thought of it as a way to get books, going through reading lists in his head over and over again, returning to the places where he felt strongest. Cuba was the restaurant kitchens and the narrow, high platform on which he moved. Whenever he cut his knuckles on knives and potato peelers hidden in the dishwater the pain always came very late.

For a long time my papi did not realise that hunger was the reason why he had to keep touching things to stop them floating away from him. When Chabella first met my papi his eyes were still too big; prolonged malnutrition is hard to shake off.

History books: Papi stubbornly scratched surfaces to look for Africa. He knew that his friends hid dismay behind their teasing, that they wondered where the black boy was in him, the snapback, the physical intelligence. But he had the snapback; it was in his head.

When my papi was Tomás's age he would not listen to the restaurant owners' comments that began: "The good thing about you *morenos* is that you can work! God, but can you work . . . on and on." He didn't listen, but because he didn't sneer, people didn't know what he was thinking.

Papi saw a *babalawo* cry. Papi saw a *babalawo* come out into the street and stretch himself out on the ground because his daughter had died. He had come to heal her because under Batista no one poor could get taken care of unless they knew someone in authority. But that *babalawo* could do nothing against his daughter's cancer, the cells that unsheathed crab claws and waged civil war on each other. The *babalawo* was dressed in civilian clothes but Papi recognised him; he had come from La Regla. Papi's uncle worked the docks there, and Papi's cousins had been blessed and made Santeros by this very *babalawo*. Papi told me that this *babalawo* was over six feet tall and white-haired, that he was very, very black. "Can you imagine?" Papi mused.

I could not.

"The other boys from the neighborhood were playing some bastardisation of baseball, but they steered clear of this priest. They took their game down to the other end of the street. They said, 'Juan, come in on Miguel's team,' but like the bookhead I was, I was on my way to the library and I didn't want to tell them. But to get to the library I had to pass that priest. He lay very still; he was like a stain on the ground. So black. After only a second of looking at him he became something very simple to me, something just hurting on the ground, something with no other thoughts. I think I could have stamped on him and he would not have understood what I had done.

"I got worried that some of those *Americanos* would come with cameras and take a picture. I was thinking, *Get up, you. Just get up, get up*. Blood was pouring from his mouth; every time he opened it his lips made this wet slapping noise and flies came near. I bent down to him, but I couldn't do anything. I saw his tongue. Well, half his tongue. He had bitten his tongue in half; the end of it was in the dust, sort of coiled up like a wet tail. The heat made it smell. And he was just trying to speak, trying to speak to the sky I think, not to me, but his mouth was full of blood."

Tomás doesn't believe Papi about the *babalawo*. "You didn't see his tongue, man. Not his tongue. Maybe you heard about that. He probably just drank chicken blood as part of a ritual or something."

Papi is adamant: "It was his tongue. His daughter died and he bit it off. I ran away from him. You shouldn't run away from grief, but my God, you must run from madness. That country. It seems that no one there is able."

What if Papi has no strength either? What if he is wrong not to live in the place allocated to him and he is *gusano*? Then Tomás is the son of a *gusano*, and, after all, worms eat soil and dead bodies. If the boy can't keep food down, maybe food is not meant for him. What can it mean, not to be in love with your country? That you belong above the earth, or under it.

One evening dinner was haphazard; *mores y cristianos* with *yuccas relenas* and ladlefuls of stew poured over. Amy Eleni ate with us, and every bite brought her a surprise—one minute she tasted mashed rice and beans, the next mashed potato and beef, the next spicy tomato.

I teased Chabella about the Moors and Christians—"The beans are black, right, so that's the Moors, and the rice is white, so those are the Christians . . . *ai*, Mami, we can't be Christians, we're *black!*" Amy Eleni backed me up; she said she reckoned that she was a Moor, and she wanted to know what Chabella was going to do about that. Mami whooped, "I didn't name the dish!"

Papi didn't say much. He ate and darted his attention from his own plate to Tomás's face. And, maybe because of the pressure of Amy Eleni's presence, Tomás gave a small cough, the beginnings of a full-blown heave. Mami still smiled, but she quieted down, became watchful. Amy Eleni knew something was wrong and she looked at Tomás, too, even though I fussed at her to distract her, poured her more water, poured her more juice. Tomás bowed his head and pressed his hands on his knees, arguing with his food, his cheeks distended. Papi twitched but kept on eating, even when Mami gave him a quick, deep, mournful glance.

When Tomás looked at him, Papi barked, *"Téngalo en. Traga lo hacia abajo."* He told Tomás in Spanish to hold it in, to swallow it down because he didn't want Amy Eleni to know what he was saying. But Tomás wouldn't hear him. He just held on to the chair and lowered his head, waiting for Papi to let him go to the bathroom.

I said, *"¡Papi! ¡El es apenas un chico pequeño!"*

Papi made a sign that I should quiet down and said painfully, *"El debe aprender."* He must learn. In English he said to Tomás, almost pleading, "Come on, T-boy, it's unheard of." Tomás didn't move or look up, but his breathing grew more laboured—he was about to cry. Amy Eleni gave me a wide-eyed sideways glance. Papi said, *"¡Tomás! ¡Dije, lo trago hacia abajo!"*

Amy Eleni studied Papi and studied Tomás and said to the top of Tomás's head, "Tomás, go on, throw up. I dares ya. If you throw up, I'll do it too."

Tomás's eyes found Amy Eleni's and he shook his head desperately from side to side, no, no, don't you throw up.

"What? You don't want me to throw up all over the table? But I will. You think you're so tough! You think you're so clever to throw up like that? I can do it too!"

Chabella said, uncertainly, "Amy Eleni—" but Amy Eleni made a fake gagging sound that was so slimily authentic that Tomás swallowed, burped, and squealed, "No!" in a single moment of delighted horror.

"We're trying to eat!" Mami said, bowing her head to Amy Eleni, her eyes full of thanks.

"What's wrong with you! Trying to throw up on the table!" Tomás demanded of Amy Eleni, his face lit bright. It was the way Amy Eleni made my brother move when nothing else would move him that brought Papi to realise something. Before he put him to bed that night, Papi picked Tomás up under his arm, chuckling as he wriggled, and walked around the house with him whispering things. I couldn't hear what Papi told Tomás. But it must have been simple, because every now and again, Tomás replied calmly, "I know."

....

Aya steps through her London door and crosses concrete slopes that balance drowsy houses on their shoulders. Night's edge blunts itself at traffic-light level. Aya wishes that she could reach that night and bring it down. Her auntie Iya could. Aya has seen her auntie Iya stop walking, stretch languorously, then leap with her arms splayed against impact and sprint up into the atmosphere on a diagonal, hot sparks snapping from her heels as she wrests clouds open. Aya walks and wishes.

A girl sitting on the pavement with her legs crossed under her, this girl holds her hands out to Aya with soft words, words sighed more than said. Her smile is numb, fragile, milk and water. A round plaster at her temple drives back long black waves of her hair. The girl smells of wild honey, jellied amber so raw that fingers delving into its centre bring up the crisped black remnants of bees. The girl is saying, "Ye-ma-ya-Sa-ra-ma-gu-a-Ye-ma-ya-Sa-ra-ma-gu-a," and she rocks, wrapped in the rhythm of her own words, rapt like a child at play.

"How do you know my name?" Aya asks the girl.

The girl looks into Yemaya Saramagua's eyes and slowly, painfully puts her smile away somewhere safe. The girl says to Aya, "I don't know your name. What's your name?"

A rainbow of blowsy silk handkerchiefs hangs from the girl's belt. And when the girl says her name is Amy, to Aya this does not feel true. Amy puts out her hand for help, and to make a beginning of it, Aya helps her to stand up.

Amy lives on the top floor of a tall house with stairs that go apologetically naked after their third rotation. Inside, Amy's warm honey smell drugs every hollow; the immediate inside rectangle of doorways, the cracks in the corners of window cases. This place is more of a home for books than it is for people; scruffy paperbacks lounge in heaps on the sofa, rickety shelves host a gap-strewn gallery of faded titles. The light, when it comes, will be full and frank; the night sky heaves against square windows wider than Aya's outstretched arms. When Amy pleads with her to stay, Aya curls up in the contours of the armchair to wait. If you should find yourself in a place that is indifferent to you and there is someone there that your spirit stretches to, then that person is kin.

In the morning comes the man that Amy lives with, and Aya feigns sleep to watch him. He is beautiful. He might be from Abeokuta, where the essence of the Ewe poet stirs and causes cool-faced people to be born, cool-faced people whose hearts are self-stoked furnaces, great anger and great love. He stows his trunk into a space at the foot of the television. His gaze lingers on Amy who, still asleep, has curled up on the sofa so tightly that she is no more than a patch of denim topped with a tangle of brown hair, and then he bends over the trunk and snaps its locks open. The trunk is filled with ash, or grey sand, and he hunkers down beside it and makes a small, distressed sound, running his fingers through it, watching the grains whirl together into twisted fronds as they touch his hand.

When Tayo straightens, his eyes find Aya. Aya stays still, but she fears her face will crack under the pressure of keeping her eyes open to just this degree. Then, as the fear grows strongest in her, Tayo turns away. He softly tells the air, or Amy, "She's very ugly."

Amy surfaces from sleep for him, says, "Tayo."

Blood mists her face in tiny, diamond buds.

Tayo kneels by her and says her name with sorrow and they lay their heads together and are hidden there in Amy's pain and in her hair. When Aya comes to take Amy's face in her hands, there is the bruise. It stains Amy's cheek in dull blue-and-brown veins, starbursting as if a finger has punctured a pressure point in her cheek and opened other tunnels.

Amy touches Aya's hand then, and smiling rigidly, she rolls up the sleeves of her long T-shirt, rolls socks down, brings daylight to bruises burnt old and deep purple, bruises clicking together around her arms like connected bangles, or another skin. Amy's blood runs and will not turn back, though Aya counters it with water, with her vanilla. Tayo watches her. A smear of ash is on his temple. She cannot bear his gaze.

"Have you come to help us?" he asks Aya, and his laughter is so sudden and so quickly spent that it divides Aya from her nerve, sends her to the door, hauls her out.

TEN

· · · · · · · · · · ·

PRESENTIMENT

(THAT LONG SHADOW ON THE LAWN)

Magalys and her older brother Teofilo are the only people in the studio, and they are dancing together between the mirrored walls; he promenades her, then draws her to him, pretends to back away from her, beckons her on. They step slow, quick, quick, slow, quick and quick, to a Xavier Cugat song. It's the kind of music I laugh at when Mami and Papi dance to it. But Magalys and Teofilo move and I see that inside this song there is something even, something near to perfection; there is a rhythm that a dance keeps.

Magalys in dance-teacher mode is scary-looking; she has added some drama by wearing a black flamenco skirt and bodice, hiding her hair beneath a black headscarf and daubing her lips with red lipstick. Teofilo, who has no place at all in my blurred memories, is half a head taller than Magalys and three years older, brown-skinned and curly-haired. He smiles with sharp-looking teeth when he sees me, but he and Magalys dance the song to the end. I clap, and Magalys comes to embrace me. Teofilo holds out his arms in an invitation to dance. We consider each other. I say, "No, thank you," and forget to soften my refusal with a smile.

Teofilo laughs; the tape rolls on to the next song. "You're Cuban? And you can't dance *el Son*? Not even the basics of it? Nobody taught you *el Son*?"

His English accent is better than Magalys's.

"She should know it in her bones," Magalys gasps, pretending shock from her place on the floor, where she is changing her dance shoes for trainers. I feel attacked, so I smile.

He takes my hand. "Come, I'll show you."

I try to back away but he is busy positioning me, straightening and extending my arm so that it matches his, wrapping his other arm around my waist to try and make me sway. I know that I cannot do this dance—there is something inside me that is slow, something that rises slowly, dips slowly. Something that does not talk back to a drumbeat.

"I don't want to," I say, too quiet. He steps to show me how to step, and I am dragged along with him. I see myself in the mirrors; I am wide-eyed and tight-lipped, and where Teofilo is not holding me straight, I flop like a dummy.

"Please! I don't want to!" I say, and I am louder than the music. Teofilo lets me go, shrugs at Magalys and turns away to switch off the cassette player. To Teofilo's back, and to Magalys, I say, "I just don't really feel this kind of music."

Magalys tucks her arm through mine, pats my shoulder reassuringly and tells me, "*No te preocupes, no es nada, no es nada.* But you should know that, though it is not quite your jazz singing, it is really not all that different."

We walk to the coffee shop across the street without saying anything else to each other, listening to the conversations around us and the traffic humming nearby and looking at each other without embarrassment, as if we are content to let the traffic be our speech.

We find a corner table and settle, carefully rolling our mugs of coffee over our palms to counteract the cold. We chorus, "So how are you?" Magalys answers first.

"I am doing well," she tells me. "Teofilo has a lot of students, so we share them and it means he gets to have longer breaks."

"Is that why you're here?" I ask her.

Magalys looks at me blankly, waits for me to elaborate.

"Did you want to come here to teach dance?"

Magalys shakes her head, her curls bounce. "Oh, no. I just came over here to see what it is like. To see if I miss Cuba. I certainly don't miss *la lucha*. I certainly don't miss having to be clever every day and having to smile at ugly men who have ranking and can allocate me more meat than I've been allocated, or more fish than I've been allocated, or a new kettle."

She sips her mocha, blows on it, sips again, says, "But," at the same time as I say it for her, as a question. She looks around the coffee shop, at the casement-framed paintings and the people chattering on the purple sofas, as if the whole shop will fall down on her if she is not grateful to be here.

"I don't know, sometimes it just doesn't really feel like anywhere over here. I look at maps and stuff and none of the places seem real. I think that's what happens when you don't belong to a country, though—lines are just lines, and letters are just letters and you can't touch the meaning behind them the way you can when you're home and you look at a map and you see, instead of a place-name, a stretch of road or an orchard or an ice-cream parlour around the corner. You know. It's okay, though. I didn't expect to know this place. You haven't told me how you are doing."

I say, "I'm fine." There is an awkward silence because we both know that I don't want to give her any more than that.

"You really scared me at that Vedado party, you know?" Magalys says, eventually.

My heart hammers in my chest and there is no room in there for me to be louder than my heart and tell her that I'm sorry about what happened to her. I drink my coffee, drink it down as if it's going to save my life, and say nothing.

Magalys says, "I thought about you a lot when you went away. I used to worry without really knowing why. I felt as if I knew you well because I had seen you fall ill."

"Fall ill?" I examine Magalys's face; she is frowning.

"Don't you remember?" she says. "We were under the table, and—"

"A woman came and started to sing," I interject, but Magalys only skips a beat before waving my words away: "You don't remember? We were under the table, playing dominoes, and all the grown-ups were at the table eating and drinking and some of them were asking where we were, and we started laughing, but then you said 'shush,' and put a finger to your lips. You started shaking, and I knew it wasn't normal shaking, I straightaway knew. Your eyes were rolling so much, and you were biting your tongue, and you were . . . I don't know—but you were staring at me and I felt as if you'd closed the world or something. I yelled so loud that everyone looked under the table at almost exactly the same time. And your mami took you away. You don't remember?"

I need to think—I try to smile and think at the same time. I close my eyes and try to fetch back that lantern-lit night, the singing, and the other girl, rosy Magalys, flailing the air. But now there are gaps ripped through the image and the singing has turned to a mashed, static whine. I want to ask Magalys what she has done to my one whole memory. Instead I say, still smiling, "That's not how it happened, Magalys."

(Magalys please see my smile see it is not a happy one and agree with me just shut up and agree with me.)

Magalys stares at me. "I remember your mother just picked you up and took you away, and almost as soon as she'd gone, some people started whispering about her and you and saying that she'd asked a *babalawo* to give you visions, to see how it would go with you abroad. The fit seemed like a bad sign."

I am not the one who had the fit—how could it have been me? Or, if I had the fit, then I had already left that place and it was you who were caught fast in illness like glue, while elsewhere the woman sang.

I need my Cuba memory back, or something just as small, just as rich, to replace it, more food for my son, for me. I think I will pretend that I am not from Cuba and neither is my son. The boy and I started a race from that other country, and I got here first.

I walk up the street from Aaron's flat to the travel agents, and I take time during the journey to stand still and gape at nothing; I don't care who sees—I do it because I need to. If I don't protest my skin will destroy me. When I rubbed cream into my skin today, the cream layered, then scratched away to show me that I am a gourd, bound in crisp servility to my insides.

With plane tickets in my bag I call Chabella, maybe to tell her about a thing that I will soon be unable to hide. When she picks up the phone, I say that I have called by accident.

....

On a dais in a London church, the Virgin Mary sits surprised by a rough crest of candlelight. The discomfiture isn't in her expression but in the fluid form her carving takes, the way peaceful eyes rest in sockets that threaten to release them. Either the wood is eccentrically soft, or this sculpture remains a tree, alert
(despite careful varnishing and a wide, warning ring of sacred space around it)
to a propensity to burn.

The rest of the church is dim and all of a piece; russet floors nascent with insubstantial pews, Stations of the Cross boarded to the tops of the very last row. Incense knots in Aya's nostrils. Her hands shake as she leans over and puts a candle to the Virgin's rigid blue shawl, willing her to catch fire. Varnish turns to smoke.

But Tayo speaks a greeting into Aya's ear, slips his arm around her waist and reaches up, gesture joined to hers, to capture the candle's metal base from her hand. He blows the flame out. She sidesteps him and he follows, plucking her away from the bank of candles when she backs too close to them. His hair is done all over bumps, plaits dragged in on themselves.

"What are you doing here?" they ask each other. Outside it is calm. The sun's gift to the day is the most benevolent yellow Aya has ever seen. Today is bright yellow like waking well after a long illness; the heart's tinny hymn postcrisis. Gold.

They walk; the wind is polite and dusts the playthings of other days from their path. Tayo lights a cigar and blows smoke at the ground. High on his cheeks, his eyelashes form fringed crescents. Aya asks of Amy, and Tayo lets his cigar fall and by so doing murders it; its battered head smoulders and collapses. Amy is in hospital, he says, because she tried to die.

The beds on the ward are narrow and high. Iron bedsteads. Everybody lies down obediently and in exactly the same way; people who slept on their sides or their stomachs at home lie on their backs here, stiff. No bed is near a window, no one has a view. A giant Pinocchio lopes in red, yellow, pink and brown along the back wall, interrupted by a heavy door that stands, unperturbed, in his stomach.

Amy, her hair dropping in a multitude of coils from a single, burnished bun, beams from amongst her pillows when she sees Aya and Tayo, though she could be smiling at the gifts—a carton stuffed to overflowing with red grapes, and sunflowers whose tawny heads are double the size of her palms.

Amy hugs Tayo, Aya, the fruit and the flowers simultaneously. The pain on her cheeks, her forehead, her hands stands out blackly, as if her veins are delicately weeping poison and her skin is a cloth placed over it to soak up the damage. The girl in the bed next to Amy's is asleep. She has a sharp little face, like a baby bird's, and she cannot walk because her spirit does not want her body and bids it disappear. Beneath the girl's covers, atrophied muscle makes her legs lithe and kneeless. The girl's mother sits beside her, reading the newspaper to herself.

Tayo slowly kneads Amy's hands between his own; it reminds Aya of her mama. But Amy turns away from him, turns into her pillow. Her body curls up foetal. She hides in her hair and quietly, quietly coughs out gummy streams of pale green. The nurses gently move her to a new bed. Amy's silk handkerchiefs still cluster over and under the brown leather belt she's tightened around the waist of her nightie, but Aya gives her a tissue; she dabs feebly at the sores that now show starker beside her mouth.

Aya asks her, "Amy, why?"

(How can you know my name and want to die?)

Amy says, "I don't know. It was just an idea, really."

Aya cannot stop looking at the beautiful bird-girl in the bed next to Amy's; the girl sleeps even though the blankets are too heavy for her, even though her mother's sad hand on her pillow is too heavy for her.

Aya cannot stay. This place is not a place that she understands, and Amy knows that. She kisses Aya and says to her, "It has been good to see you again, Yemaya Saramagua."

ELEVEN

1% THANATOS INSTINCT, 99% AIR

Amy Eleni's flat is a deconstructed chest of drawers—all on one level, all as is to be expected. The medium-size sitting-room box sits in between the medium-size kitchen and the bedroom, with its high double bed and the black television and VCR on the table beside it. In the sitting room is a non-scent, a pale, clean sofa, light curtains. There is waiting-room magic here, a polite insistence that these rooms are in fact a space you pass through on your way to somewhere else. You're not to trouble yourself to look at the walls, since there are no pictures there. You're to wipe your feet, but keep your shoes on.

You would never guess that Amy Eleni is a teacher. Actually you wouldn't guess anything about her; you'd think she was suicidal and had given most of her stuff away.

Amy Eleni doesn't buy books; she buys shoes instead. She takes books out from the library—ten at a time—and lives on them, around them, all over them. She spilt coffee all over a library book and said to me, "See? Me and books—I'd better not even try to live with them. Life is over there, behind the shelf."

Amy Eleni doesn't have a shelf in her flat. So, because I had no idea what she was talking about, I was immediately suspicious that her hysteric had her. But before I could say anything, Amy Eleni jumped on me, smothered me with her hands and shouted, "Why are we friends? You really need to read—"

I surfaced and covered her face with my hand.

"Shut up! I'm not *taking* any more recommendations!"

Melded together on her sofa, drunk on *fragolino* and watching TV, Amy Eleni caught me peering around, in a mood to dismiss, thinking, *how bare this place is.*

She said, "Look, I just don't have a lot of things."

For this week's showing of *Vertigo*, Amy Eleni is wearing a smooth grey pencil suit and heels, entertaining me with the reminder that, apart from the fact that they're both blond, she looks nothing like Madeleine Elster, the doomed woman in the film. Madeleine Elster is sleek and taut, like one long nerve at red alert, and Amy Eleni is short and of far softer stuff, all whirls and coils and curves, her hair, her body, the gradations of colour in her irises. Madeleine Elster looks a little more like Amy Eleni's mother. Amy Eleni goes to make us some Horlicks, calling from the kitchen that she's adding soy milk to mine because it's supposed to be good for developing bones and teeth and stuff.

"I would've thought that would be cow's milk," I say, watching the opening scenes of the film: Scottie's fall; his resulting trauma, the way it seems he can't even look down at his own feet without seeing swirls.

"I teach English . . ." Amy Eleni reminds me.

"Give me cow's milk, woman."

In the voice she reserves for a creepy phenomenon, Amy Eleni says, "Imagine if that baby wasn't a baby at all, and that this is one of those strange pregnancies you read about in the *Fortean Times*? What if all you've got in your stomach is this limp piece of dough and it just keeps expanding until—boom?"

She's joking, but I don't like it. I feel cold.

"Don't say that!"

"What?" Amy Eleni comes back in and hands me my Horlicks.

"What?" she says again, when I take it without saying anything. I sniff at the mug, as if my nose can tell me the difference between soy milk and cow's milk, as if my nose can tell me which is better.

In the evening, I use a hand mirror to supervise my earrings. I boil tonight down to flip-switch decisions: hoops or dangly earrings; long skirt or black dress; to sing well or to sing badly; to tell Aaron now that I'm going to Cuba next month or to put it off until I can sound sane when I say it. I've missed band rehearsals and Michael is pissed off at me, so I have to be early tonight. Aaron is in the kitchen cooking up a batch of *jollof* rice; I hear him hissing as the onions sizzle. He isn't fully aware of his kitchen soundtrack, his tendency to imitate food sounds.

"You shouldn't cook—you're tired," I tell him, watching the clock. "I could have made you something."

He comes out of the kitchen expressly to point his spatula at me. "But I want *jollof* rice, and you can't cook it. Anyway you should eat some of this," he says, "it'll be good for our boy."

I suck my breath in, find lightness to speak with. "Who says it'll be a boy?"

"I knew you'd say that," Aaron sings. I am supposed to want a girl child; he is supposed to want a boy child.

The phone rings. It's Amy Eleni, and I'm immediately stricken with guilt for not having called her first. She says, "Oh, hi, Maja. Is Aaron around?"

She doesn't sound cold or angry at me, just busy. I think. Or maybe she is angry. I pass the phone to Aaron and wander around looking for my shoes, thrown off course by the call, trying unsuccessfully to listen in.

Aaron comes back into the sitting room, hangs up the phone and sighs. "There goes my free Sunday afternoon—I was going to try and sleep right through it," he says.

"Did Amy Eleni sound angry with me?" I ask.

"No?" Aaron tries. He doesn't want to be involved. He tries to tiptoe past me.

"Then what? Why would she ask to speak to you before me? Are you seeing her tomorrow?"

"Calm down. I'm her friend too," he says. He bends and hands me my other stiletto. "Maybe you should start wearing flatter shoes now. Her school's running some mentor scheme, and she managed to get some guy from Shell—can you imagine, a Shell Oil man? A more ethical mentor doesn't exist, I'm sure. She got this Shell guy to agree to mentor three boys in her form and take them out tomorrow for a first meeting, but the guy pulled out, so . . ."

I pretend to be confused. "So why did she call you?"

"Yeah, shut up," he says. "I'm a good role model. Excellent, in fact. If I survive this year I'll be well on my way to becoming a psychiatrist, so shog off. Anyways, these boys are Ghanaian, so she thought I'd be perfect."

I scrutinize him, but I can't tell what percentage of what he just said is a joke. He must know that if he mentors these boys, he is not showing them what a Ghanaian can do with his life, but what a white guy can do who chooses or refuses Ghana at any given moment. I change the subject.

(You are no more Ghanaian than I am Cuban. So what if you can number your memories and group them in years one to eighteen? That country will not claim you when you are broken, when you have forgotten the trick of breathing easily and you will have to learn how to resuscitate yourself.)

But if I say this, he will take offence. Because if I *do* say it I will mean it to offend.

"Did you get to talk to Miss Lassiter about the leak?" I ask instead.

He shakes his head. He leans his forehead against mine.

"If I were to ask you to marry me," he murmurs, "what would you say?"

I baulk, but I think I manage to not let him feel it.

"Okay, first of all, I have to go and sing in a minute and you're trying this? Secondly, I'd say, *querido*, I can't marry you yet." I can't be a wife yet, not even Aaron's. I need to sit down and have a good long talk with my personal hysteric before I become a wife.

"Why?" he asks, very seriously.

"Z."

He doesn't want to smile, but he smiles because he has to be grown up about it.

———

Tonight there is no choice between singing badly and singing well: I cannot sing at all.

Onstage, in the smoky dark, I shut my eyes, place my fingers around the microphone as if in prayer, and I cannot remember anything—not just my Cuba, but even the words to the song and my place in the music. The band realises what is happening. They change temperature; they ease down from standard swing and into a mellow instrumental, and Sophie begins a gentle, improvised solo. I scramble offstage as quickly as I can. I do not cry until I'm outside, and even then I fumble for the tears, as if this crying is just something I'm doing in a blackout while I'm waiting for the light to come back.

Aaron follows me into the bedroom when I get back. He fiddles with my things. He slaps my hand when, in retaliation, I reach for one of his chewing sticks. I catch sight of myself in the mirror. I am concerned. I look as haggard as I feel.

"I am very ugly these days, aren't I?" I say.

Aaron looks at me; he makes a good job of his surprised expression. "Ah, you don't know how you look to me."

I stay out of his reach, smiling tiredly. "Is that a direct quote from a Drifters' song?"

Aaron groans. I peel off my jumper, turning away a little so he can't see my stomach. I step out of the skirt I reserve for fat days; it drops to the floor like a flattened pom-pom. Aaron hasn't gone away.

"This isn't a striptease," I say.

He is still waiting. "What?"

"This is the first day off I've had in ages where I'm not half dead," he says.

I don't look at him. I do not want to talk. I want to rest first of all, and then I want to try to sing again, try to find a tone that my vocal cords and my aching throat will let me stay with. Or maybe I want Amy Eleni with me under a tent made of blankets, chin in hand, talking to me with her clear eyes narrowed. I don't want Aaron—he doesn't know.

"You don't want to spend any time together?"

He is flinching a little, as if we are having a fight. We're not having a fight.

"I keep thinking you'd rather go back to St. Catherine's or something," he says reluctantly, when I don't reply. "You've put something down between us. It's invisible, but it's very strong."

He comes to hold me then, and I realise that I can't reply because I've been weeping those easy tears that Chabella passed down to me. He doesn't hold me any differently—I thought he would have care for my stomach, but he is as sure as ever that his touch is good for me and my son.

"Tell me why you keep wearing this," he says. He runs his thumb lightly, lightly down the ridge of my polo neck, and I hold still and I let him.

But I can't say. What do I say, "My mother . . . ?" Do I say, "The hysteric . . . ?"

Gelassenheit.

I lift my head from his shoulder and touch my lips to the skin that crinkles over his Adam's apple. My teeth latch onto him and I clamp down hard, so hard that my teeth find each other again through his skin

(he *shouts*)

and I am not thinking anything in particular, just that I have to hurt him.

It's to do with Magalys, who said there was no singing in the garden in Vedado. Such words are surgical; a pole separates a man's brain and he survives, but no one knows him anymore. With my Cuba cut away from under me, without that piece of warm, songful night, I am empty of reasons. Aaron's hand smacks my forehead, instinctively batting me away from him, and I recoil like he wants me to, painfully sucking at my teeth which are laddered with blood. He stares at me with his hand to his neck; my own hand is at my neck. He is breathing hard; I am breathing hard.

"What is wrong with you?" he asks me.

I wipe my mouth.

Aaron rubs his neck, puts me into strong focus, and I am so nervous, too nervous, as if I am fourteen and this is the first time I have ever talked to a boy about anything serious. He draws me back to him, and when I bite him this time, he clenches his fists around me, but he doesn't let go, and he doesn't cry out.

Mami and her habit of unhappiness. Mami dazzled and shaded in a strip of kitchen tile and flowered tablecloth, candlelight prising her gaze open for the dark. In the kitchen she makes some more of her prayer flowers.

"What, you think I don't make them anymore? You think I'd forgotten?" she asks me. "I make them on the third day of each month, on the day that should be given to Elegua."

The blinds are drawn down against a night storm that screams black noise and thorny rain. Chabella shivers and says quietly, "This house will blow away."

I ask her if there are hurricanes in Cuba; her reply is simple silence.

I talk to her softly, talk secrets to her, but she won't answer me. So I keep talking anyway, to keep myself awake for her, because I see how the muscles in her long neck are strained, how she bites down and swallows even though there is nothing in her mouth. The window frames bounce against the gales. Chabella says, "Lord Jesus Christ of Nazareth," without looking up. She is just as fleet at her prayer-making as she's always been, just as expert, squinting at the paper heaped between her spread elbows, selecting a piece and swiftly folding, twisting, pinching the crisp layers between her honey-soaked fingertips to form broad petals topped with fractured spires.

When her flowers burn, she stretches and sighs.

"It still works," she says.

I watch the petals curl under the blaze that takes them to the centre of the bowl, and I don't know what she had expected. Did she think that rice paper was no longer flammable? Take a prayer and put it in a photocopier, collect the copies and smile because you have more to go around, cry because when you lifted the lid of that machine, something blank and coarse fell out.

Chabella outstares her flames.

"My father was kind to people because he didn't expect them to be good, only interesting. And people are always that, no? If somebody stole from him he didn't mind as long as the thief was impeccably audacious. If someone lied to him, he didn't mind as long as the lie was too wild to be believed, or too subtle to be suspected. Your *abuelo*, God rest his soul, was so tall that he couldn't sit down on buses because there was really no room for his legs. But he was good about it; he stood up instead and lowered his head so that it didn't slam against the bus roof, and he just smiled and watched people like a big bent hook in a paint-spattered T-shirt.

"My father allowed me to throw tantrums and flounce and switch moods, and I never had to explain. When I announced that on Mondays I was going to eat only green things and on Tuesdays only brown things and on Wednesdays only yellow things, he said, 'Fine, you must do what you feel,' even though my mami frowned and said, 'You are making her strange, you will let this girl run mad.' His girlfriends said to one another that he was spoiling me and that he would get no one to marry me. But he was just letting me contradict myself while I still could.

"My father was almost perfect. The only thing wrong with him was that when he didn't understand, he got angry. And he didn't understand me because he stopped listening to me. I was the 'feelings' child. Everything I did was a feeling, and it did not count. It is so difficult to talk about demons and gods and spirits without it seeming that you are mad, or sarcastic, or simple, or talking in pictures, or trying to confuse. Or trying to be interesting. It is difficult to talk about demons and make it understood that even if 'spirit' is the best word available, it isn't the right word.

"Maja, let's talk like mystics: let's say I never had a mother. 'I always ran home to Awe when a child, when anything befell me. He was an awful mother, but I liked him better than none.' Who wrote that?"

I stare at her. "Is this a quiz?"

She laughs at me. "No, *querida*, I only mean that I can't remember who wrote it."

I lay my head on my outstretched arms and Mami strokes my hair. Honey from her fingers webs behind my ears, but I don't move. So what if my hair gets messed up; Mami has stayed still for worse. She told me that once, at a Santeria mass, she sat with open eyes while rooster blood mapped her face.

Chabella was brave because she didn't have a plan. She isn't a storm or a leader or a king or a war or anything or anyone whose life and death makes noise. The problem is words. There is skin, yes. And then, inside that, there is your language, the casual, inherited magic spells that make your skin real. It's too late now—even if we could say "Shut up" or "Where's my dinner?" in the first language, the real language, the words weren't born in us. And unless your skin and your language touch each other without interruption, there is no word strong enough to make you understand that it matters that you live. The things that really say "stay" are an Orisha, a kind night, a pretended boy, a garden song that made no sense. Those come closer to being enough.

TWELVE

THE SOUL SELECTS HER OWN SOCIETY

There is a leak in the hallway too; from a dim green patch the ceiling is crying a thin stream of tears.

Miss Lassiter has said that she doesn't know where the leak is coming from. Aaron, not being a plumber, has tapped her pipes, has said "Hm," has made a phone call. All we understand from what the plumber tells us is that this is an old house

(AARON: "Yes?")

and that the repair is going to cost more than five hundred pounds.

(AARON, jovial: "No! Come on, no no no.")

He laughs pleasantly and tells the plumber that he's going to get another quote.

I say "Aaron, *please*, I need the leak stopped now, now," but Aaron is intractable. He doesn't know that the leak is killing me. Haggling is fine in Accra, but he can't do it to me—not here.

Someone knocks on the door, knocks so hard it booms. I twitch (it is nothing to do with the door)

and that makes Aaron twitch.

He checks the sitting-room clock and tells me, "It's Amy Eleni's boys." He rubs my arm, *Don't worry*. He shouldn't do that; my hysteric is the boring girl in the corner that you ignore—if you talk to her she won't shut up.

The boys crowd in, these are people's sons. Their heads are close-shaven to expose peachy nicks on their scalps. They're wearing Timberland boots and heavy-cut jeans that crash down to their toe caps. A uniform always prepares me for a crowd, so that at first I think there must be more than three of them. They look around, elbow one another, refuse my offer of tea, and crow, "This is boom digs! Sonic booooooom, know what I mean?"

Aaron introduces them as Kobe, Kweku and Kevin, his voice fitting smoothly around the Ewe names. Kevin shuffles his feet and wearily insists, as if continuing an argument that started before his birth, that it's not his fault his parents gave him an English first name: "The teachers jump on it as soon as they see it in the register; they ignore 'Akwasi,' " he says. "I think they're a bit relieved not to have to say it, really."

Aaron manages to locate his coat, picks up his camcorder carry case and says a few words to them in confident Ewe. They look at him with flattered, embarrassed smiles and reply with accents less certain than his. Aaron's accent, normally a quirk unique to him, now makes a skewed kind of sense. Somehow that hurts me; I would have preferred the accent to have stayed a quirk.

When Mass is ended and we have genuflected toward God, I tell Mami I'm going back to Habana. She is confused. She waves and smiles at other friends who are trickling out of the church, presses the Father's hand, indicates that she can't stop to talk today. She says, "Oh, but Maja, you can't go."

I touch Mami's face, I ask, "Why not."

"Better talk to your papi."

Mami and I walk home holding each other's hands tightly. Chabella is wearing big furry gloves, and I am not. Chabella insists that my hands are cold. I say no, but she keeps lifting my hands to her mouth to blow warmth onto my cracked palms.

Chabella says of Tomás, "Somehow he is just too tender. I know some will think that isn't how a black boy should be. I am afraid that the other boys will punish him for it, his tenderness."

I can't find it in me to tell her not to worry. She should worry.

When Tomás was nine or so, I sometimes babysat him and his friend, Jon. At that time they were intense about conker wars. They waged their wars under the kitchen table, both lying flat on their stomachs, heads bowed toward each other as they struck each others' forces in skirmishes and temporary sorties from behind fortresses, strategising with shrivelled conker soldiers. Tomás's strategy was probably immaculate; all his work is, his diagrams and graphs and essays. But Jon won every game because it seemed that Tomás's overall strategy was to let him win. Jon, his hair falling into his eyes, got frustrated with winning and swung with more force, harder and harder, his conker smashing against Tomás's knuckles. But Tomás just winced and let him win and win.

These days after school Tomás comes home with a group of raggedly uniform boys who live around the way. Tomás walks amongst them with his hands in his pockets, smiling and shaking his head as they whoop and hang off lampposts. He is careful talking to the other boys; he is kindly. It's as if he's trying his best not to let the others know that they are not real, that he is talking to himself.

Some schools think being quiet is a sign of genius-level intelligence. Last year Tomás's school put him on the Gifted and Talented programme to help him get to a top university. His friends were annoyed; they were losing him to books and extra homework, and he was getting to be a good striker. But Tomás found that in his Gifted and Talented classes his hearing became so faulty that he couldn't understand anything except for the end-of-lesson bell. He couldn't hear, and he panicked and froze. Chabella worried that he would become completely deaf. I worried that he would become completely deaf. His teachers said it was frightening, uncanny, *unheimlich*; that they could shout out his name within five paces of him and, unless he was looking directly at them, he didn't turn a hair, or show any understanding.

Chabella withdrew him from those classes after a meeting with his Gifted and Talented English literature teacher, even though Papi pointed out that it was most curious that Tomás could hear well enough to watch *Pinky and the Brain* on TV before dinner. Tomás's weekends took their old shape once again; he went back to playing striker on the local football team, a position that Jon had kept warm for him. He also resumed his post as Papi's book assistant, lying on his back in Papi's study shuffling through notes with a fluorescent marker, typing out references when Papi's fingers felt too stiff.

But even if he is Papi's boy, there are things that Tomás will ask only of Mami. It's the same with me. Sometimes there are things that you need to say and you know that the right person to say them to is the person whose logic works two ways; the person who can sit through Mass without staring sardonically at the boy in the dress who waves incense in their face.

Chabella was making guava *pasteles*, hands working a mass of pastry and sweetener when Tomás came back from football huffing and sweating, the collar of his tracksuit top turned up around his neck in a funnel. He looked urgent, the way he used to when he was smaller and would come to Mami during an argument with another boy, tug at her arm and say, "Tell him."

He sidled up to the counter and tore off a hunk of dough. Chabella clucked. "Tomás, why? You'll only throw it up."

I laughed. "What's the point of feeding him at all, then?" And Tomás ignored me and said to her through a sticky mouthful, "Chabella, it's getting stupid. We're supposed to learn our names really early, no? Like, a few months after being born we're supposed to respond to our names or whatever."

I was leaning on the counter, reading and breathing in Chabella's sweetened steam. I looked up and said, "Are you trying to tell us you're retarded?"

Chabella flung a handful of sweetener at me, and she missed. "What's wrong with you? Don't say these things, they'll come true!"

Tomás plucked more dough out from under Chabella's hands.

"Listen Chabella, really it's getting . . . I don't know. When someone nearby calls a name, I have this thing where I look around at them as if they're calling me, it doesn't matter what name they call out. Just now on the road this boy shouted out 'Oi, Jack!' and I turned around to him and looked him in the face and he said in some properly nasty voice, 'Oh, are you Jack?' And I said, 'No, sorry—' "

I called out to Tomás, "You should have put your hand in your pocket and said, 'Who wants to know?' Or you should have said, 'Depends who's asking . . .' and *then* put your hand in your pocket. Then you should have narrowed your eyes and made a clicking sound with your tongue."

Tomás rolled his eyes. "Yeah, standardly I should have said that. And then he would have pissed himself laughing. This boy was tonk, trust me. Anyway I said, 'No my name isn't Jack,' and this boy was all like, 'Well don't *watch* that, then,' and I was thinking, but this happens all the time, it happens all the time—I just keep looking around when someone calls, as if I haven't learnt my name or something. One of these days I'm going to end up smeared into a wall."

Mami didn't look up. She blew on her rolling pin, tapped it on the counter, bent over her pastries to inspect the frills she'd drawn into their edges. Only I could see, over the top of my book, the tension on Tomás's face. Mami didn't look; Tomás placed his palms on the counter and leant far over into Mami's way. He kissed her cheek, he swung, he waited for Mami to look. But when Mami turned to him, her gaze got lost somewhere on the way to meet his; her eyes were guilty somehow. She fed him some guava and told him, "It's okay, London baby. You must trust yourself. Tomás is not your name; it's just a tag we gave you until you find something you like."

....

Late in the night Aya sits still, her head resting against Amy's. She is knocked comatose by the twin thicknesses of Amy's hair and honey.

Tayo has dragged out a drawer from his cupboard; he lays it carefully on the floor, he bids Aya look. His eyes are full, too full, brimming.

The drawer foams damp white; at first she thinks, snow?

No—row after immaculate row of drowned paper flowers. They pull at her heart, these flowers, they do not ask for light the way that real flowers do. She puts her hands out to make them well again, and as she touches them, one by one, they dry out and crackle under her fingers. Rice paper.

Aya asks, "They're yours?"

He is vehement: "No."

When Aya holds the flowers close to her face, she sees that each has a black word bled into it in spidery writing. On each flower, the same word.

"Then I want them," she says.

He recoils. "They're not meant for you."

She asks who gave them to him, and he shakes his head.

"A her?" Aya asks.

"Mm."

"And you parted?"

"Not exactly. Kind of. Well, she doesn't know."

"How can she not know that you've parted?"

He shrugs.

Aya hugs the flowers. She tries to hug all of them at once but her arms do not have enough space between them.

"She knows," Aya says.

In her bedroom, in the morning, Amy says, "Yemaya, I have the trick of crossing heaviness with lightness. I could jump in the air right now and not come down. I wouldn't go any higher, either. I'd just stay there. They'd ring bells and tell lies: a soul has gone to heaven. Yemaya Saramagua?"

When Amy leans over from her bed, there is no more early light; Amy's face is desperate, her granite eyes disappearing under eddying water. She scratches at the bruises on her arms, trying to lift them away, bringing down blood instead. Aya tries to help her to lie down again, but Amy will not. "Amy, what is it? What is it?" Aya asks her.

"Ochun, Ochun. Please say it. Yemaya Saramagua, you must know my name," Amy weeps. She bites Aya to make her let go. Aya won't let go. Finally Amy lays still and rattles out a breath that sounds like her last, sounds like her heart is broken.

"I should never have left. Why doesn't anybody know my name? Why doesn't someone come for me?"

THIRTEEN

·······················

THE HOUR OF LEAD

I offer up Saturday night for a vigil. I flip through travel brochures. The purple UV lamps hurt my eyes. According to the brochures, Habana Vieja is old and beautiful and majestically crumbling, and Miramar has great beaches. Everything is very picturesquely blue or a very surly brown, and set on a slant that sands down the sky's edges. Cubans are, apparently, very friendly if they feel their gestures are reciprocated. Do I count, am I like that too? I thought everybody was like that.

I try to balance my saints' medals on my forehead as if they are tokens that I can swap for something overhead, and I wait for Sunday morning Mass. I think, *No, it is not true that Mami would try to inject me with visions. Not like that, not when I was so small.* It is hard to know. I do know that Chabella loves me because she can look inside me against my will, and it seems people can only do that if they love you. But Chabella is from a different country to me; she is wound around and around with her Brigitte and my *bisabuela* Carmen. I've had *Mork & Mindy* and *The Cosby Show*. I've had gaps between the things I see and the things I know, the dilemma of getting a comb through my hair on mornings when my personal hysteric makes my arms droop and refuse to work.

I stare at the Orishas from the distance Peckham affords me, but Chabella grew up in a small white house in Querejeta, just off a ring road where trees are sparse and the traffic makes humidity fly in low circles. From her window she could see the Hotel Nacional waving its flag to welcome small crowds of hatted, suited, feathered, colourful Americans. From the first, she swears that all she ever wanted was to be gone from there.

There is one dog-eared photograph of Chabella at ten; we have never resembled each other physically, she and I. Light clusters in Chabella's huge irises, and she is sitting on the marble steps inside her house, her posture perfect, her hands clasped, her hair combed up high and tied with a ribbon. She is smiling the way a china doll smiles, and to me that means she is not happy. China dolls, their cheeks flushed vicious, always look as if they have been threatened with dismemberment and posed, their limbs arranged. They would take life if they could. A few days after that picture was taken, Chabella tried to run away from home for the seventh time, and that day her father, Damason,

("Your *abuelo*, God rest his soul," Chabella stares at me until I cross myself)

lost his patience with her and beat her. But escape wasn't meant as a personal insult to Abuelo Damason.

Chabella was the youngest of his four children, and closer to her father than to Laline, her lawyer mother, who disappeared beneath portfolios and was preoccupied with women's rights. Chabella and Abuelo Damason spent afternoons in his studio fascinated by feet, the whorls of taut skin. They stomped in vats of paint before dancing across vast sheets of expensive paper. He danced alone, then she danced alone, then they both danced together. They wanted to see whether the idea of dancing was contained in the feet, or, if not, what feet really meant. The tracks they made were linked, ungainly shapes, ridiculous, bright and strong, like the first images of their kind.

Abuelo Damason also had a lot of women back then. Sometimes Laline let her smooth veneer chip, and at night she would scream at Chabella's father that he'd better stop making a fool of her with his girlfriends. "They were the kind of women who cluster around when a black Cuban becomes successful—all kinds," Mami said. Women who hated her, smiled at her, gave her sweets, and stole the hair from her combs so that they could have roots people work spells to make Chabella leave hold of her father's heart. Chabella's first real memory was of falling off the swing in the house's back garden and cutting her knee, and then crying because her father wasn't there. My pretty, light-skinned *tía* Dayame, the next sister up from Mami, was combing her hair in front of the sitting-room mirror—when she saw the wound she simply shrugged and said, "Good."

Maria, the family's maid, cleaned Chabella's knee with something special, and told her that she'd better be more careful. "If you leave your blood on the earth, it gets hungry for more," Maria told her, and then when six-year-old Chabella trembled, she reassured her by saying that there were at least three spiritual protectors observing her; one of them was an ancestor, another one was an Orisha. Maria told Mami that she was lucky. In those circumstances, it was true.

I grow so tired that my head droops and my mouth opens and I begin to think that I am my Chabella and that I am the woman who was singing the song that made the garden in Vedado so wild. St. Bernadette and Jeanne d'Arc fall heavily into my lap and I try to make merciful Mary, the mother of God, appear to me through the strength of my own heart.

I don't want anything from her. I just want to know that I am the one that brought her.

My neck aches, and lines run straight up from that pain to my temples. Another line makes a trampoline from my stomach to a place above my head.

The pages of the brochures feel like money to me, brittle, symbolic—if I tear a page even slightly, I will not be able to go. Outside on the street, people are drunkenly cock-crowing. They sound close. I keep expecting to see faces squashed against the window. Aaron tells me I need to rest, and he tries to make me lie down with him. When I won't, he says, "Okay wait, I'm just going to get my Jung, then I'll be right back. I'll stay up with you."

He's lucky that he didn't promise; he doesn't come back. I know he's spread out over the bedcovers, staring, sleeping, with *The Archetypes and the Collective Unconscious* beside his lax hand. The leak has grown louder, but he is able to sleep through it.

Sophie calls and softly asks me if I know when I'll be able to sing again. I tell her I'm not sure, and that it's fine if they want to find someone else until I'm ready. She doesn't argue. When I put the phone down I walk back to the sofa slowly, tracking liquid with my fingers; warm, gelatinous arrows of blood are running down my thigh. But my period shouldn't come. There is no reason for my period to come when I am pregnant. I am bloating, my stomach is touching my lap like sacking, and there is a smell that maybe Chabella would recognise. It is a bad, natural smell; logical, like rotting.

....

Amy's dress is a plum divided; the deep-red taffeta skirts are the leathered skins, and the gleaming bodice is a layered tapestry of rich fruit flesh. The dress suits her completely, despite—or because of—the belt she's slung at hip level, heavy with multicoloured scraps of silk. With every step she takes, a billow of her honey scent rises. Outside the day is chill and gloomy; cold sits still on the ground and in the air and sticks frosted leaves to the earth.

Amy wants Aya to know:

that she had thought she had settled for being just Amy,

that if it wasn't for . . .

(she rubs at a bruise, at her bandaged arm)

she wouldn't know that this was a lie.

Tayo leans over the bathroom sink, fingers curled around his torso, incubating agony. He spits out a string of needles; the pain is irregular but larger than his mind. Afterward, he rinses out his mouth to lose the metal tang and mumbles in the bath, knees drawn to his chest. Water slams his curls flat against his head.

Another time he plugged up the sink and ran the tap until it overflowed. Then he lowered his face into the water—first just grazing it, a dip as if he were simply rinsing. Then, after a moment of shallow breathing, he dived for full, jerky immersion, clamping one hand onto the back of his head, fighting. As he drowned, Aya felt the water scuff her lungs. But before she could go to him he had already lost against himself. He surfaced, coughing liquid, to lay his head down on the side of the basin as the water dripped onto his bare feet.

....

FOURTEEN

FLOODS SERVED TO US IN BOWLS

I don't think my son is there anymore.

I killed him by being so jealous, by wanting him before I under-
stood what he is. Or I ate too much crap. Or my body is built like
Chabella's and I must lose as much as twice before I can begin.
I keep mistaking my heartbeat for his.

My heart

(his heart?)

my heart?

(mine)

my own heart,

beating me down like a belt.

I am still bleeding.

Shhhhhh. God already knows.

I am not special. Maja you are not special.

Sleep, then get up again, and so on.

The kitchen smells of toasted coconut; Mami has been baking
before church. At the table, Papi has drawn up a chair and is sitting

at Tomás's shoulder, leaning his chin onto his fist as he watches Tomás write his homework. Usually Tomás fidgets and shrinks if someone is in his space for longer than a few minutes. But Tomás's arm, spread over his paper to shield it, is gently touching Papi's. Papi nods at us, and when Chabella and I come at him and Tomás from separate sides to kiss them, he says, "And how are my Kingdom Kids?"

Tomás looks at me directly and I see that his lip is swelling under a deep pink cut. There is bruising on his temple. I narrow my eyes at him, but Papi pulls me awkwardly onto his lap and asks, "How are you and Aaron? You know, last night, I had a dream that I was in a big, cosy den in Lapland or somewhere, smoking my pipe—
(Mami shouts and flaps a napkin at him)
And it was snowing hard outside, so hard. But suddenly there was this tiny rap on my door, and I thought, 'Who could that be?' So I opened up, and there were two beautiful children, one little boy and one little girl—the boy was sturdy, curly-haired, a little older, and quite a lot taller than the girl, who was so beautiful I couldn't look at her for long. She was wonderful; a princess. If you'd seen her, Maja! Anyway, I let them in, and they warmed themselves, and I gave them *cucuruchos* and hot tea, and they said some very intelligent things about Communism, and then I said, 'Now, who do you belong to?' and they said, 'What do you mean, Abuelo?' *Abuelo*! Imagine! 'So,' I said. 'So, so, so.' They called me *abuelo*! They were my grand-children . . ."

I hold myself very still. I am wrapped in layers, long jumper over long skirt, scarves, but any motion might bring Papi that smell that is all over me.

"Hey, yeah, right, keep dreaming," I tell him.

Papi says, "You are breaking my heart. And you're disturbing Tomás's homework. You and Chabella need to clear out and let Tomás's discovery of his love of history continue as before."

"History makes me want to kill myself," Tomás mumbles.

I take the seat next to Papi and look from him to Mami. "Papi, I have tickets to go back to Habana next month, but Mami says you don't want me to go."

Papi looks at Mami as well, as if my going is her suggestion and her fault. Papi taps Tomás on the shoulder to make him look up. "Tomás, I want you to listen to this as well."

Tomás looks at me as if he wouldn't mind if he died right now. Tomás looks at me like, *stop this*, but I won't.

Papi turns his eyes to me.

"Why do you want to go back?"

"What's wrong with me going back?"

I see Papi's hands; they are quivering.

"Do you think I brought you here for a joke?" he asks me. His voice is very low. "Do you think that I just brought you over to England for a long holiday? There are reasons why we are not living in Cuba, Maja."

"And these are?"

"That it's not safe; that staying there is accepting the lies of a regime that in its aimlessness will destroy the country," Papi says. His tone is that of the teacher soothing a gormless pupil.

"You want me to stay away to make a *statement*? A statement that doesn't affect anyone, that doesn't reach anyone's notice but mine?"

Mami wrings her hands.

Papi says to her, "I suppose you want to go, too?" He says it with too much calm, and maybe that is why Chabella doesn't reply. Out of respect for Papi, Tomás is not writing, but he is not looking our way either.

"Why do you want to go?" Papi asks me again, a hand to his forehead. This thing I want is a problem that he is trying to understand. There are no texts he can turn to for this problem.

"If you were asking me about Turkey or Morocco or America or Spain, it would make more sense! Like if you were saying, 'Why are you interested in going to Turkey, there's nothing in Turkey for you,' I'd understand. I'd still go, but I'd understand why you were asking me. But what you're asking me now—I mean, how can you ask me why I want to go when I don't understand what it means to have left?"

After that he will not let me speak.

"It means that you are free. That is what it means. I brought you here so that you could live in a place where the people who are in government do not affect whether or not you can eat what you want to eat, see films you want to see, read what you want to read. I brought you here so you don't live in a place where politics can actually bust your door down, or make you disappear. Turbulent times, Chabella and I know, turbulent times.

"Maja, unlike your mother, I did not grow up in a nice house. I grew up in a tenement in Habana Vieja, and when I turned fifteen, I didn't have a nice party but I was happy because it meant that I could pretend I was sixteen a little bit more convincingly and ask for a better wage when I had finished washing restaurant dishes. Why are you testing me like this? The idea of a library that I could borrow any-thing from seemed like a dream to me.

"When those boys came around, I believed more than anyone that what Fidel, Raúl Castro, Che Guevara, Camilo Cienfuegos, Juan Almeida, and the others would do would be a great thing—the greatest thing for Cuba. I mean, Juan Almeida was black! A black revolutionary! My God, I thought, yes, we have a share in Cuba. They say it's not a black man's country, but it is! My heart overrode my mind. They were already saying suspicious things, those boys, saying things along the lines of 'We don't want to identify with any ideology because we want our worth to lie in our actions,' et cetera, but *el corazón hace caso omiso mi mente.*

"What they are doing now is bad, of course. Yes, go on, nod and shrug. You know, you know it all, and yet you want to go back—but only a few days ago, they detained a man just your age because he criticised the government for not doing anything about finding his schizophrenic brother who had gone missing. And they were proba-bly the ones who got rid of his brother; after all, the brother left a note saying he was trying to leave the country via Guantánamo—" (Who are They?)

"Papi, I know all this. I know," I say.

Tomás has left his chair and has wrapped his arms around Mami. Tomás looks at me and shakes his head; I am to forget this. It is my job to keep the peace and hold my peace and all the peace is on my shoulders.

"Look. I'm not here to fight anybody. But I have the tickets and I am going. I just thought I'd tell you."

"No, Maja. You are not going. I say you are not going. Let it sta let what I say stand. You say you know, you know—no, you don't know anything. Look at Cecilio Haber, only just out of jail. Why? Because he did something that would be perfectly acceptable over here in a free election—"

We are talking over each other; my words slip into his, but I know he hears me. I'm saying: "I'm going, I'm going, I'm going, I don't care what you say . . ."

I sound like a person who doesn't think. I am all fingers in my ears and la la la. It's the hysteric doing it, or maybe just me, or maybe all along it's just me. Today it's hard to tell.

Papi rubs his hands together—he has finished, he is certain. "I am sorry, *querida*," he says. "But let me tell you about the people of Abeokuta in Africa, where my family and your mother's family may once have come from.

"The story goes that the township was established when a company of slaves managed to escape the slave gatherers and fled west of Lagos. They did not know where they were going, but they passed some caves in which a spirit dwelt. They were afraid of the spirit, but less afraid of the spirit than they were of losing themselves. And that spirit repaid their trust, and it took care of them and showed them fertile land where they could live. I ask, I always ask, Where is that spirit? Why did it only go with those slaves who escaped? Anyway, forget about going. You're not from there anymore."

He talks about the spirit. He talks about the spirit but he doesn't know. Papi thinks "spirit" and in his mouth the word becomes *Geist*, a train of reason that chugs on and on and drags us all behind it without our understanding. But I want to make Papi understand about ba memory and St. Catherine's, that strange, safe Old Testament feeling that was there in the night, peace in the centre of a locust swarm. The sting that catches you before you have a name for it.

As if he knows what I want to say, Papi tells me, "I did not want to raise . . . 'spiritual' children. Spirituality doesn't protest injustice, it just bears it. I don't want that. I want you to think."

It must be something in my expression that makes him reach for me now. But I stand up.

To Mami I say, "Why don't you tell him? Why don't you tell him about all your flowers and your crying?"

Mami covers her mouth with her hand and says nothing. She looks sick.

I sit at Tomás's dressing table with all his tiny paint tubes in front of me, and my tears have dried on my face. I look at my brother's reflection in the mirror. His hands are on my shoulders. When he sees what I'm looking at, he self-consciously touches the wound on his lip and hisses, "Shut up."

"You should leave that school," I say. "Tell Chabella and she'll find another school."

He picks up one of the paint tubes. "You want some on?"

It scares me, the thought of him choosing his armour already, the thought that already he is hiding. Tomás balances a tube on his palm, squints at it with one eye closed.

"I run almost twice as fast with this stuff on, you know. I run like no one knows me, like no one can hold me."

I turn back to the mirror. Tomás bends over me with a blanched pearl on his fingertip, and he coasts it over my skin, gentle.

I watch my face begin to disappear under his hand.

At first I think that I will not be able to take Mami's collar. I expect the beads to fight harder to stay with Chabella. Pricked by the sharp reproof of her scent, I reach under the pillow on her side of the bed and open her incense box, and the collar falls out as if it is glad to go with me. No one discovers me, no one says, "What are you doing?" but I jump anyway and my fingers knot into each other as I yank down the fold of my polo neck with one hand and fasten the collar's clasp around my throat with the other.

All she had to say to Papi, "You don't understand. Just like you don't understand about my altar, you don't understand about this."

But she didn't say anything, my mother, my son's mother once removed.

I find Aaron sitting on the doorstep of the house in his big blue Windbreaker. He is eating noodles out of a plastic tub, and there is sauce all over his chin. He smiles up at me, notes the face paint with his finger.

"That was a long Mass," he says. "Are you cheating on me?"

I tweak his nose. "Yes. His name is Father Rodriguez. He gave me a message for you: those who wish to be saved must share all that they have."

He motions for me to sit down with one hand, jabbing with his chopsticks to make sure that I don't kick his camera, which is set on the step below him.

"How was it mentoring the Ewe posse?" I ask him.

He smiles and says, "Not one of them has even the makings of a hang king in him." He feeds me a long noodle strand, and I cup my hands around his face to make it secret that I'm kissing him.

"You're tired," he says, eventually, and I say no, but my eyes feel as if they're receding into my skull and I am already beginning to wonder how I will pick my limbs up in order to take them inside.

Aaron snaps the lid back onto his noodle tub. "There was a message on the answer machine when I got back," he says. "From a Sister Perpetua."

Sister Perpetua, who is so sure that darkness is part of heaven. St. Catherine's, where darkness comes for me and it is not hell. He looks at me, waits, as if I have to say something to reassure him that I'm staying with him, but I just say, "Oh."

"She said—"

I force myself to say it softly: "I'll listen to it myself."

He smiles unhappily; his eyes search me.

Sister Perpetua's message is simple: she felt moved to speak to me, and she wants me to know that I am always welcome to visit, that I must come if I need space to think.

I don't want to think. I thought I wouldn't be one of those pregnant women who touched their stomachs, but I am touching, wondering do I still feel pregnant, trying not to let myself know that I'm wondering.

Aaron stays outside and stays outside and stays outside. It is cold out there and fast becoming night. I want Aaron to come in to me. But I just stand at the window, looking up and out into the street, and all I can see are his legs, dressed in dark jeans, stretched a long way over the grey steps.

On the window, dusk is formed into a mushy hand shape, a single print. I stare at it, then switch on a lamp and lift my hand to the print. I cannot understand why someone has pressed their hand so hard against the window. I cannot understand why there is only one handprint. The interior is solid, like a mist breathed against the glass, and there are no skin patterns, no fingerprint patterns. This print has been left by a cold glove, a morgue glove. I tell myself that it's not true, it's not true, it's not true.

I say, "Aaron," as if he could hear me through the glass, and of course he doesn't notice that I am calling him, and so to bed.

FIFTEEN

THE KING WHO DOES NOT SPEAK

No Kayodes in the somewherehouse, and so Aya hears nothing but the cedar beams whispering until Mama Proserpine strides out into the hallway to find her. Because it is a mask day for Aya's mama, and because Proserpine is not wearing a mask this mask day, Aya averts her own gaze. Proserpine's wooden mask is secured atop her head in bows of downy lining; her cloak fastens in tarnished bronze links at her throat. Proserpine multiplies and a carnival of cloaked women bend their fractured gazes on Aya.

But no, it is only the mirrors, mirrors everywhere Aya looks.

"Proserpine, why did you bring the mirrors down?"

Proserpine's sigh is refined, tolerant. "Proserpine is not my name."

Aya climbs the stairs to the Kayodes' rooms. She is slowed by flashing mirror surfaces that stir the air in an ascending chime. The house gives way to a spiky maw that snaps at Aya as she opens doors and doors and doors to take down mirrors. Her own aghast reflection runs at her, looms at her, flies from openings to toss her into foreboding until she cries, "Who's that, who's there?"

The mirrors are studded with the blunt stems of her watchmaker's seeds, which have staggered into mahogany life; their petals all point one way. The attic, nude and luxuriating in its new dark, welcomes Aya by spattering her with moths. Aya sits with her back against the door and places her hand over her juddering heart.

But the hard flowers are here too—she didn't forget the attic when she was planting them. The flowers point: Aya is meant to go still higher.

She puts her head out of the attic window. The branches scrabble to attention, she winces as snow scuttles across her face and eyes.

"Yeye?" Mama Proserpine's call climbs from the kitchen to the rafters.

Aya looks up, sees that she has never understood the somewherehouse's trees. Their branches brush the ground, yes, their branches fountain in twiggy brackets from earth upward, but
(their roots are buried in the sky)
clouds crawl lazily away from the black suction that the roots, wide and thick as doors, drive into the blue.

Snow crumbles onto Aya, snow salts her.

All of the watchmaker's signpost flowers are straining upward, pointing out what it is that she seeks, up, up. In shattered minutes from window ledge to rough tree trunk, she has fought her way up to the snow's uneven red centre, a V that looks less and less like light and more like blood. Snow unfolds itself in bolts on and around her. Inside her is a happiness that threatens to unzip her and step out singing.

Then her skin finds a limit: other skin, a cheek against her cheek. She tries to climb back down to safety, but, as if she does not own or control her hands, Aya releases the branch. She does not fall, but her tears start immediately. Compunction, for he is terrible.

Him. He leans forward to her; he is the one who has caused the trees to grow contrary, to grow from his heart. He is a great cuspate blade primed to flay her, he is a hammer bringing sun down to gloom.

He says, "Daughter."

"I cannot."

"Cannot——?"

"I."

Aya weeps and she looks for herself, but there is no one there.

Papa says, "What do you want of me?"

"I."

"You poor child," her papa says.

Her nerve a million times denies her. Papa waits and they breathe together, but Aya cannot speak. Such oppression. It pulls at her eyeballs. He releases her. Aya falls through the tree's tentacles with her arms spread wide; she is shadowed by falls of snow . . . until a new heat lances her and with trembling hands she learns that she is dangling just above her window, her stomach impaled on an ice-whitened branch. Oh, blood.

Mama Proserpine, swimming in place in an ocean of black silk, leans out of the attic window

(too far——she could fall)

to try to help her, and Aya, unable to gesture "no," cannot yet say that this pain brings her *ache* to the front of her mind.

Sleet races leaves down from the tree roots; sleet covers Aya's shoulders, chills the hot blood she's losing. The way her limbs are splayed now she is more honest in her agony than she has ever been before. This is what she really looks like, humble before him, her father. This is how he has always seen her.

Kneeling down before three mirrors that Mama Proserpine has fetched and propped up against the attic wall, Aya touches her lips, her forehead, her cheeks; they are daubed with blood from her fingers.

Once, she heard the word "welkin" used, and "welkin" became a word she loved, but did not hear again. Welkin describes old, high fascination. It describes supple colour that catches and jails the eye—blue sky in summer when it spreads itself out like a magic carpet and it seems a person could step up onto it. The welkin tint is caught in Aya's eyes, is swept over her lips, lights her whole face. Her fingertips wind a dance of shudders down her throat, stroke whorls around her nipples. Drugged with content, her hand slides down to her lap.

"Where are the Kayodes?" Aya asks.

Proserpine squeezes another bloodstained rag into her bowl of water, and a green herb smell stretches its fronds over them.

"They went."

"You took them home?"

Proserpine nods and flattens another rag over Aya's stomach. Aya doesn't feel it.

"Are you Mama?"

"Yeye, don't do this."

Aya peels off the hot rag and drops it into the bowl. "What happened to your face, your skin? What happened to the way you walk? Why don't you wear your mask on a mask day?"

Mama settles herself opposite Aya. She sees Aya is uncomfortable and she pulls down her mask, adjusts it. The mask is a white hand that cups Mama's face.

"I was weary. So I went to your papa, and he took my *ache*."

This new Mama's eyes flicker behind her mask.

. . . .

Aaron wants to tell his mother about my son.

"I haven't even told *my* mother."

He says, "Well, let's tell her as well. What's the problem?"

"No problem, there isn't a problem." I am sarcastic. I do not let him hold my stomach, or even brush against it. Because he performs examinations—that is what he does—when he touches me now his fingers become probes, his fingers tell me he doesn't trust me. I reject his name suggestions: Gabriel is a stupid name, the other boys would have kicked him to pieces over that name anyway, my son, if he had lived.

I can't get the sanitary towels out of the house fast enough. So Aaron finds out about the bleeding, about the dark syrup my son sends me. He holds up one of my scented sanitary bags between his fingertips and we both look at the sodden cotton whirling around inside it. For a moment I can see the anger he talked about before. It's there on his face. Then the flash fades and he is left with a scared face and I am left with a nervous giggle that he doesn't understand. Aaron wants to know why I didn't say anything.

Is the baby . . . gone?

Have I been to the doctor?

What is the *matter* with me?

I want to know too, maybe.

Dr. Maxwell has big pink cheeks. In her family I bet she is the youngest child, the well-fed child who got morsels from her mother's fingertips whenever something special was cooking, who had her cheeks pinched into prettiness by tens of doting fingers.

Aaron takes the scare out of the visit to her. The heel of my hand, that part where the veins are most traceable—Aaron kisses me there while she talks about our options. I wade through the ultrasound, through six glasses of water and clear, cartilage-thick gel and the probes, and my son is still there
(or some thing, a small wonderful curl that represents him—he is turned to hide his sex) and later Dr. Maxwell says my bleeding was just an extra egg, just an extra egg, that sometimes that happens.

Throughout the scan Aaron cannot catch his breath for gladness, he cannot see straight for crying—who is he fighting?

I think I am sleeping too much.

My eyes open and I think: *daytime*. Other times my eyes open and I'm certain it's nighttime. I do not say a lot, because of the leak. If I speak, the leak speaks louder. The water does not want me to be heard. Aaron wants me to know that I am exhausted. But there is no reason for me to be exhausted. I am about to ask him, *exhausted from what*, but before I can, I am asleep again. It cannot be a good thing to keep falling asleep like this, falling asleep without my choosing or my control. No dreams. But when I manage to fight into waking for long enough, the woman's song comes back to me so clearly now (and yes she did sing in Habana, she really did—Magalys has lied).

My son is strong, a greater strength of coffee than both I and Aaron. No one will be able to drink right down to the bottom of this boy, if only I let him be born.

Aaron is here again trying to feed me soup, trying to feed me tomato kedgeree but all I see is bloodied fish. Aaron smiles, he tries to keep me cheerful. I take a long time gathering coherence and then I ask him if he sees anything when he sleeps with his eyes open the way he does. His smile is his answer; it protects him from me and I lose him inside it. I am beginning to understand that at the end of this time there is going to be a need for strength, that as the skin over my stomach pulls tauter my centre descends, and one day I am going to have to push. I don't know how anyone survives it, the thought or the happening. I will not.

I try to talk about the leak. Aaron says I need to be patient about having it fixed. That leak, it is too cruel, it bypasses me and talks to the other one who is not me. I am not being stupid or petty and I am not playing the girl card when it happens that I cry and say, "Please get that leak stopped." Aaron says, "Soon, soon, I promise."

I am trying to make sure that I live. Living is not a thing I can do alongside the leak. I have taken to crawling in my sleep. When I wake, I laugh at the carpet burns pulling at the skin on my knees. I am trying to get away from the woman who walks above me, walks from room to room even as I crawl. The leak

(Cubans are very friendly if their gestures are reciprocated, Miramar has great beaches, don't forget to check out the Varadero, oh look what has happened to this Cubana, if nobody told her she was Cuban would she even know? Yet *siempre el dramático*)

the leak is out of proportion and out of control. The leak is tears. And tears are prayers, but I think Mami only says that because she is best at tears.

St. Catherine's: that place with its bell tower and sweet, long-spaced chimes; its trees; the Sisters; the way the light there is different. Having someone who knows me a little see that place could be worse than letting someone read a book or hear a song that has worked witchery on me. St. Catherine's is the kind of place that someone could use to suddenly know me a lot better, and against my will. Amy Eleni is driving me up there, because with Amy Eleni I don't mind so much. I wouldn't want Aaron to see that place.

Today Amy Eleni is wearing a terrible hat I bought her for Christmas years ago—she calls it that, "The Terrible Hat." It's a patchwork fleece hat, as ugly as sin, but warm, which I knew she'd like. I sit beside Amy Eleni in the front seat of her car and hold my seat belt a little bit away from me so that I don't feel so restricted. London slips away and is not missed; trees and sky begin to gently blend, there is more air. Amy Eleni plays Billie Holiday and we listen to her blessing that child that's got his own. Also, we quote lines from *Vertigo*. We swap so that neither of us has to be Scottie for longer than is fair; Judy gets all the best lines.

"That film is cleverer than either of us," Amy Eleni says when she runs out of quotes.

"Yeah," I say. I have run out, too.

Things are more serious than Amy Eleni and I realised. We are not equal to this pregnancy thing.

"So what's been the matter with you lately? Do you think you're the first woman ever to get pregnant or something?"

Amy Eleni keeps her eyes on the road, doesn't waver as I look at her and tell her plainly, "It's the hysteric. You know. Everything's become absolute. I get this feeling that either I or this baby is going to die."

("Okay," says Amy Eleni, "that's why we need to get rid of the baby.") She brakes so hard that the tyres scream and I bounce in my seat, fall forward, and the top of my head is numb numb because I've smashed through the windscreen and the noises my brain makes, the noises, for almost a second I am blind.

No I'm fine. My belt, my seat-belt thing. I'm fine. Except Amy Eleni is staring at me, her eyes like rounds of bottle glass. Except I heard Amy Eleni speak, but she did not speak, or it was not she who spoke.

I am beginning to understand something about the hysteric, how sneaky she is, how she can repeat in Mami's voice, "A white girl is never your friend, she works to a different system." I can see how my personal hysteric and I could conspire and do something to my son and make it Amy Eleni's fault. This thing, this mistrust I did not know I had, it could go far, too far. Hysteria has got nothing to do with an empty womb.

"Calm down! Something ran out across the road. A stray or something. I didn't hit it," Amy Eleni says, starting up again once she is sure that I am all right.

"Please turn back," I whisper.

"No, I'm taking you to St. Catherine's. You wanted to go."

Nothing but trees and the cold outside.

"I've changed my mind! I don't want to be in the car with you!"

Amy Eleni's eyes narrow, but she checks her rearview mirror and turns the car around, she turns the car around, thank God.

"You think I don't understand this pregnancy thing, and you're

right, I don't understand it. But please do me the courtesy of thinking it's because I've never been pregnant, not because I'm gay, not
because I'm not going to have any kids. I saw your face when you
found out I'm an egg donor," Amy Eleni says, flatly.

I don't say anything to her. I look out of the window. I want to
drown her out in case she says anything else; I would turn up the
volume of the music, but I don't want to touch anything in her car. I
just want us to be safe. I don't know what "us" means; there are com-
binations—me and my son, me and Aaron. And there's me and Amy
Eleni, the friend who came and made it so that I needed no other
friend. Green changes back into grey, the pavements return.

When she drops me off outside Aaron's flat, I get out and say to
her, very carefully, "I can't see you for a while. And we can't talk
about this baby anymore. It's not your fault—it's mine."

She just nods and rolls up the window.

Sleep, get up, et cetera.

I want my papi to come for me. But if he comes with reason I
will turn him away. I don't want the everyday Papi who lives out of a
suitcase of ideas and cigars and woollen slippers. I want my papi of
emergencies, the Papi that I can reach when we're both quiet and
straining to catch each other.

Papi caught chicken pox when I was twelve. Tomás was three,
and Mami's main concern was keeping Tomás away from Papi so that
no one died. I hadn't had chicken pox yet, but I volunteered to be
chief nurse and snuck into Mami and Papi's bedroom to check on
him even when Mami banned me from doing so. Papi was very
quiet, very patient. His eyes, peering out from the tufts of

chamomile-soaked cotton wool that Mami had left on his face, were pale red. I loved him so much more because he didn't have anything to say about his chicken pox, my brave silent sufferer; I sat up beside him in bed and hugged him carefully. I wanted to catch the pox from him because I thought it would help him by dividing the spots in half. I took his temperature with increasing daring, leaving my hand against his forehead for so long that I thought I was sure to succeed. His fever ran so high that entire week that it seemed certain he would spontaneously combust. But when I knelt by his pillow and told him so, he laughed breathlessly and asked me what I knew about spontaneous combustion. So I showed him books—the best picture was of a man's leg resting at the foot of a chair, a few inches away from a hill of ash. The leg, dressed in a kneesock and training shoe, looked jaunty in its independence, as if it was about to launch itself toward the ash and kick it in every direction. "There's a man who spontaneously combusted," I said. "I bet he didn't say anything when it was about to happen. I bet he knew what was going on, though. He must've felt hot."

Papi agreed with me.

The next morning I woke up before the sun did, gagging with thirst, feeling as if my tongue had been scraped with a rusty spike. I kept spitting dazedly into my hand to see if there was blood. My pillows were sucking me in.

"Papi, Papi," I shrieked, and he came. When he saw me, he tutted as if it was my fault I felt sick. He said, "Oh, Maja."

I tried to stop spitting into my hand. I knew it was ugly, but I couldn't help it; my hands were seamed with glassy, bitter-smelling bubbles.

Papi ran his fingers over the red rash on my forehead and kissed me all over my face, and said, very low, very serious, very kindly, "*Gracias, m'hija, gracias,*" until I settled against his shoulder, content that he was grateful. Papi comes to conclusions suddenly and works backward, once he's there at the beginning of a thought he understands.

Papi: ordinary boy or extraordinary boy? When Mami used to cornrow his hair for him he would think of something and get impatient halfway through and wander around the house looking for the book with the paragraph that was perfect for that starburst of thought. Even if Mami worked quickly she could only get half of his head done at once, then for the rest of the day he would go around with his fingers marking several places in several books, one half of his head neatly plaited, the other half a mass of curls with an Afro comb quivering in it. He looked like a retired rapper in denial. Eventually he'd stop in front of a mirror, tut and say, "Chabella, I thought you had finished? Somebody needs to take these plaits out."

Chabella started enlisting me to cornrow the other half of Papi's head so that we had a better chance of making his hair presentable. But one day he defied us. He went out and came back with his head shaved. He stood dramatically in the doorway and crowed, "Ha!"

My papi loves salt so much he can eat it sprinkled over thinly sliced tomatoes; if he feels his blood pressure rushing he reaches for more salt in case it's his last. My papi is so fond of conclusions that he reads the last three chapters of a novel before he reads the first. My papi dreams of small children who will call him their *abuelo*. But all that means is that if I want revenge I will have them call him "Grandsire," curtsey or bow, and ask if he will take one lump or two.

Only with Papi can I forgive at the exact moment that he hurts me. It is as Chabella said: there is nothing wrong with my father except that he stopped listening to me. But Awe is not my mother, Chabella is, and she is not on my side. I thought she was fighting Papi and sugar and England with her tears and flowers, but really she has been fighting me, too.

The doorbell rings so urgently and so many times that it wakes me. I go to the main door barefoot, rumpled and disoriented. Papi has sent Tomás to pick up my plane ticket. When Tomás comes in, I see that he's surprised by how dark the flat is. He draws in a deep breath and says, "Why does it smell so damp in here?"

I could tell him about the leak, but instead I say, "Because it is England."

He is abashed, as if it's his fault that I'm not going to Habana. He shuffles his feet while I go through my bag for the tickets. I am slow finding them, but I do not think to withhold the plane tickets because I do not think. When I find them, I hand them to Tomás without taking them out of the envelope.

Tomás says, "Maja, I did try to talk to him for you."

I hug him and he resists at first, then he folds into me.

I say, "Why couldn't Mami talk to him for me?"

Tomás lets go of me and says, "Mami's ill."

"What's wrong with her?"

He pauses, fumbles for the root of the problem.

"She can't find her Santeria beads."

I am laughing now. I can't give a reason for it, but my brother wants to know why. His face comes very close to mine and his hands form fists; I press a hand down on my chest as if somehow that will silence me, but instead my hand falls onto my stomach, and we both look, we both look at the bump. Tomás eases away. His voice is shaky. "She's lost her beads. It's not funny. Papi and I talked about getting her some more, but apparently they'd have to be consecrated and all this stuff and you know that's enough to send Papi mad because he doesn't trust *babalawos*. But this thing with Chabella . . . oh. You should come. She's . . . I don't know. She tutors and she cooks and she makes those paper flowers and she just sits there and she's so sad. It doesn't sound like anything. But. You should come."

I cross over into the bedroom and bring Tomás the collar. When he sees it, he sits very still and looks as if he has forgotten how to breathe. He thinks I am heartless to still be holding the collar after what he has told me. He doesn't understand that Chabella and I are fighting. I hold the collar out to him, draw it back.

Tomás whispers, "Please give it back. You don't know how sad Mami is."

(No.)

"Why are you blaming her? It was Papi who said you couldn't go." When I don't reply Tomás says, "You're pregnant, aren't you? Why didn't you say anything to us?"

I will not answer him.

"Hormones," Tomás says, to goad me.

Tick, tick, no answer. But as soon as he leaves, I call home. Mami answers and her voice is hoarse and thin, and I think, *fight me better than this.*

And she does. Chabella says that she is fine. She does not talk to me about the collar. I say I have been tired lately, and of course she is concerned and of course she thinks she has something that will help. Should she bring it over? I say "No" louder than I mean to.

Amy Eleni is brusque with me when she calls. "Now, tell me what's the matter, Maja."

I am sitting up in bed with my head against the headboard; the phone is pinned between my shoulder and my ear. My arms feel weak. I didn't want to speak to her, but Aaron gave me such a look when he handed me the phone. I tell her, "Nothing. I'm pregnant. Nothing. I'm going to die."

"Shut up! Aaron's worried sick. You tell me you don't want to see me, you act all fucked up, but because I'm your best friend you know I can't just let that stand. Another thing: you sleep all the time."

"Okay, it's sleeping sickness."

"Didn't I just tell you to shut up?"

I shut up.

Amy Eleni says, "I read my class a wonderful poem, a stunning poem, the Elizabeth Jennings love poem about stargazers, and the only comment I had was anonymous—it came from the back, and it was 'I don't get it, man.' They think they have to 'get' it. When I talk about Shelley, this same kid at the back shouts out, 'Who's Shelley?' When I talk about Marvell or Donne, this boy or deep-voiced girl shouts out, 'Who's Marvell? Who's Donne?' When I talk about Shakespeare, this little shit at the back shouts out, 'Who's Shakespeare?' I look and look but there's about eight of them with their hands over their mouths. Their last teacher was male, and he cracked after someone spat on his head; he couldn't identify the culprit and everyone thoroughly denied it, so maybe they're expert liars or maybe they got this man so nervous he imagined saliva. They're trying to . . . well, anyway, I won't do it, you know?"

Suddenly I am telling Amy Eleni about Magalys and Papi and Mami. I talk for a long time.

Amy Eleni says with certainty, "Listen Maja, I think you're pulling a *Vertigo* on me with this distraught chat about oh, something missing in your Cuba memory and how you feel so trapped by your dad not letting you go. The reason why you're not going is that you know it's not what you need—what you need is here. If you really needed to go back, you'd come to the regretful conclusion that it's none of your dad's business and you'd go anyway. Wouldn't you? There's nothing between you and yourself. If Madeleine Elster or Judy really needed to kill herself, then between that person inside her telling her that she had to go and Scottie saying, 'Hey you're pretty and I like you so don't die,' Scottie didn't stand a fucking chance. The Elster chick, or Judy, or whoever, she could have just shot herself in the head if it all got too much. But she didn't. She *let* Scottie get in the way."

I listen to Amy Eleni breathing on the other end of the line, and I listen to the leak. I listen to the African news channel that Aaron is watching next door; I don't listen to what the newsreader is saying, but to how she is saying it, her tone of perpetual astonishment.

I sleep. I wake and put Chabella's collar back on to make my sleep uncomfortable, to give me a better chance of waking. Some-times Aaron is there. More often he is not there. When he speaks on the phone to Geoffrey, he speaks in Ewe because he doesn't want me to know what he is saying. The smell of damp collects in my bones.

I warm myself up some tomato soup and before I can sit down to drink it I've become carbon, the black before a diamond shows itself. My senses turn crystalline and abrade one another until I lay down my spoon. If this spoon should scrape against the bottom of the bowl just once, and I should hear it scrape, I am not sure of the result. I am not sure where the hysteric and I are going to go when that bad sound comes. I hold the spoon away and I breathe and do not eat.

Aaron looks at me over the top of his own bowl of soup, and the circles around his eyes are so dark that I begin to think I am reflecting him.

"You have got to eat," he says. His voice is very hard. It hurts. He stands over me and drags my wrist so that I have to put soup into my mouth. I let him; with his hand over mine there is less risk of the bad sound coming. A spoonful at a time, we do it. The cold in this kitchen never ends, the steam off the soup is nothing. Whenever I think I am going to spit soup in Aaron's face, he knows, and he warns me with his eyes.

I say I've had enough, and Aaron looks into the bowl. It is still more than three-quarters full. Aaron says, "Don't be selfish." He jams the sloppy spoon into my mouth. It isn't deliberate when the metal strikes my teeth—but the metal does strike. I take the spoon myself and continue the work. Aaron watches me swallow; he is sad that he has to do this, but he is strong. In his eyes I am a throat working down red juice, I am a shaking hand and a spoon and beyond that his baby.

(Herr Doktor please die as I cannot have you think of me this way.)
I am so ashamed of my tears that I am going away, not up and out,
not inside, I don't know where, just away. My shame brings me escape velocity, brings me *Gelassenheit*. I love my son, so when Aaron is
gone, I do not throw up to spite him. I let the soup stay. I let us have
the soup.

Aaron has to go when there is a cardiac arrest and he is on night
cover; he has to go for fourteen hours at a time on a lot of days. He
has to be gone, full stop.

Amy Eleni has tousled her hair up with gel. I peek into the sitting
room and watch Aaron wrap his arms around her; she nips his
cheek, talks to him for a moment
(the first thing she says is, "This place smells worse and worse all the
time."
I think he offers her words about the plumber, or time, or something, because the second thing Amy Eleni says is, "She will lose her
mind in this smell you know."
I don't hear the third thing)
then she comes through to me.

She has brought me an armful of coffee-table books about Cuba,
two torches and a grab bag of salt-and-vinegar crisps. I refuse to let
the books remain in the bedroom.

"But these are good, I promise," she says. "I meant to give them
to you for your birthday, but this is an emergency. Anyway, shut up."

Amy Eleni has inscribed the inside of the first book: *Friends make
the world strong and beautiful. —JOSÉ MARTÍ*

We crawl under the covers with torches, Amy Eleni lies flat on her stomach, I lie on my side. Our breath tickles the pages, and we stare at Cubans and the words that they have said to the photographers, the words printed alongside the monochrome and sepia images of bearded men waving out of the windows of long brown cars, houses with tiled floors and open wooden shutters and pictures of Che Guevara beside pictures of Jesus, leathered women in aprons churning butter, a queue of uniformed girls following a nun down the street with their buckle-shoed feet caught in variations of the cha-cha-cha, each grabbing the other by the ponytail.

My fingers turn the pages to salt and vinegar, but they stay on a page where a black Santero woman strewn with the beads of her gods lets her laughter throw her head right back. She is a big woman, and a diamond-patterned headscarf covers even bigger hair in a turban wrap. Behind her on the wall, in blurry focus, is a wooden crucifix, and the words next to her picture don't matter.

I decide to be proactive about the leak. I take pen, paper and the Yellow Pages and sit down on the floor by the phone to find and write down the telephone numbers of four plumbers in the area. Understanding what I am reading takes longer than it should because something seems hilarious to me, but I don't know what it is. The laughter is there and there's no bottom to it. I try strategies. I try to dissect what could be making me laugh; I try to remember if I've just seen anything or heard anything or there's anything in the room that I'm not fully registering. I put the phone book down and I search the sitting room for hilarity. The sitting room is nothing but books and lamps and videotapes. At the window I see that the day is recovering from rain and I see that Aaron has left a plantain skin on the windowsill.

I try to stop smiling because smiling is another way for this laughter to seethe out from between my teeth. I try to outrun the grin and I go to the front door and back again, but when I stop, the world whirls and the sloshing in my ears tells me my water levels have gone awry. There is already too much water inside—my son swims as he sleeps; when he is awake he surges toward a sound. I want my son to try at leaving me a little, so, for him, I found my voice this morning and sang. I think my son likes my voice. It disordered me to track his movement with my thumb. My voice came differently this morning—there was a raspy range to it before that has gone away. Now I'm sounding impossibly light and singing nonsense lullabies that very quickly seem as if they had never been, like bubbles blown and broken at second breath. But my son heard, and he swelled his walls in one smooth rush. He strained so eagerly that I understand that he doesn't know that his walls are me. I wanted Aaron to know. I called out, "Oh my God! Aaron!" and then I remembered that he had already left for the day.

Still believing that I am about to start laughing, I look at phone numbers, but each number stands independently of the others, smug mathematical symbols. Today my handwriting comes out so small that when I try and call one of the numbers I misread my 5's for 6's and my 6's for 5's and call the wrong number. The second time, I call the right number. But there is some problem with the way that I'm describing the leak, and the man I'm talking to gets exasperated and hangs up.

After that I sit and hold myself very tightly in case I start to laugh. The leak is making me laugh; the sound, the way the water droplets smack each other, like clown shoes. Someone will fall over soon, and even if it's me, it will still be funny. I snort and stuff my fingers into my mouth so that the joke doesn't come loose. I should go to sleep. At least that way I will not be laughing. I don't want Aaron to have to come back and find me laughing and make me stop. It's as Amy Eleni says, there's nothing between me and myself and I may have to end up letting Aaron intervene.

No, I should go to bed. I leave the numbers on the notepad by the phone and I write to Aaron, very carefully, that he should *please call today.*

In bed, by accident, I say, "Ha ha."

And then it's all over and it's rhythmic, it's

ha ha ha

ha ha HA HA HA HA

HA ha

HA ha

and again,

I cannot hear the leak while this "ha" is being forced out of me.

I laugh until I'm bent almost in half and the bones in my knees bounce against my stomach. My mouth is dripping because I haven't had enough time to swallow. I'm upside down, I can't understand what I'm seeing and I think I need to climb over my knees somehow if I want to be in an upright position. But there is a living end to the laughter after all—this is good news. Maybe the laughter is my son's. He is a serious event, but not all that serious. He is not the first baby that was ever born. I take Chabella's collar in my hand and it corrugates my fingertips, hard wood in a trickster's colours. Elegua's humour is inscrutable.

Carmen, you are born again, but you are born without your tongue. Find it. Be who you were before before.

But Elegua doesn't go backward, he makes things change when they need to. Chabella trusts what the German language has enabled her to call her spiritsoulmind; Chabella takes any risk that involves it. But if she should fail . . . what poverty! The goal is that Carmen is not born again. The goal is that the lost tongue stays lost, but new tongues grow. No one need be maimed.

I am asleep when Aaron gets back, but he moves around and it wakes me. The dark is too thin. Aaron has the bedroom door wide open and all the lamps in the sitting room are on. His face keeps escaping the light, but I think he's looking at me.

He says stiffly, "Maja. Do you not want this baby? Is the problem that you don't want it?"

I sit up with a hand over my eyes. Aaron's question has pushed him to me straight from washing up in the kitchen; his hands are still dripping soapy water and he is holding one of our soup bowls.

He says, "Just tell me."

"Why do you think that I don't want the baby?"

He says, "Just tell me, just say something about it."

A tremor comes through his hands and he can't hold the bowl anymore, he bats it toward the ground as if he thinks it is a ball that will come back up to him. There is not much sound, but I flinch as the china shatters. Some of the pieces roll, then rest. Automatically, he says, "Shit, sorry," and he bends to pick pieces up with his bare hands. Automatically, I say, "Use tissue, you'll cut yourself."

He does not listen. He balances a row of brittle blue claws on his palm before taking them away, coming back to rescue more. His hair is in his eyes. He does not get cut.

I say, "The leak. Please call the numbers, get a plumber here tomorrow. Call the numbers."

Crouched on the carpet, Aaron tilts his head and says, "What numbers?"

I lie down again.

"I left them on the pad."

"Those are numbers, eh? They look like a series of decimal points."

I get up to rewrite the phone numbers so that he can see them, so that he can make the phone calls for me. But my note has already been ripped away from the pad.

I took a third-class degree. It was better than I'd expected, especially considering that I had actually handed in my dissertations on a block of wood. But I didn't know how to tell my parents about my results. I had misled them from an early age. I had given them to understand that I was clever. And they were both first-class students.

So I completely lost my nerve.

"It's . . . a two:three," I said, when it was time to tell them.

Chabella, who had clasped her hands in anticipation of good news, lowered them again and frowned.

I didn't back down, there was no point now. "A two:three," I insisted.

Papi threw up his hands. "What in God's name is a two:three?"

"You know," I quavered, holding my certificate behind my back. "You can get an upper second class, a middle second class, and a lower second class. A two:one, a two:two, a two:three . . . ?" Papi and Mami surrounded me, hugging me, kissing me, cackling.

"So it's a third-class degree, then," Chabella said.

Papi said, "Thank God—at least it's finished. All the drama, all the crying, all the painting things black, the praying of the rosary instead of revising. A degree. You've got a degree, Maja Carmen Carrera! You passed! You are to some extent educated! And you didn't even notice while it was happening!"

Amy Eleni was very flushed when she showed me her certificate. She had taken a first-class degree. I thought, *Of course*.

"Please don't give me any shit about this," she said, before I'd even opened my mouth.

When we got back to my house on graduation day, Amy Eleni, mortarboard in hand, kicked off her high-heeled shoes and put them in her handbag so that the black toes peeped out of the top.

Our parents were in the back garden drinking Pimms and lemonade, Amy Eleni's mother looked vaguely astonished by the drink in her glass. I told them we were going to church, and Chabella beamed. Amy Eleni's father looked at us, his eyes that special shade of blue that Amy called "accusing ultramarine," and was entirely unable to hide his pride. We almost changed our minds about going to church.

When we got out onto the street, Amy Eleni walked beside me barefoot, gowned, her hair in her eyes—people around us kept looking for cameras, as if we were on a photo shoot. We stared at the people who stared at us, caught them in our double headlights, stared with the conviction of newly educated, non-crap-taking female youth—they always looked away first.

The church ceiling seemed higher because of the incense, grey arms uplifted to exalt. Except for Father Gerald at the front, who sat with his eyes closed and his hands folded over a missal on his lap, the church was empty. He didn't turn around. We had had our baptisms, our Holy Communions, our confirmations here. This church, from window to window, from wall to wall, seemed tied in for me with a desperate battle to avoid the Spirit—to be holy, but not yet.

For my confirmation name I had struggled to find the saint that God might love the least. The list was whittled down according to time and manner of the saint's death—early, gory deaths were sure signs of excessive favour—stigmatic-yes-or-no, mystic-yes-or-no and whether or not that saint's corpse had been exhumed and found to be uncorrupted. I wanted God to know the situation. I wanted to be more than just good friends, but nothing heavy until I was ready. I settled for being St. Ignatius of Loyola's namesake, and suffered a few weeks of hearty laughter and being addressed as "Sister Ignatia" by everyone else in our confirmation class.

Amy Eleni chose Sophia and debated extending her given name to "Amy Eleni Sophia." Her mother let her be confirmed in pearls, a black veil and a black, watered-silk dress with a stiff bustle. People in my class sniggered at her overdressing. But nobody knew what a victory that confirmation was for Amy Eleni. Her mother didn't attend the Mass.

Now Amy Eleni bent over the wooden prayer box, the box into which parishioners who wanted Father Gerard to pray for them had slipped their requests. She tucked it under her arm and walked out without a sound, leaving me to tiptoe behind her as best and as quickly as I could.

"I don't know what to do next," she panted, when I caught up with her and cried outrage. "The stuff of life to knit me blew hither, here am I, right? From Cyprus à la my mother to England and school and university, there's been a conspiracy of me, a me trying to work into a pattern. Now I feel like I'm out, graduated, so . . . what? I don't know which way I want to go yet, but I need to know if I'll be allowed to get there. I don't know if I can . . . yuck. I suppose I want to know if I can trust people with my dreams."

It wasn't an explanation, but coming from Amy Eleni, it was enough. We opened the box in my bedroom, tipped out a cascade of white paper slips, and read aloud to each other prayer after prayer, request after request, until we ran to the end of them. Speaking the words, I felt as if we were unsealing the wants behind them, releasing spurts of chalky tomb air with every sound. I felt as if we were granting wishes because we heard them and then they were free to be possible, the way a priest sits in a box and listens and becomes Jesus.

The sun went down and left its rays clinging to our skin. I looked out of the window and saw that our parents were still in the garden, laughing and talking and blowing dandelion petals, oblivious beneath a dark orange sky that threatened to swallow them.

It seemed like everyone in our church was praying for one another. There were so many wishes that people not be hurt, so many offerings of thanks for others, so many short pleas to save lives or offer a new grace to die with. Amy Eleni looked dizzy and small with all these slips in her hands; she had not expected this.

Near the end of our reading, I recognized Chabella's handwriting. She had written: *Please pray for Juan Carrera to be happy. Please pray for Juan Carrera to find whatever he came to this country looking for.*

I didn't read it aloud, but it was the first prayer I put back into the box; I had to do that so Amy Eleni wouldn't see it. It was the only bitter prayer in there, the only prayer that betrayed its writer.

"I'm going to go and find Sara," Amy Eleni told me, wriggling off the bed with the resealed box under her arm. I lay flat and began tracking shadows on the ceiling, pulled my polo neck up so that it covered the bottom of my chin, began my great, private worry about my life.

Amy Eleni paused at the door, turned, studied me, came back to me. She stood over me, sweetly serious, and I hauled myself up by degrees, matching her look for look; the inches between our faces grew warmer as they fell away. She dipped her head to kiss my mouth, and whispered against my lips, "Happy graduation." Her eyes were closed, and mine were wide open.

．．．．．．．．．．．．．．．．．．

When Aya visits now, Amy's wrists are newly, tightly rebandaged, her eyes are crayoned round with waning purple, and she is still so pale—even her lips have shed colour. She throws her arms around Aya and hugs her, so light a pressure that Aya thinks she might be imagining it. "Please stay a while," she says. "I loved it when you came to see me. You seem to care."

"I can't help it," Yemaya says, simply. Amy laughs, but Aya is serious. Amy is only laughing because she is pretending that she can switch her caring on and off, admire different books, love different people, discard her own life.

Aya moves about the somewherehouse, finishing her self-appointed task of returning all the mirrors that Proserpine brought down. The attic, reluctant to have the mirrors back, gives vent to floorboard groaning. Mama has put the Kayodes' rooms in order; their winding cloths are unpinned from the walls and heaped onto chairs. Their chessboard is gone. Their cupboards are pleasantly bare, the shelves are free of dust and expectation.

Aya had expected to find complicated packages of newspaper, braided trails of string, or some other closed thing that the Kayodes might have used to keep their speech amongst themselves. She had not expected to miss them as much as she does. She draws a hand over her eyes and picks up a mirror that rests in the arms of the rocking chair. She has asked Tayo to follow her here, and he comes—but hesitantly. The somewherehouse's cedar beams breathe *wheeeee* to bring their smell in after him. She wonders if the house will not keep him. Tayo hesitates, then draws her close to him, sits in the rocking chair and takes her onto his lap, pushing her hair aside to whisper into her ear, "But what are those figurines downstairs supposed to be?"

He has to close his eyes for her so that, with a fingertip, she can spirit ash away from those spaces where he is softest.

"What figurines?"

And after all people are sitting in the basement

a boy, a man, a woman,

withered, rheumy-staring from a carousel of spiderwebs.

Aya looks at Tayo and lets him see in her eyes what is happening. He says feebly, "Yeye, it's all right. They're not real," He is far more frightened than she is.

High-heeled footsteps clatter above; Proserpine has come in though the front door.

Aya decides quickly. She breaks an old chair, catches its leg up in her hand and goes to put an end to Mama Proserpine.

"Yeye!" Tayo grasps her wrist and tries to follow her, but she eludes him and the basement door is locked tight as she passes into the hallway—she makes it so.

Proserpine turns a pale stare of appeal on Aya. In her arms, caught up in her cloak, a rooster tramples air in a fright of feathers.

"Yeye, listen—"

The rooster escapes Proserpine's arms as Aya comes at her. Aya is like thunder. Blood wells from Proserpine's lip; she is dazed, delayed.

Aya cries to her, "You told me you took them home. But you killed them."

"Yeye—"

Aya says, grimly, "Shut your mouth. Don't ever address me that way. Proserpine, I saw you from the first."

Aya has the chair leg to Proserpine's throat. Proserpine has not cowered, though one of her eyes has swollen shut. The gaze of the other eye, the bulge of surprise in it—that drives Aya outside of herself. Aya's hand is a hot-red clutching, the wood splinters it, and she doesn't care. Her next blow snaps the chair leg clean in two.

"Yeye," Proserpine wails. "Don't you know how long it took you to find this place? When you got here, the Kayodes had only just arrived."

"Which Kayodes? The ones you killed?"

Proserpine spits a messy tooth into her cupped hand.

Aya asks, very quietly, "When?"

Proserpine smears down the wall until she is crouching, the heels of her shoes broken. Aya bends to hear her, her face knitting itself ready to spit. And Proserpine tells her about the Kayodes now, Proserpine tells and tells. With each repetition the story is truer.

By the time Aya asked her where the Kayodes were, the Kayodes were already dead. Because while Aya was gone through the London door, the Kayodes began starvation. But they didn't know what the feeling was—they didn't know that the ache meant "eat."

Proserpine cooked for them, so many desperate meals: she cooked *amala* and *ewedu*, *eko*, *moin-moin*, *bistecca*, *ajiaco*, fish-and-chips.

The Kayodes tried to feed on the smell, they breathed in until their lungs let the scent escape. But then one of them always said to the other, "Proserpine must not waste this food. Proserpine must give this food to someone who needs to eat."

Soon the Kayodes grew too weak even to talk to one another.

In the basement they sat and stared and waited for Aya's papa.

They were certain that Aya's papa would not forget them.

Then they were less certain.

Then they grew bitter.

And then they died, one immediately after the other, click, click, click, like three switches breaking a circuit. How afraid the third one was when he saw the dying moment begin in the first.

SIXTEEN

VENTURED ALL

(UPON A THROW)

Aya and Proserpine strain and sweat and dig a shallow grave around the back of the somewherehouse, in a spot where the grass and trees dip at the same point. Proserpine weeps. Her hands claw at Aya as if she is a closing door with home on the other side. Aya is suffocated by icy leaves. She leaves that place, leaves that woman.

Aya watches Amy untie the knots that secure her handkerchiefs to her belt and spread the silken squares out, full-length, over her bed. Picking one up at the corner feels like pinching a beautiful nothing between the fingertips.

"Do you want them?" Amy asks.

Aya lets the handkerchief settle back onto the covers.

Amy turns her bruise-hooped back to Aya and brushes the handkerchiefs onto the floor before she climbs into bed.

"Look what Tayo gave me," Amy says, after a moment. She opens her hand and a saint is in it; a medallion with dainty piecrust metalwork running round it. The saint is a woman with a long nose, hair demurely covered by a shawl, hands crossed on her breast.

"It's Our Lady of Mercy," Amy says. She closes her hand with a grim smile and draws her saint back under the covers. She gets lost in a dark memory that she doesn't say aloud.

The handkerchiefs are waiting on the floor. On her way out, Aya wonders, for less than a moment, what it would be like to own these handkerchiefs, to leave an aftermath of honey perfume. In Tayo's room, the white pointed tips of wet flowers spill over the tops of every drawer in his cupboard, as if the cupboard is crammed with people who are reaching their hands up and willing their fingers to escape the trap.

But early in the next day the fresh air in the room is spent, and the carpet around the chest of drawers is ringed in charcoal dust.

Amy is gone.

In her absence, Amy's room, baring itself between hills of glass-bead necklaces, socks, books and shrugged-off cardigans, is filled with grey light. Tayo, one hand clad in Amy's green silk handker-chief, stands at her dresser as if he is awaiting some news or appear-ance. He is so angry that he does not know what to do with himself, how to stay inside his skin. He shakes his head, bares his teeth to maul the air, but he doesn't leave the room.

He says, simply, "Where is she?"

"You love her?" Aya is serene.

"Amy," he says, "is missing. And you're asking stupid questions."

His smile is unguarded, also it is antique somehow

(yes, yes, who are you to me? almost I know)

his arms come down around her, draw her to him; she arcs under the pressure of his hand. His *ache* comes to her loudly. It comes through his chest.

"We have to get Amy to come back." Tayo's wish is spoken into her hair.

Aya closes her eyes against him. She will not go.

"Please," he says.

In the attic of the somewherehouse, Proserpine is hanged. She is like a pale, black-sheathed pendulum caught on a ceiling beam, in a quiet space behind the door that will not trouble anyone. As long as they stay outside, as long as they avoid looking to the left and catching sight of a bare, dapper foot, toes achieving the perfect pirouette. The mirrors report the hanging first; they are stern and reproving, then they make eulogy in softened light. Dozens of refracted Proserpines, faces forced up by frantic throats.

Proserpine not Mama, Proserpine not Mama.

Why, then, has Mama's face returned to this woman?

Her eyelashes, settled on her cheeks, spike the black clouds of her hair.

Tayo is downstairs—Aya hears muffled thumps, as if he is moving things around. The somewherehouse's cedar beams whisper to her of their alarm, but she ignores them and turns away.

"Tayo, don't come up here," Aya calls, and shuts the door.

Her papa, high, high in the roots and the snow, must know of this by now. Downstairs, the somewherehouse has thrown off its disguise. The house recognizes her with a sniff—about time. Aya falls to her knees, winded. All of the running that she has ever done, all of that fleeing for freedom from the Regla house, just to find La Regla house unfolding before her again. This hallway lit with a galaxy of gas lamps.

Tayo stands in the centre of the hallway and looks up at the domed ceiling, the rich stains that form the creation fresco. Young river, wild-eyed rooster, bulging palm kernel—poised intent on a beginning against the sky. They reach the big window at the end of the hallway and Aya leans out, touches the trees; their leaves rustle under her hands with well-fed laughter, sated by the sun and the warm earth. But Tayo is afraid. Aya tries to take his hand. She tries to bring him with her into the next room, but Tayo will not come. His smile is as hard and dark as mud clay. Aya frowns and calls Tayo's name, gently calls on him to explain, but Tayo says, "No, not him."

He backs away from her, holding his arms out to her; she follows him step for step, down, down into the dust, the basement. Step for step, she tries names, old names, newer names, until she remembers her mama's tale of the trickster who left the family for change.

She asks, "Elegua?"

"No!"

"Echun . . ."

He is crying hard now, the shape of his face buckles as if under blows.

"Oh, Echun," Aya says. "Echun, why? What's wrong?"

"Yeye," he says. "I know who I am. Shhh, I know. I know. But I have to be different. I have to be stronger. Needles and drowning; your papi is trying to make me kill myself. But . . . but I can't let him take my *ache*, no, no, he cannot have it all, he must leave my *ache* with me."

He opens the door for London—the Lagos door is nailed shut.

And he has matches. The basement cloth is slippery underfoot, he has wet them with something moss-smelling, something unordinary. Aya goes to him, but he holds her away with terror, as if she is a chemical rag that will stain him. He keeps saying he wants her, but that she is her father's eye. It is funny how afraid he is. Aya stops fighting him. She wants to spit at him, she wants to scratch him and hurt him, she wants him to die, she wants to go with him. She is drawn to him, sure and true, by her own instinct, the instinct of the runaway to be away, always away, always leaving, and running, running, running for home, hoping never to get there. Echun is beautiful, she sees that again. Of course it is because he is a trick.

"Give me the matches," Aya says.

He does not trust her—he gives them up to her only slowly. He is ready to fight her. Without taking her eyes from his, Aya strikes and lights a match.

"Go," she says, and drops it. Heat throws a swift and screaming shape between them.

Aya strikes more matches. These flames are hungry, glad, lean. They move in colourless crests.

"Shut the door," she says.

She does not see his face as he does; from behind the fire she cannot be certain whether he closes the door quickly or slowly. She thinks, *Poor Echun*. It doesn't matter that he wants to keep his *ache*; her papa will take it back. What matters is that Echun doesn't want her enough to risk being found.

Greedy Echun. There is much that Aya would have risked for him.

Aya climbs higher to escape the noise of wood breaking beneath the flames. She dreams of what happens next after the fire has taken her bones. She squints through veils of smoke, follows the trail to the top of the house, lies down under the sweeping glass ceiling. And Amy is there, Amy in her baggy dungarees, but she has changed. Aya pauses long and looks her fill at Amy in the Kayodes' rocking chair: Amy's Ochun-lips take a straight and sober line; her Ochun-skin, newly hazelnut, glows; her open eyes contain only the tenderest blessings of darkness, her hair is plaited into thick, shimmering vines. Aya doesn't touch her—she leaves her be.

Fire climbs the stairs.

There is more time, but not much.

If you are lucky, you lose a mother to get another.

If you are lucky, you shed a body to climb inside another.

Sometimes a child with wise eyes is born. And some people will call that child an old soul. And that is surely enough to make God laugh.

....

This morning I wait for the plumber. I wait and wait and the plumber doesn't come, and while I wait I try to mend the leak with my calm.

Indoor rain. It does not stop, I don't know what it means— something has opened somewhere and the rain is just there. Raintalk.

I phone Aaron. He answers so quickly that I barely realise I've finished dialling and I think he's called me. He says, "What's wrong?"

I pace the sitting room, heel to toe. "Did you call?"

"Did I . . . ?"

"Aaron, did you call a plumber?"

He says, very slowly, "This is why you're calling me?"

He is too loud. I wince and hunch my shoulders; my eyes are fixed to the phone pad, the imprints my writing has left on the paper beneath.

"The plumber isn't here yet. How come?" I say.

"Maja," he says. Disbelief brings him down to baritone. But I walk myself into the bedroom, asking him, asking him. He says, "Listen, I forgot to call. I forgot. I'll do it tonight. I'm bringing back some stuff about Lamaze classes. I think you dismissed them too quickly when Dr. Maxwell suggested them."

I have found Aaron's jeans, folded into his top drawer. He is talking about birth pain management, and in my palm I have my crumpled list of phone numbers from his pocket, the figures so small that they disappear into the crinkles. I have had to work at the paper with my fingernails to open it out. Aaron has folded and rolled my list of plumbers until it has taken on the hard, round unity of a shell.

This is how small my hysteric makes me; this is how far she takes me from speech when it is important that I speak. This is why she must be dissolved.

It is early, or late—4 a.m. I watch Aaron shaving at the bathroom mirror; he hums the guitar undertow of a Kofi Amese song. And he is careful; his lip wrinkles thoughtfully as he stops after every scrape to consider his chin. It was Papi who gave me the impression of shaving as an early-morning daredevil ritual, the will-he-won't-he-slit-his-throat in a wash of soapy lather. Papi winked at the mirror-me, then turned his head from side to side, judging what work was needed. Then he tilted his head upward, and flashed his razor up and over his jaw, flaying hair from his face in two or three simple strokes. I was certain that he would bleed—it was impossible for his skin not to open up under such provocation. He laughed when I squeaked and jumped high, holding out my hands with a will to catch his life and throw it back into him that way. Then he told me—in a deep African accent that I never tired of his assuming—that my mother had worked a very strong juju for him so that his throat might be cut but he would never die.

When Papi's hands began to knot up and loll heavy on his lap, he said that he'd decided to accept the dignity of facial hair. His razor rusted in the bathroom cabinet because Papi wouldn't let Chabella throw it away.

Aaron says to me, "That plumber's coming back tomorrow."

With one hand to his face, preparing his cheek for the razor, he laughs at me. He begins to say something else, but starts whistling another highlife song instead. When I come to kiss his other cheek, he smiles at the mirror-me as if he knew that that was what I was going to do all along.

Last night Aaron came home with a single nappy pressed flat in its plastic wrapping. It was tiny. I said, "There's a child in the newborn bay that's missing that."

Remorse came into his eyes with a speed that made me suspicious. "I should give it back?"

There being nothing for me to say to that, he opened the pack and widened the nappy's waistband with his thumbs. When he looked at me and held the nappy up for me to see properly, his gaze was sceptical.

I laughed at him. "What? You thought a baby wouldn't be that big, or that small?"

His thumbs were still hooked into the elastic. He stretched them wider and said, "Maja, come on. To come to this from the womb, where there wasn't enough space to properly wave your arms and legs about in the first place. I mean, look at this thing. Look at the shape of the leg holes. And the way you have to tape the waist in. He'll think he's been moved to a higher security grade prison. He'll make frequent escapes and we'll have to lock him up again."

I remembered to tell him about the kick my son gave me in exchange for a song. He lay his head on my lap and murmured things to my son, things in Ewe not meant for me. Everything was still; everything in the room, every part of me was trying to listen to Aaron's words and wanting to understand. I took his hand, ready to travel my stomach. But he sat up and said gently, "Maja." He meshed my fingers with his, touched his lips to mine.

I go home because Papi and Chabella want me to go to Tomás's sports-day race with them. The first thing I do when I get home is go upstairs to my black-and-white bedroom. I stand at the window. What I like best about my room is that in the late afternoon, if I am tired, I only have to wait. Then, sunset. Since light refuses to waste itself, it slips onto me, all over me. I lie down on my bed and I don't have to do anything else. Something else breathes for me. But Chabella will not let me stay in my bed. It is hard to know what is important to Tomás, so we should not take this risk, we should not miss his race.

Chabella sits by me and insists I rise. That's exactly how she says it: "Rise." Her hands caress my face; her voice is thinner than tracing paper.

"Tomás told me that you've lost your collar," I tell her finally, because it is either that or cry. I remember how heavy she told me the collar was, and how in my hand it weighs hardly anything.

At the running track, Mami sits between Papi and me and links our arms through hers. No one else's parents have come. The swing seats behind us are aswarm with kids in PE uniforms, some of them splashing water over their faces and gurgling loud encouragement to their friends in other events. The long-jump competition, at the far right of the track, is made mysterious by its distance—a boy with impossibly long legs wades the air and lands with a stiff snap. When

Tomás's race starts, we lean forward as one, peering into the dense pack of boys sprinting two hundred metres. Chabella and Papi can't pick out Tomás until I tell them that he's the one with the white zigzag masking half of his face. Tomás's head is lowered; he is ready to ram the whole world. He hurtles straight through the centre of the boys keeping pace with one another, his feet blur as he peels back space with his legs. Tomás is the most beautiful black boy there, the most beautiful boy there. Chabella and I scream for him, Papi stamps his feet, but we are lost beneath the school crowd who are chanting with one fast-fermenting voice for someone called Joseph. Tomás, two other boys at his heels, lifts his head to look at the stands. He oversteps, kicks out too far, swerves and folds onto his knees. The other boys buffet him as they swarm past, and he is on his feet in an instant, but an instant too late, and he is fifth to the finish line.

The crowd says, "Joseph, Joseph," but when Tomás shouts out, they hear him. Two girls behind me loudly agree that Tomás is a sore loser.

It's as if Tomás comes home separately from us; his body sits next to me on the tube, but when I try to hug him, he is like a mannequin, his half-face cool and incurious.

At home, I knock on his door.

"Ask him if he wants dinner," Chabella hisses from below.

"Tomás? Do you want dinner?" He doesn't answer.

I sit down outside his door and tap, low, to let him know where I'm sitting. A long second, and then he taps back, just a little higher.

He tries to talk to me but his voice won't let him. The school was screaming "Joseph," and after all he is not Joseph. If they were quiet, or if they had just made wordless noise, Tomás could have soared through on his own call.

Disappearing; Tomás is the kind of boy who can do it if enough people tell him to. I don't know why Chabella and Papi keep calling him the London baby. If you put a name to this boy he'll die. Chabella and Papi mustn't do it anymore—it bothers him, it's different from calling him *el enano* and they know it.

Tomás is crying now, and he doesn't care if I hear it.

The house is silent in the early afternoon. I look at Bisabuela Carmen in her place at the centre of the family altar, behind flickering candles—I lose myself in looking at her. She appears to be watching the Holy Child of Atocha very suspiciously from the corner of her eye. How blood works, the things that pass across. I'm not sure what there is of Carmen in me, and I worry about what she, a *babalawo* who could read messages in blood and salt, might tell me if I really opened my heart to her and asked. She might fill me. Candle flame heats my fingertips as I run my fingers along the rows of faces.

Mami has been cooking the way she does when she is nervous. She has made an enormous batch of chicken *ajiaco*, more than Tomás and Papi and I could ever want to eat, this is a catering-size pot. It sits, squat and morose, still bubbling on the back hob, covered only slightly so it can cool. I feel as if we are beginning here again, and if I step out through the back door and into the garden I will find my brother, four years old, bundled up in scarves, kicking up leaves and happily colouring in bear shapes.

Upstairs, Papi and Chabella are asleep. Papi's breathing barely disturbs his chest; Mami sleeps with a glow on her. I am smoke, the sign of her fire. She doesn't know that she's alight.

I am staying overnight for Tomás, as if I'm back to watching him for cot death.

His door stays closed—he doesn't come out for dinner; he doesn't come out for the *pasteles* that Chabella has made especially for him. Papi said that we must call him once, then leave him be. The boy is not a drama queen—if he's hungry, he will eat.

I watch late-night television, listening out for the stairs to creak, nodding sleep away until my chin dips in and out of my glass of lemonade. On-screen, two hamsters begin to chase each other around a maze. Tomás looms behind me in a mushroom cloud of blankets and touches my elbow. I don't jump. Ever since I left those two sleep-girls behind me in Hamburg, I keep thinking that they will come back. Ever since Hamburg, I have been ready.

I take my blanket and wind it around me. Tomás and I pad through the kitchen, a tight squeeze through the doors because we are holding hands and mashing into each other. Tomás fetches Mami's black lanterns from the shed, and even though the cold night knifes us, we fall into the garden deck chairs. We wrap our legs in our duvets; we tuck our hands inside our dressing gowns. The wind knocks my hair lopsided.

We watch the lanterns scattered around us, the tea-tinted wax inside them holding up their flames against all comers. The wind comes, some rain comes, two murders for our light. But the flames stay so we can see each other's faces. I smile because Tomás is smiling. He looks exhausted, cosy, as if he has come in from some long journey and collapsed in front of a fireplace, but the candle flame isn't enough to warm us. What warms us is the way the light stays and stays, dances limbo, touches the bottom of the glass then shimmies up again.

Mami's collar is in my pocket, working itself loose from old string and old care. Tomás says something. His voice is hoarse and I don't catch his words. I ask him, too loudly, what he said. He puts a finger to his lips and we quieten, in case we disturb them, our guardians and guides, our Orishas in the house, the ones upstairs asleep.

ACKNOWLEDGEMENTS

ED

Thank you **BENTE LODGAARD** for That Chat in Oslo.

Yay (and much love to) **ALI SMITH**.

Yay (and much love to) **SARAH WOOD**.

Yay (and much love to) **LOA./LORNA OWEN**.

BOOGIE/J/JASON TSANG—best friend to be had anywhere in the world, and father of TOH at T Street. Boogie . . . I don't know what to tell you, man. Thank you.

ANITA SETHI, thank you for the support and the ultra-late-night chitchat.

PTAH HOTEP, thank you for the transatlantic cheerleading, best of Ps.

Thank you **ROBIN WADE** for keeping everything together.

Thank you **JULIET LAPIDOS** for your attentive reading, especially re Aaron.

Thank you **ALEXANDRA PRINGLE**, you are the king, the king.

BEATRICE MONTI-REZZORI, thank you . . .

Thank you for feedback and general jest, **ANTOSCA**.

PAM HIRSH and **LORRAINE GELSTHORPE**, it probably wasn't apparent on my face at our supervisions, but I think you're both awesome and idiosyncratic teachers. You helped me to finally find value and interest in SPS. I'll remember that. Thank you.

CHOOP/RUPERT MYERS, re your removable E drive—I'm much obliged. Also thanks for the very sight of your Florentine jumper.

CLAUDE WILLAN, shut your face and you better don't open it again EVER (also . . . um . . . thank you for the support, the feedback, the sarcasm, the rallying insults).

With equal measures of love and dread, my thanks to **ALEX SHILOV**, **RAY/RACHEL DOUGLAS-JONES**, **HAZEL CUBBAGE** for bringing jokery to Third Year.

Thanks and love to **'TONY BABATUNDE OYEYEMI**.

Thanks and love to **MUMMY** and **DADDY**.

All remaining thanks and love (lots!) to **MARY BIOLA "WE DON'T PICK UP THE PHONE AFTER SEVEN . . . A.M." OYEYEMI**.

A NOTE ABOUT THE AUTHOR

HELEN OYEYEMI was born in Nigeria in 1984 and has lived in London since the age of four. She is the author of the highly acclaimed novel *The Icarus Girl*, which she wrote before her nineteenth birthday; *The Icarus Girl* was short-listed for the 2006 Commonwealth Writers' Prize. Helen Oyeyemi graduated from Cambridge University in 2006 and is at work on her next novel.

A NOTE ABOUT THE TYPE

The text of this book is set in Perpetua, a typeface designed by Eric Gill and released by the Monotype Corporation between 1925 and 1932. This typeface has a clean look with beautiful classical capitals, making it an excellent choice for both text and display settings. Perpetua was named for the book in which it made its first appearance: *The Passion of Perpetua and Felicity*.

6/7/19 - 7/9/18